ME ME ME

# DAVID HUGGINS

# Me Me Me

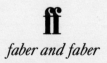

*faber and faber*

First published in 2001
by Faber and Faber Limited
3 Queen Square London WC1N 3AU

Typeset by Faber and Faber Ltd
Printed in England by Clays Ltd, St Ives plc

A CIP record for this book is available from the British Library

ISBN 0-571-20936-x

2 4 6 8 10 9 7 5 3 1

For my Mother

# Chapter One

'I started writing this book over twenty-five years ago to tell the story of myself and wrote over five thousand pages.'

Kirk Douglas, *The Ragman's Son*

The pilot took the plane into a holding pattern over Los Angeles, and the sight of the Santa Monica pier called to mind a blonde woman I once saw roller-blading there. Banded by a fluorescent bikini, her lean tan body had pricked my teenage lust at fifty yards, but when she came up close the flesh on her face looked like brown candle wax dripped over a skull. More than sixty years old, her hair was the colour of sulphur. I'd flown out on that trip in a haze of youthful optimism, and had celebrated my eighteenth birthday at a restaurant on Sunset Strip with my grandfather, the actor Donald Tait. 'The world's your oyster,' Grandpa had told me that night, with no idea how cold, grey and slimy my life in the British theatre would ultimately become.

Thirteen years on, the fuselage shuddered as the pilot made his final descent, and the smog looked worse than it had on that earlier visit – thicker, more toxic. But then, of course, so did I.

My cab driver took La Cienega instead of the freeway, and when he pulled up at some lights in the flats, the peculiar smell of Los Angeles came in through the open window, an aroma of jasmine-scented garbage. Having forgotten to bring my sunglasses, I squinted to make out the street signs – Horner, Alcott, Pico – and to re-read my grandfather's letter. '*I know how busy you must be*,' he'd written in his elegant, looping hand, '*but I'm horribly behind with my memoirs and could really use your help editing them. Is there any chance you*

1

*could come out here for a few weeks? The book's so overdue that my publishers would be happy to pay you for your trouble.'* This was the first solid offer I'd had in months, and knee-deep in debt following the bankruptcy of the experimental theatre group in which I'd worked since leaving university, I'd jumped at it.

Reaching Beverly Hills, I asked to be dropped on the horseshoe-shaped driveway of my grandfather's house on North Canon Drive. Dwarfed by the soaring palms that lined the road, a man in a baseball cap was watering some oleander by the archway that led through to the inner courtyard. Thinking him to be Pedro, the pool man, I called to him, but he turned to me with the soft, frightened face of a stranger. A small sign staked into the lawn between us bore the words 'Edison Security. Armed response', the very blades of grass making death threats, so I told him my business before dragging my suitcase on its squeaking wheels to the front door, sensing his eyes on my back.

Handmade out of hardwood and plugged with wrought-iron studs, the Spanish colonial-style door weighed a ton but still looked fake, as if you could push it open with your little finger. A smiling sylph in a halter-top and cut-offs answered the bell and introduced herself as Julie, the new housekeeper.

'Hi, Ralph. How you doing? It's really great to meet you,' she said. 'I've heard so much about you.'

My grandfather had mentioned Julie in his letter, but from his description of her as *'a wonderful cook from Iowa who runs the house to perfection'*, I'd imagined a spinster in her fifties, buttoned to the neck. With long brown legs and long brown hair that she wore in squaw-like plaits which fell down her chest, Julie wasn't yet thirty.

The dark, cool hall was bigger than the entire basement flat I'd been renting for the past six months in east London, and my eyes strained to adjust from the glare of the day as I followed Julie through a series of arches that led into the library. I felt dry and empty. Opening the shutters, she said that she was going upstairs to fetch my grandfather.

'Look,' I said. 'If he's resting –'

'Oh, no,' she said, cocking her head to one side. 'He asked me to tell him the moment you got here. Really.'

Watching her run up the curved staircase, I was apprehensive. Over the eight years since I'd last visited my grandfather, we'd exchanged the odd letter and spoken on the telephone regularly but never for very long, and I'd found it all too easy to paint an upbeat but untruthful picture of my work as a writer and a director with the Direct Debit Theatre Company. Grandpa had little idea of the difficulties we'd faced in recent years, let alone that the company had finally gone bankrupt, and he continued to imagine that his grandson was enjoying a creditable career in the London theatre. Having grown up in Britain himself, Grandpa retained an enduring if misty-eyed affection for its institutions, and had referred to me as 'the white sheep of the family' while I was at Oxford University. It was a joke my father had suffered with a tight smile at the time, but now, consigned by events to the role of spear carrier in the tired repertory production of my own life, the joke looked to be on me. A year after Direct Debit's disbandment, I was still trapped beneath my own little rain-cloud of failure and worthlessness.

As I waited in the library, the ground began to rumble, leading me to fear an earth tremor until I recalled the elevator that I'd been forbidden to play in as a child. When the grinding noise stopped, the concertina door rattled open.

'Ralph, my dear boy. You made it. Bravo.' My grandfather's voice, the kind of gravelly English baritone that can still be heard in the House of Lords, resounded down the corridor. Then he appeared propped up on an aluminium cane, and his face, once described in *The New Yorker* as that of a good-looking gargoyle, lit up. 'It's simply wonderful you're here at last,' he boomed. 'You're looking marvellous.'

'You too, Grandpa,' I cried, my failure to match his ebullient tone making me feel even more of a charlatan. I'd always pictured my grandfather as being taller than me, so it felt strange to have to bend down to kiss his sloppily shaved cheek and to feel his spine through his cashmere blazer, curled over like a question mark. Julie hovered at his elbow as he brandished his cane.

'I despise this bloody thing, but my knee's seizing up all the time,' he said. 'You go on through to the den, dear boy. I'll follow you. I want to hear your news. All of it.'

Taking a deep breath, I steeled myself to confess Direct Debit's bankruptcy, but before I could begin, he told me that his new physiotherapist, an ex-Marine named Merle, was working wonders with his leg. 'He has healing hands, dear boy, healing hands.' On my last visit, my grandfather had carved wood in his workshop and swam his lengths in the pool every morning, a sprightly sixty-eight-year-old, but now he walked with difficulty.

Once in the den, Julie and I helped him into his favourite armchair, where he sat surrounded by photographs of himself in some of the hundreds of roles he'd performed over the course of his career. The room was unchanged since my last visit, and I was touched to see that the framed print of my graduation photograph still had pride of place on the table by his chair.

'Get that bloody stick out of my sight, would you?' he barked at Julie. 'I can't stand to look at it.' Frowning at him, she placed the cane behind the sofa. Grandpa winked at me to let me know that he'd only faked his tantrum for my enter-tainment, and in a stage whisper, declared that Julie was a perfect angel, making her blush beneath her tan. Slicked straight back from his forehead, his thick white hair was in need of a trim. 'Lucky we never had the elevator removed, isn't it, dear boy?'

'Absolutely,' I said. 'I always wondered what it was doing there. I mean, since it's only a two-storey house.'

'The chap I bought it from was bedridden.' Holding my gaze, he gave his words time to sink in. 'That was thirty-five years ago. Can you believe it?'

4

My grandfather shook his head as if old age was the most unexpected thing that had ever happened to him. He was scared, scared of dying, but he couldn't say it, and his unspoken fear chimed with my own anxieties as to where my life was going. Years of Californian sunshine had turned his face into leather and his full lips had been thinned and purpled by old age, but his pale eyes were bright as a teenager's, and when Julie left the room, they shone as he tracked her behind.

'She's really wonderful, Ralph. A godsend. I'm so lucky to have found her. I've been through half a dozen helpers since Mrs O left.' Mrs O'Connor had been Grandpa's housekeeper for twenty years, and her *Star Trek*-mauve hair and long yellow teeth had terrified me so much as a child that I'd gone to elaborate lengths to stay out of her way. 'Christ,' he said, 'I can't believe I let myself get frozen into this ghastly city. Would you be so kind as to mix me a drink?'

Although Grandpa liked to give certain words an American twang, this tic only served to point up his peculiar achievement of having preserved his English accent over half a century of almost continual residence in the US. Once I'd handed him his J&B and water, I rolled down the blinds against the glare of the sun, and seeing the new pool man raking over the gravel beyond the terrace, I asked after Pedro.

'Pedro? He got deported back to Mexico,' Grandpa said. 'Nothing we could do about it. Six, seven years ago. Terrible business. Something to do with tax, I believe.'

I asked about Pedro's family, but Grandpa didn't seem to hear. 'My God, it's good to see you again, Ralph,' he said. 'My *grandson*. It's been far too long.'

'It has,' I replied, gulping a Dr Pepper in an attempt to rehydrate after eleven hours in the Boeing Company's moisture removal tube.

'Thanks so much for taking the time to come out here. It means a great deal to me,' my grandfather said. 'What with my publishers being on my back and everything. I suspect

5

they're worried I'll be joining the heavenly choir before they get their hands on the book . . . Well, we'll talk about all that when you're over the flight.'

We smiled at each other, and when my grandfather closed his eyes, I began to unwind. Such time as we'd spent alone together had mostly been passed in this room, watching old movies and televised baseball games on the various visits I'd made to California in my teens and early twenties. Having moved to London at the age of four, I'd never managed to grasp the rules of baseball, but Grandpa loved the game. Although he liked to play up his Englishness for all it was worth when it suited (a framed fan letter from the Queen Mother was turning yellow beside one of his Tony awards on the mantelpiece), his accent had long been the only noticeably un-American thing about him. By taking US citizenship in the 1960s for tax purposes, he'd precluded the possibility of an otherwise inevitable knighthood and, never a tea drinker, hadn't revisited London since deeming it 'filthy' in the early 1980s. 'Precious few people are born in the country where they truly belong,' he liked to say when pressed on the matter.

Dozing, my grandfather was surrounded by so many play-bills and pictures of himself in various roles that the plaid wallpaper was barely visible. The photographs of his memorable, bumpy face dated from the London stage of the 1940s to colour prints with his co-stars in *Brannigan*, the US police series in which he'd played the lead. One glance at various film stills from the 1960s, the high point of his career, left little doubt that he'd leave a lasting mark on the world, an achievement that forced me to reflect on my own meagre efforts. A snap taken twenty-five years ago by Arnold Weissberger, the theatrical lawyer, showed Grandpa with his arms around his two acting offspring, my father Larry and my Aunt Eleanor, and I was examining his children's forced smiles when he opened his eyes.

'By the way,' he said, 'does your pa know you're here?'

6

I'd called my parents by their first names since I was five years old, so the word 'pa' threw me. 'Who? Larry?' I asked.

Grandpa nodded.

'I left a message on his machine but I don't think he got it,' I said. Not having seen my father since his last brief visit to London three years previously, I'd been looking forward to spending some time with him and was disappointed that he'd not returned my call. We hadn't spoken in six months, but as far as I knew, Larry was still living in Laurel Canyon with his third wife and, according to my mother, living off her. Like Grandpa, he was endlessly optimistic about marriage.

'Well, you may as well hear it from me that the two of us haven't exactly been seeing eye to eye lately,' Grandpa said. His disagreements with my father had never been a secret, and our sense of shared grievance was one of the corner-stones of the special bond we claimed to share, but Grandpa seemed disinclined to discuss this latest rupture. Staring out of the window as if I wasn't there, his blazer bunched up around his shoulders with each breath he took. 'I wish I could get away from here,' he said finally. 'Hit the road and just bugger off, you know?'

Chuckling mechanically, I wondered how much time he'd spent on his own in this room over the past few years. To change the subject, I asked him about my Uncle Bruce.

'Oh, Bruce is at Ojai fixing up the house,' he replied. My grandfather had a holiday home in the country north of Los Angeles, and I'd spent some happy times there as a child. 'You'll see him this evening, and we'll make a trip in a few days to see how it's all going. You'll hardly recognize the valley, the country's so green. A demi-paradise. But tell me, my boy. What's happening with your company?'

My mouth drained dry, because nothing was happening. Still desperate for artistic and financial recognition after a decade of hard work and penury, we'd decided to mount a short season of our group-generated work in a disused east London film studio. Unable to obtain sufficient corporate sponsorship or even an Arts Council grant, I'd finally pledged the small trust fund that Grandpa had set up for me at my birth (in a never-to-be-repeated moment of generosity) to underwrite the costs. It was a risky, last-ditch attempt to establish Direct Debit in the public eye. Our flagship production, a play loosely based on *Locus Solus* by Raymond Roussel, won a clutch of good reviews in the national press, the best of which I sent to my grandfather, but we sold few tickets and the season bankrupted the company two weeks before my thirtieth birthday. We told ourselves that there was no shame in this (after all, the founders of The Living Theatre, in which Joe Chaikin began his career, went to jail for non-payment of taxes). But the very week our 'theatre' went prematurely dark, I received Grandpa's response to the reviews I'd sent him. *'You are launched,'* he'd written, *'and I exult in your triumph.'* These words had, literally, choked me.

'Ralph, are you all right? I asked how things are with your company.'

Grandpa was staring at me, and I should have told him the truth then and there. It was an ideal opportunity to put the record straight, but I couldn't quite do it. A year on, the bankruptcy was still too distressing for me to talk about freely, and in any case I didn't want to let him down.

'Sorry. I was in a daze,' I said. 'Yes, everything's going swimmingly.' Grandpa wanted more information. 'Whoever put us forward must be practically certifiable,' I added. 'But the play's won an award and transferred to the West End. The Fortune Theatre. We're playing to packed houses. There's a strong possibility that it might come to Broadway in the autumn.'

The words had shot out of my mouth before I could stop them. Thrilled to think that his genetic investment had risen in value, Grandpa billowed with pride, but all too quickly I felt only burning shame. My lies were indefensible. All I can say is that to grow up as an only child in a family of actors was to experience childhood as a sort of botched adult, as a

8

dwarfish voyeur. From an early age, I learnt that success was all that counted and to say what I thought the grown-ups wanted to hear. It's no excuse, but that was exactly how it was with Grandpa in the den.

'Who's bringing it to New York?' he asked me, clutching the arm of his chair. 'Which producer?'

'Nothing's been signed as yet, and it's bad luck to talk about it,' I replied, calling on the time-honoured magical thinking that pervades the theatre.

Superstitious himself, my grandfather dropped his line of enquiry without another word and then, to my relief, Merle the physiotherapist arrived, dressed head to toe in dentistry whites, his doughy face topped with a silver quiff. Julie led me upstairs to the room directly over the archway, where I'd slept in a narrow single bed as a child, feeling as safe then as I ever had anywhere. The smell of old wood was reassuringly familiar as I laid myself out on the covers and closed my eyes. Honoured that Grandpa had asked for my help with his memoirs, I felt doubly bad about tricking him and even more uncomfortable because I'd been acting a part from the moment I'd told the lie. Like lizards disappearing into cracks in the wall, these thoughts troubled me as I fell asleep.

Waking with no sense of the time of day, I went downstairs feeling lost and nauseous, and found that years of sunlight had bleached the geometric pattern from the yellow wallpaper in the kitchen. Drinking a cone-full of water from Lake Arrowhead, I jumped when the hum of the refrigerator broke the silence. Beyond the screen door, the azalea and gardenia in the back yard were drenched in the flat pink light of late afternoon, and a splashing sound from the bottom of the garden led me to Julie, who was swimming lengths in the pool, her body a deep brown distorted shape in the water. I called to her.

'How does he seem to you?' she asked, blinking rapidly to clear her eyes. Their lashes were as thick and black as the spines on a sea urchin, and her wet hair lay flat against her fine-boned skull.

'Grandpa? Wonderful,' I said. 'In marvellous shape.'

Julie beamed with pleasure. 'It's great for us all that you're here,' she said. 'He's been brooding lately. About this book, mostly. I'll bring him down in an hour or so and give you both dinner then, if that's OK?'

When she pushed back into the water, I went into the pool house, a single-storey structure with sliding glass doors and a mansard roof, to get myself a Dr Pepper. Taking it out to a lounger in the shade of the ficus tree, I watched Julie's head bob along above the concrete sill as she breaststroked up and down the pool. A recently sprayed rose bush glistened by the garden wall and the air smelt of hibiscus. Except for Julie, nothing moved in this hushed perfect world and it was hard to believe that, only twenty-four hours earlier, I'd been in my cold London flat playing 'If only . . .' with myself over the collapse of Direct Debit. Kicking off my shoes, the tops of my feet were very white, as if I was looking at them under-water.

Julie finished her lengths and rested her chin on the lip of the pool. 'Isn't it beautiful? This is my favourite time of day,' she said. 'You want to swim, Ralph? The water's perfect.'

Her delight in the natural world compounded my own jet-lagged disaffection. 'Maybe later,' I said. 'I'm still a bit fuzzy from the flight.'

'You know they never change the air on those planes?' she said. 'My cousin had a job at Des Moines opening them after they flew in from all over. He'd push the ladder up to the air-craft and give the all clear, then run like hell because when the doors opened there was this terrible stink from inside. Really the worst smell imaginable, he said. After nine or ten hours, the air's so bad –'

Flipping the tab on the Dr Pepper, I noticed a crescent of darker brown aureole peeking over the cup of her bikini top, which Julie adjusted with no trace of embarrassment.

'Wouldn't you prefer a fresh juice?' she asked. 'I could fix some for you.'

'This is fine,' I replied, taking secret pleasure in the fizzing, sugary poison.

'You'll feel better tomorrow. Your cells just need some time to repair themselves after the flight,' she said. 'God, I just love working here. Your grandfather's really a great human being. You must be so proud of him.'

'I am,' I said. 'And I'm glad of the chance to spend some time with him. Do you have family here in LA as well as in the Midwest?'

Her smile tightened and her eyes went small. 'I no longer have contact with my family. I guess the temple's my family now.'

As she spoke, Julie pushed back into the pool, as if re-enacting her escape from the family plot. 'By the way, Ralph. Congratulations.'

'On what?'

'Opening on Broadway. Donald told me about it.'

'Nothing's been finalized yet,' I said, standing up so quickly that a hundred tiny stars burst around my head. 'It won't be for months.'

'Really? Well, why not be positive? I just know it's going to be a big hit.'

Retreating to the pool house, I braced myself against the ping-pong table and took some deep breaths, feeling like an idiot. Who else had Grandpa told? Only back in Los Angeles for a few hours, I'd already jeopardized my chance for what I'd hoped would be a fresh start.

A car pulled up in the back yard and it was some comfort to see Uncle Bruce appear beyond the end of the box hedge. A kindly, bear-like Californian in his forties with a free-form moustache and tangled hair, Bruce lived above the garage at North Canon Drive in a self-contained apartment, did odd jobs around the house, and sometimes mislaid his mind. Once he'd just curled up in a ball under his bed and refused to come out for two days; another time, Larry had apparently found his brother asleep on a median strip in Brentwood, untroubled by the rush-hour traffic thundering past five feet from his head. On such occasions Bruce would be admitted to a clinic for a week or two until his medication had been adjusted, but for the most part he gave the impression that his life had been one long happy dream.

When I went out to greet him, he hugged me hard enough to squeeze the last of the airline's pre-breathed air from my lungs.

'Hey, Ralph. I've been counting the days.' Once inside the pool house, Bruce took two Coors from the refrigerator and made as if to throw me one, but I shook my head. Following Direct Debit's bankruptcy, I'd been on the wagon. 'It's so good to see you,' he said. 'And you're going to be helping Pops with his book?'

'That's the idea,' I said.

As Bruce sipped his beer, I could tell he was struggling to think of the next thing to say. He was transparent that way, and even though he'd been my favourite uncle when I was a child, I knew it would take us time to get close again. Years ago, my father had explained to me that Bruce had a mental age of twelve and that he wasn't expected to develop further. The Coors had left some foam on Bruce's moustache. Wiping it away, he told me that he'd shot two coyotes on the property at Ojai the previous night, and I nodded wisely, unsure if it was bad news that they'd been there in the first place or good news that he'd killed them.

Climbing out of the pool, Julie waved to us, displaying an unselfconsciousness that had been confiscated from me at my English boarding school and never returned. As she walked back up the garden path in her bikini, I asked Bruce how long she'd been working for Grandpa but, lost inside himself, he remained silent. There were times when you had to ask my uncle something twice to get an answer.

'Six months or so,' he finally replied. 'Julie's a wonderful girl. Just wonderful. A godsend. Takes real good care of Pops.'

These were almost Grandpa's very words, and it sounded as if his son had learnt them by heart. 'Say, Ralph, can I show you something I made?'

Crossing the back yard, we passed a dusty pick-up parked beneath the jacaranda, and I noticed some varicose veins on the back of my uncle's hairless calves as we climbed the wooden staircase at the side of the garage. Stepping over the junk that cluttered his cramped apartment, Bruce pulled back a tarpaulin to reveal a lump of wood some three foot high, which he'd carved into the shape of my grandfather's head and shoulders, thrice life-size but instantly recognizable.

'I did it myself,' Bruce said. 'Gonna give it to Pops at his birthday party. Think he'll like it?'

At first glance, it called to mind the sculptures that fill the art and craft shops up at Ojai, the harmless effluent of a hundred early retirements. On closer examination, the carved face hummed with the unsettling animal–magical quality Picasso had found in certain tribal masks from the Congo. With its wide leering smile, Bruce's carving was a labour not of love but of slavish devotion.

'I've never seen anything like it,' I said. 'I think it'll knock him out.'

'You mean that?' Bruce asked. Heading back across the yard, I obliged him with a string of fresh intensifiers until Julie emerged from her quarters on the far side of the archway with her wet hair coiled up inside a towel turban.

'Bruce, may I speak with you a moment?'

Hearing the little whip in her voice, he strode obediently towards her, bowed his head as she said her piece, and when he rejoined me, taking small steps on the balls of his feet, his centre of gravity pitched so far forward that each pace seemed almost a pratfall in the making, he seemed cowed.

'I raided the refrigerator for the trip to Ojai, and Julie's just a little pissed at me,' Bruce said. 'As usual. You want to come to the store?'

Heading south in my uncle's pick-up, Beverly Hills seemed as strangely uninhabited as it had on my previous visits, and North Canon Drive was deserted save for a pool man using a blower to shift clippings from the lawn of a new Williamsburg colonial. Bruce pulled up at the lights, and when he told me that, despite Grandpa's problems with his knee, his overall health was excellent, I felt my guts fill with slush. Determined though I was to put my grandfather right on the matter of Direct Debit at the first opportunity, it was agonizing to picture myself actually making the confession.

Juergensen's had long gone, but Mrs Gooch's on Crescent Drive was now selling organic produce under the name of Whole Foods, and once we'd collected Julie's order, Bruce and I went for a malted at Nate 'n Al's, an unreconstructed diner on Rodeo Drive that had been a childhood favourite of mine. The counterman greeted Bruce as a regular, asking after his father before going into a routine from one of Grandpa's rare comedy films. Laughing at the tired punchline, Bruce introduced me as Donald Tait's grandson and, his eyes already swivelling towards the next customer, the counterman lied that he remembered me. As Bruce and I made our way to a button-backed booth, a dozen people checked us out only to be disappointed. We were nobodies.

In the past, dinner at North Canon Drive had been a formal affair in the dining room, but my grandfather now took his meals in the den on a collapsible table. Bruce didn't eat with us that evening, and as I chewed Julie's bland chicken casserole, Grandpa said he'd asked his son to take the manuscript down to the pool house.

'I thought it would be a quiet place for you to work,' he said.

This suited me perfectly since I'd be able to smoke there with impunity. Praying for the courage to put my grandfather right about Direct Debit, perhaps even to make him believe that it had all been a misunderstanding, I asked him about his book.

Grandpa frowned. 'Wait until you've looked it over,' he said. 'We'll talk about it then.'

When he dropped his knife on to the carpet, I picked it up and passed it to him, but he managed no more than a cold nod by way of thanks. Detecting a glint of the cruelty my father was always complaining about but which, as a grand-child, I'd so far escaped, I found it impossible to confess my lies about the play and the loss of my trust fund. As the silences stretched, I asked myself if I was really obliged to tell my grandfather the truth. He was old, his world had shrunk, and in two weeks' time I could simply break the 'bad news' that the transfer to Broadway had fallen through, affecting the customary grace of the good English loser.

The telephone rang, and Julie came through to tell Grandpa that John Blumenthal wished to speak to him.

'Again?' Grandpa growled. 'Tell him to fuck himself. Tell him I'll do as I bloody well please.' Rolling her eyes, Julie left the room. There was a pause and I felt compelled to ask who John Blumenthal was. 'Wretched coat-hanger maker who lives up on Stone Canyon road,' Grandpa said. 'You used to go over there and play with his step-children.' I dimly recalled a French château-style house in Bel-Air. 'John and I had a lot of fun together once upon a time,' he added. 'But now he thinks I screwed his wife, and that I'm going to kiss-and-tell in the book.'

'And did you?' I asked. 'Screw her, I mean?'

'Ralph, I made a picture with her in 1974, and to tell you the truth, I really don't remember.' I asked whether he was kidding. 'I'm not,' he replied. 'And from where I am now, I can tell you that life's not much more than a dip in the bathtub. Have fun while you can, and if you want to do something, do it, dear boy. Just do it.'

After dinner, I swooshed my tray through to the kitchen and complimented Julie on her cooking.

'Oh, it's nothing. Not like writing and directing a play.' she said. Suffering a sharp stab of loss for my years with

Direct Debit, I asked her if Grandpa was always so angry. 'Oh, his bark's worse than his bite,' she said. 'And I think he really quite enjoys playing his little games with Mr Blumenthal.'

I couldn't put a face to the name, so Julie fetched a copy of *People* magazine from a stack by the back door and found a photograph of John Blumenthal's most recent wedding. A scrawny sun-baked ancient, Blumenthal appeared to have married a Barbie doll of indeterminate age on a bluff by the ocean, witnessed by a gaggle of superannuated celebrities whose faces had been not so much lifted as launched.

Back in the den, Grandpa asked me to pick a movie for us to watch, and seeing as over half the video cassettes on the shelves featured a Donald Tait performance, I took care to choose a Western in which he'd played one of the lead roles. Nursing his decaffeinated coffee, Grandpa perked up as the opening credits rolled and enjoyed himself until the attrition rate on screen began to prefigure that of real life. A young actor playing a cavalry officer took an Indian bullet, and as he tumbled down into an arroyo, Grandpa's mood dropped alongside him.

'Lung cancer,' Grandpa said. 'Fifteen years ago.'

Sipping his coffee, he made a slurping noise that sounded like *Weltschmerz*. When an eager Ronald Reagan galloped on to the screen to deliver a message, Grandpa cursed beneath his breath.

'Are you all right?' I asked.

'Sometimes I think I'm just about ready to go,' he replied. 'To cease upon the midnight with no pain. Without you and Julie, I'd have nobody at all.'

'Come on, Grandpa,' I said. 'You've got a lot to look forward to. Your birthday, the book –'

Nailed by the dead-eyed look he'd employed when playing heavies in his films, I shrank back in my seat.

'A hundred years ago there were thousands of theatres all over this country playing Mr Shakespeare to packed houses,' he said, flicking some cookie crumbs from the folds of his shirt. 'Now what do we have? David Mamet?'

If Grandpa thought so little of Mamet, I had to wonder as to his true opinion of my own work and was glad when Julie joined us. Gliding silently across the Persian rug to sit at her employer's feet, she was enviably impervious to his mood, which by that time had run through me like the tines of a pitchfork.

Twenty long minutes dragged by.

When I glanced at my grandfather, his head had drooped forward, his eyelids had lowered, and I was glad to hear some air blow through his lips because it meant he was still breathing. Staring at the screen as if participating in a successful mind-control experiment, Julie's face glimmered in the blue-white light.

# Chapter Two

'The barber, plunging at once into talk, began to
shave with a less attentive hand, and with a sudden
sweep of his blade – pop! The pimple was beheaded!'
André Gide, *The Vatican Cellars*

My grandfather's autobiography isn't yet available for public scrutiny, so in all fairness I feel I should preface my initial
reaction to his manuscript with a further word about myself.
When I was a child, every adult I met asked me if I planned
to become an actor when I grew up, but even though my
mother, my father, my grandfather and my aunt were all
actors, I always answered 'No.' Did I already think it strange
that an adult should make a living pretending to be somebody else? I doubt it. The first four years of my life were
spent in Los Angeles and it had seemed perfectly normal that
my grandfather should appear on television dressed as a
pirate or a detective, or that from time to time my father
might drive along Sunset Strip counting the number of times
his own face appeared on the billboards.

Until I reached puberty, I'd no wish to join 'the profession'
myself, but over the next few years, much to my surprise, I
developed a secret longing to do just that. Having resisted the
temptation to take part in school productions despite my
teachers' entreaties, on arriving at Oxford I felt ready to reveal
my talent to the world. Imagine then the humiliation I suffered
when I auditioned for a small role in an Oxford University
Dramatic Society production of Lorca's *Yerma*, only to fail to
win the part. The director was right to have turned me down.
I simply didn't have the gift: too shy and lacking assurance, I
preferred to hang back. But the hurt went deep, and the
memory was still painful when, early on the morning of my

second day in Los Angeles, I discovered six piles of foolscap arranged on the ping-pong table in the pool house, and I picked up the title page of my grandfather's autobiography:

To Be!
A Player's Odyssey
by
Donald Tait

Settling down by the ficus tree, I'd no sooner scanned a few pages than I was extremely alarmed. In his letter Grandpa had led me to believe that his manuscript was almost ready for publication (indeed, he'd implied that it was already destined to spend eternity in a thermostatically controlled display case in the Getty Center). But as I searched through the piles of paper in the pool house with trembling fingers, I realized that Grandpa's reminiscences had been typed up exactly as he'd spoken them into a tape recorder. Little further work had been done on the resulting text, which was prolix and disordered, and appeared to follow only the vaguest chronological pattern. A typical page began with an affectionate sketch of Deborah Kerr that led on to an anecdote about a Broadway producer which in turn inspired an analysis of the shortcomings of Capri as a celebrity holiday destination in the post-war years.

The towering stacks of paper on the ping-pong table had looked like various draft versions of the manuscript, but they were in fact sections of the same work. My stomach rose as if it had been pumped full of helium. Ignoring the ongoing pressure of jet lag behind my eyes, I multiplied the number of words per line by the number of lines per page and, with a rapid heart, estimated that the complete text ran to several million words. A horde of secretaries had worked on the typescript, and it seemed unlikely that even my grandfather himself had read all of it. Just as I'd lied to him about Direct Debit's London season, so he'd misled me over the state of his memoirs. It was editing that I'd been brought over to do,

not writing, and Grandpa's reticence on the subject the previous evening was now all too understandable: the job
would take months, if not years, to complete. Little wonder
that he'd sent me an open ticket.

Grandpa's pell-mell story was hard to follow, but individual passages intrigued me. On a childhood journey to visit
the American branch of the Tait family, he'd witnessed the
Depression at first-hand, and from his clear-eyed description,
I could almost see the hobo jungles from the train window
and smell cabbage cooking in the iron pots. *'Men in rags were
living alongside the tracks in makeshift shanty towns, and they
stopped what they were doing to stare at our train as we shunted
by. They were half-starved, and my uncle put his hand over my eyes
so I wouldn't see them.'* Grandpa had been born in the north of
England, the son of a glove manufacturer who emerged
between the lines as a remote and cold-hearted patriarch, but
for the most part family life in Lancashire was depicted,
albeit in mawkish terms, as an endless carnival. *'We spent the
long summer afternoons playing badminton on the lawn, and there
were always cream teas to be enjoyed with Nanny holding court.
Time went more slowly then, and it was all very heaven.'*

Aside from a teenage crush on the actress Gladys Cooper
(*'one of the great beauties of her time'*), there was little explanation
as to why my grandfather had fled to London at seventeen to
become an actor. A former chorus girl and *'the sweetest, kindest
mother the world has ever known'*, my great-grandmother had
encouraged her second son's theatrical ambitions against her
husband's wishes. *'Desperate to see me established as a juvenile,
that darling woman even pawned her jewellery behind my father's
back to help me buy a new suit to attend auditions.'* Even so, it had
proved very difficult for Grandpa to get a foothold on the West
End stage in the 1940s. Starting in the box-office of the Apollo
Theatre, he'd slowly worked his way up to the post of
Assistant Stage Manager, scraping a living in dreadful digs
before graduating to walk-on parts. Between jobs, he'd been so
broke that he'd been forced to scavenge scraps from the dust-

bins of smart restaurants ('*Sometimes only a half-chewed pork chop stood between me and the terrible pains of hunger*'), and to sleep wearing his overcoat and scarf against the draught from a broken skylight for a whole winter ('*I can still hear that cold east wind whistling in my ears*'). Although a brass band struck up some Elgar in my inner ear as I read this, Donald Tait's determination to succeed was evident in every word, and his struggle made me feel even guiltier for having blown my trust fund. Or simply for being me.

Just too young to fight in the war, my grandfather had finally got his break playing Cosgrave in *The Brass Farthing* for Binkie Beaumont ('*London loved the play, the production and, in all humility, my performance*'), and this had led directly to a small role in a Hollywood film. But as Grandpa would later quip into his tape recorder, 'Slowly Comes the Dawn *found the sunset terribly quickly.*' In the transcript's margin, he'd pencilled a note that, during the course of the filming, he'd met and married my grandmother, an actress from San Francisco (who'd died in 1964), and that she'd borne him a son, my father Laurence.

What Grandpa didn't mention was that, unable to find enough work as a bit-player in Hollywood, he'd deserted them both soon afterwards, and having recrossed the Atlantic, fell for a debutante during the run of a comedy in the West End some two years later. My grandfather dismissed his second marriage as '*another youthful folly*' (he was already twenty-eight at the time), ungallantly implying that his young wife's pregnancy had forced his hand ('*In those days one did the right thing*'). The brief reference to this marriage failed to touch on the nervous collapse his second wife suffered (divorced and left with two small children, Eleanor and Bruce) after he'd done precisely the wrong thing by returning to the United States in the mid-1950s to forge a successful film career. Grandpa's disastrous emotional life during that period had turned our part of the family tree into something of a monkey-puzzle, and if I hadn't already been familiar with the chain of events, I'd have been hard-pressed to decipher it from the manuscript. Even for an inquisitive, and salaried, grandchild, *To Be!* was an irksome read.

In the kitchen, Julie was folding a copy of the *Herald Tribune* into the wicker pannier of Grandpa's breakfast tray, but when I picked up a brown pot containing a minuscule knob of butter, she reacted as if I'd stumbled on damning evidence in a murder investigation.

'I can't get him to give it up,' Julie said. 'I've tried, I promise. It's so bad for his cholesterol.'

Brewing coffee for me (she preferred herb tea herself), Julie asked if I'd care to see a videotaped documentary about the temple she'd helped make, and resigning myself to a very dull hour, I agreed.

'If you enjoy it, perhaps you could write a few words for me?' she said. 'I want to get it shown on television.' Julie told me that she'd spent a year at Sri Rampa's temple in India, obtaining an entirely new set of spiritual values. Puzzled as to why she'd ended up in Beverly Hills, I learnt that Sri Rampa had recently established a second temple in Los Angeles and that Julie had only taken the job nursing my grandfather to help fund it. 'The people here need us,' she said. Ever cynical, I could guess what Sri Rampa needed in return.

Recrossing the yard, I saw the pool man polishing the black and silver coachwork of Grandpa's Bentley, and went over to reintroduce myself. Delighted to hear that I was from England, Ernesto's hand felt like warm rope.

'Michael Owen,' he said, his smile revealing a gold tooth.

'Who?' I asked.

Ernesto used two fingers to describe a goal scored by the diminutive England striker in a recent international football match. 'I played for my town in Salvador when I was seventeen years old,' he said.

'What made you come north?' I asked, expecting a woeful tale of state-sponsored terrorism.

'My wife is a United States citizen,' Ernesto replied.

*

At lunchtime, I was racing through the manuscript when the intercom buzzed in the pool house: Grandpa was in the library and wished to see me.

Bolt upright in a wingback armchair, he was wide-eyed with anxiety. 'I can't stand the tension, my dear boy,' he said. 'How far have you got?'

Perching myself on a sofa, I told him that I'd read about 200 pages.

'D'you think there's something there, Ralph? Is there a book in it?' My grandfather's eyes bored into me, and I felt the full force of his undiminished will pressing me into complicity. Given my propensity to tell my elders what they wanted to hear, my answer was a foregone conclusion.

'Of course,' I said. 'But it's going to need a lot of work.'

Grandpa's shoulders dropped. 'Marvellous. And d'you think you can do it?'

I coughed. 'Sorry, do what exactly?'

He blinked, the word 'ghostwrite' threatening to materialize in letters of cotton wool between us.

'Um, lash it into shape,' Grandpa said. 'So we can show the publishers three chapters by the end of the month.' That gave me under three weeks. 'Come on, Ralph. They've got me over a barrel on this because I told them I was nearly there with the damn thing. I know you can do it.'

'I'll try,' I said. 'But I can't promise anything.' Grandpa hollered in delight and I had the unpleasant sense that I'd thrown away an advantage. 'I'll need to, er, retype almost all of it,' I added.

'Of course you will. It's a shame I never got the hang of a typewriter myself.' Or pen and paper, I thought. 'Anyhow, it's all in that contraption over there,' Grandpa said, indicating the PC on the table by the door. 'Think you can use it?'

I nodded. The IBM was a museum piece from the 1980s, but by chance I'd typed my first play on a similar model.

23

With my pride shattered following the devastating reversal of the OUDS audition, I'd pounded out a short piece based on some texts by Gertrude Stein which my college dramatic society staged. It was a wretched play, but at least it served to introduce me to a number of fellow students committed to experimental theatre as an instrument of social change, and the following year, we put on a much-improved version of my play which won an award at the Edinburgh Festival. Naming ourselves Direct Debit, we hit the road on leaving university, and over the next five years, fuelled by little more than idealism, I'd written or co-written a dozen plays for the company on my IBM. Now my grandfather was asking me to use one to work on his memoirs, and I felt inordinately sad about the way things had turned out.

The following day, Grandpa was driven to a recording studio in the San Fernando Valley to read a few pages of Keats' poetry on to tape for a Federal Arts programme. Returning at lunchtime from that 'faery land forlorn', as he described it, to eat a light meal in the den, he enquired after my progress on the transcript. Having surmounted my jet lag and speed-read a huge chunk of the text, I wanted to start work from the point of Grandpa's return to London in 1950. This section was concise and reasonably coherent, and he'd detailed the indiscretions of various notables with a relish that was likely to whet the appetite of Shaugnessy King, his publishers, especially since most of the people he'd disparaged were now too dead to sue for defamation.

Hearing my proposal, Grandpa frowned. 'What are you saying, dear boy? That there's something the matter with the opening as it stands?'

On the back foot, I suggested that it might have taken him a little while to really find his voice and, after some mild bickering, finally won my case by promising to work on the beginning of his story as soon as his publishers' immediate needs had been met. Nevertheless, our conversation was strained as we ate Julie's lamb cutlets with the Frank Cooper's mint sauce I'd brought over from England, and it crossed my mind that Grandpa had only asked me to work on the book in the belief that a grandson would be easier to control than a professional writer. Despair gripped me: not only was I now faced with the miserable prospect of repeated skirmishes over the text, but I was also acting in bad faith since it seemed unlikely to me that the book could ever be published.

From the start, I'd doubted that Shaugnessy King were as frantic to see the manuscript as my grandfather maintained, and rather sensed that the eagerness he imputed to them was in fact a mere projection of his own desire to make a pre-emptive strike on posterity. But when Grandpa told me that he'd received an advance of $500,000 for the book (a sum he regarded as niggardly compared to the spoils obtained by other, lesser stars), I could well understand his publishers' desperation to recoup their money. Yet this seemed a remote possibility. Grandpa's stain on the silence had already been ten years in the making, and all too easily I could see myself working on it for years to come, ghostwriting the life of a man who might well have become a ghost himself by the time it was ready for publication.

That evening, almost fossilized with boredom, I wandered through the downstairs rooms feeling like a parolee confined to the house by an electronic tag. My father still hadn't responded to the messages I'd left on his answering machine in Laurel Canyon, and I had to assume he was away. My second cousin Danny Tait, the television actor, Grandpa's great-nephew, had recently bought a house in Malibu, but he too had failed to get back to me. All the old friends in my address book were out of town or their numbers had changed, and there were no new listings for them.

Two of the oak bookcases in the library were devoted to showbusiness biography, and a paperback copy of Kirk

Douglas's autobiography found its way into my hands. The first few pages lifted my mood, because if this kind of writing could become an 'International No.1 Bestseller', Grandpa's memoirs might not need as much attention as I'd feared. In the night, I persevered with *The Ragman's Son* until Douglas's 'breathtaking shots', 'exclusive restaurants' and tireless self-promotion led me to turn off the light. Lying in the darkness, I heard a grating sound outside my door, and stepping out on to the landing, saw that Julie's door was ajar.

'Hey, Ralph,' came a voice from the bottom of the stairs. 'Can I get you something?' Julie was wearing a kimono and holding a glass of milk. Shaking my head, I told her that I was just having trouble sleeping. 'Me too,' she said. 'May I sit with you while I drink my soya?'

Once inside my room, Julie sat on the end of my bed with her legs curled beneath her. She'd unplaited her long brown hair, which reached the small of her back. Wearing boxer shorts, I took the chair by the window and sat sideways so as not to expose myself.

'You look tense,' she said. Shifting herself on the bed-spread, Julie fiddled with a blue stone that she wore on a chain around her neck and told me that Sri Rampa himself had given it to her during the course of a private audience in India. 'He created it in his hand,' she said. 'I was about to leave and he just made it for me.'

'Sure,' I said. 'And how long were his sleeves?'

Julie laughed. 'Right now, at this very moment, you and I are communicating in one dimension. What if I told you that there are thirty-one other dimensions, Ralph? Dimensions that you're not even aware of?' There was so much to say about this that I didn't know where to begin. 'Sri Rampa's a Holy Man,' she continued. 'He has this incredibly strong aura and he's so close to the Divinity that people feel his presence as a kind of physical force. Pilgrims come to see him from all over the world. I was incredibly lucky to get to meet him in person.'

'I can believe that,' I said. 'But please don't tell me he can make jewellery in the palm of his hand.'

For some reason, Julie thought this was hysterical. 'Like I said, Ralph, thirty-two different dimensions.' When she stretched over to place her glass on the bedside table, the kimono outlined her breast. 'Are you feeling tired?' she asked, swinging her legs off the bed.

'Not really,' I said. 'I guess I'll read for a while.'

'I could give you a massage. You look stressed.'

I tried to put up a struggle but Julie persisted, so I lay face down on the bed as instructed. It was the first time anyone else's hands had been on me in months, and she loosened my knotted shoulder muscles with firm fingers, but when she moved round the bed, her brown legs passed inches from my face, and it all went wrong for me. As Julie worked on my arms and began to pull my fingers, my cock swelled almost painfully against the mattress, and I tried to picture horrible things to make it go away. Boarding-school food. A dead dog I once saw in a ditch in Mexico. Kirk Douglas. Nothing worked. I had to get her to leave.

'Mmm, that's great,' I said. 'Thank you, Julie. I think I can sleep now.'

'Nonsense. I haven't even started yet. Turn on to your back.'

Putting her hands under me, she flipped me over. I tried to raise my legs but wasn't quick enough. Seeing my erection tent my shorts, Julie smiled.

'Don't be ashamed,' she said. 'It's perfectly natural. I'll be right back.'

Julie left the room, and I was desperate. A medical student had once told me that if a nurse bathed a male patient and he developed an erection, the nurse would give it a firm slap to make it subside, so I picked up Kirk Douglas's autobiography and gave myself a thwack. If my grandfather had invested in the hardback edition, it might have worked, but Julie returned to find me sitting up on the bed with *The Ragman's Son* held aloft, mustering my courage.

'Relax, Ralph. It's OK,' she said. 'I need to make love too.'

Julie whipped off her kimono, and I watched speechless as she draped it over the lampshade, bathing the room in a green watery light. With a tiny waist, round behind and small high breasts, Julie had a dancer's body. She clambered on to the bed stark-naked, holding a bottle of aromatherapy oil, half of which she proceeded to smear into my torso while humming a tune to herself. In a thin voice, I asked her for the name of the song, but she ignored me, and when I tried to get up, she pressed me back down with her splayed hand, the ends of her long dark hair dragging across my chest.

'Have you ever practised *carezza*?' Julie asked. 'Your chakras are way out and it might help realign them.'

*Carezza* was a healing love technique that she'd learnt in India. My aura was kind of weak, she added, slithering on top of me to roll a prophylactic on to my penis with a degree of expertise that bordered on the professional. Then, all of a sudden, I was inside her.

'Hey, relax, Ralph. The whole idea is that you don't come, OK? We want to harness your energy. Marshal it, not squander it.'

Julie's breasts nosed through the curtain of her hair. When I put my hands on them, she told me not to touch her but rather to imagine a flower opening and closing with each breath I took. It occurred to me that she was insane.

'It's all in the breathing,' she said.

Her pelvis was moving gently back and forth, as if she was using me to stir herself. Julie said something and I asked her to say it again, but she pretended not to hear me. Her tan, matte skin was extraordinarily soft and smooth, and I got harder and harder. When she stopped moving, the muscles in her vagina contracted, holding me still and very tight. Stripped to the waist, Kirk Douglas glared at me from the cover of his autobiography, which was propped against the pillow.

'Are you coming?' Julie asked.

Bewildered, I shook my head. Leaning all the way back

like a limbo dancer, Julie moved up and down my erection. Her hair tickled my calves. After a minute of this she came back up to face me, catching her breath.

'Try to imagine the flower opening and closing,' Julie said. 'At the base of your skull. Where it meets your spine. A big pink flower with beautiful petals. See it open to the sun as you breathe in, and close up when you exhale.'

Julie went still again, but every time she took a breath, her vagina squeezed me. I struggled to hold off an orgasm, but each time her flower opened and closed, I was losing more ground.

'Julie –'

Leaping off me, she pressed a thumb hard into the root of my penis, just above my testicles. It was excruciatingly painful, but the immediate danger was averted.

'Let's try again,' she said. 'Empty your mind this time, and when I say so, only think of the flower, OK?'

Climbing back on top of me, Julie moved her hips in a circling, clockwise motion. Then she went the other way. Her thumb seemed to have done the trick, and when she told me to think of the flower, I managed to picture a rose, speckled with dew, opening and closing against the stone wall of an English country churchyard. But it was impossible for me to sustain the meditation for more than a few seconds.

I opened my eyes and saw Julie's breasts in the green light, their nipples hard. Breaking all the rules, I grabbed them and bucked up into her. Julie gasped and made a rapid jerking movement. Shuddering, she sighed with what I took at the time to be irritation, but looking back, I'm not so sure. Although I contributed nothing more than a flesh peg to the proceedings and can therefore take little credit for any pleasure she might have received, I think it's possible that Julie enjoyed a small orgasm. In any case, she dismounted me, her face flushed and slack, murmuring that perhaps we could try again another time.

'In India we'd make love like that six times a day,' she said. 'Sometimes more. It can really open your channels, you know?'

My erection wobbled as she took some deep breaths and then she was gone, leaving me no closer to the godhead.

The next morning, Julie acted as if nothing had happened between us, and we circled each other a little warily. Neither regretting our attempt at *carezza* nor wishing to repeat it, I sensed that Julie felt the same way. To her intense irritation, Bruce had prepared a cheeseburger for himself on his return from Ojai, stinking out the kitchen with the smell of burnt fat, and the ensuing tension brought back the atmosphere of our house in Chelsea before my father finally left us. In my mind's eye, I can still see the avocado stone, transfixed by three cocktail sticks, sprouting a white tendril into the brackish water of a glass beaker on the kitchen windowsill while my parents and I ate *boeuf bourguignonne* in strained silence.

That afternoon, Julie put a call through to the pool house from somebody called Scott Newton. Scott was an editor at Shaugnessy King in New York, and Australian. Learning that my grandfather was taking his afternoon nap, Scott said he was pleased that I was working on the book and that he'd dearly love to see some material when he flew out to Los Angeles in two weeks' time.

'Your grandfather's a bit coy about showing us what he's written, Ralph. In fact, it's getting to the point where some people here are beginning to lose faith in the book, and I really don't want to let that happen.'

'Don't worry. I'll be able to show you three chapters when you get here,' I said. 'On the London theatre in the 1950s. There's some really good stuff in there.'

Unimpressed, Scott asked me to prepare the 1960s and 1970s sections first and wondered if I could e-mail him a sneak preview of the material as it stood. When I told him that I'd need to discuss these matters with my grandfather,

Scott reminded me that my fee hadn't yet been agreed. Disliking Newton, I was nonetheless struck by his determination to get his hands on the copy. Before hanging up, he asked if I thought there was any chance Donald might be persuaded to change his title.

'There's a general feeling here that *To Be! A Player's Odyssey* might be a little recherché for our market. That we might do better with something more sales-led like *Tait: Actor*. With a colon, of course.'

'Of course.'

'We think it has a ring to it. By the way, is there any mention of a Gene Bailey in the manuscript?' The name was new to me, and I said so. 'Nothing too important,' Newton continued. 'But call me if you come across it. A possible legal snag. See you in a fortnight, OK?'

Replacing the handset, I noticed Bruce over by the pepper tree, naked save for an athletic support, red-faced and sleek with sweat.

'Hi, Ralph. How's it going?' he called to me. 'I just won my tennis match.' Stepping out of his athletic support, my uncle threw it on top of his tennis clothes and dived straight into the pool. Five minutes later, he emerged from the water and came into the pool house, dripping wet, to grab a towel from the stack.

'What you got there?' he asked me.

'Grandpa's book,' I said.

Transfixed by the computer screen, Bruce was bathed in the light of what was for him a Holy text. 'It's great that you're helping Pops out,' he muttered.

Betraying his sense of exclusion, Bruce's tone dismayed me because my uncle needed me to be his ally, not his rival for the role of Grandpa's helpmeet. Newton's query had pricked my curiosity, and keen to discover Gene Bailey's identity, I'd begun searching the various floppy disks on which about a quarter of the manuscript had been backed up. Asked if he knew the name, Bruce's eyes emptied and he shook his head, so I showed him how the software worked, and invited him to search one of the documents for me, but he was soon bored.

'You should visit with your dad, Ralph. He wants to see you.'

'You talked to Larry? Is he back?'

Bruce looked blank and I repeated my questions, but he'd retreated into a world of his own, forming shadows on the far wall with his hands.

After dinner, Julie complained about some dishes Bruce had left in the sink and raised her voice to him. Julie and I had been over-polite to each other all evening, but her treatment of my uncle seemed unfair, and when he'd left the room, I tried to explain his behaviour to her. Hadn't she realized his limitations?

'I know what you're saying, Ralph, but sometimes he just doesn't try at all,' she said. 'And it upsets your grandfather, the way he can't seem to do anything right.'

'That's just not true.'

Julie took hold of my arm. 'Hey,' she said. 'This isn't about Bruce. It's about you and me. I had fun last night, but it was a mistake. My spiritual teacher at the temple says we can't do it again. Period. But I'm hoping we can still be friends. OK?'

I nodded, much relieved, and later that night found myself in Julie's room watching a video of happy people chanting under the beneficent gaze of a smiling bearded gnome – Sri Rampa. Julie was likeable but happily crackers, and I was more than satisfied with the way things had worked out, especially when she let slip that she'd only made love to me because she'd thought I was lonely. To seal our pact, I wrote a glowing endorsement of her film.

By the end of the first week, life with my grandfather was beginning to suffocate me. Even when I wasn't working on his book, his image was everywhere in the house, rendered in oil, cartoon sketch or in shades of grey by Karsh of Ottawa, and his eyes monitored my every waking moment. Only a day trip we were planning to Ojai promised some release.

An hour-and-a-half's drive north west of Los Angeles, the house on the side of the Ojai valley provided Grandpa with a refuge from the city's heat and pollution. Julie adored the little town because of its association with Krishnamurti, an Indian guru who'd lived there for many years, and she considered it to be a very spiritual place, a view doubtless reflected in the exorbitant land values that prevailed in the area, according to Bruce. Anxious about my uncle's work on the property, a concern fanned by Julie's frequently aired doubts as to Bruce's competence, my grandfather had decreed that we'd all make a visit.

The excursion was planned with military efficiency, but at the last moment, Grandpa decided we should take the Bentley, claiming that it was 'in need of a good run'. Wearing his golfing hat and a blazer, he backed up to the passenger door, and Bruce and I helped him into the car, taking pains not to knock his head on the roof. My grandfather cursed when he dropped his cane on to the driveway, and across the street, a neighbour in a grey tracksuit gawked at us before retreating into his Modernist bungalow. Climbing into the back of the car alongside Julie, I knew every whorl and curlicue of the walnut panel on the back of the front seat from seemingly interminable childhood car journeys. From behind, Grandpa resembled a little boy dressed in oversize clothes, and only his large ears indicated his true age. Soon enough, an eighty-foot cut-out of a wine bottle on Santa Monica Boulevard inspired him to recite Keats.

'O for a beaker full of the warm South,
Full of the true, the blushful Hippocrene,
With beaded bubbles winking at the brim,
And purple-stained mouth . . .'

A voice-over contract with a Napa Valley wine producer loomed large on the horizon.

'Your Aunt Eleanor called this morning, Ralph,' said Grandpa. 'Did I tell you she's going to be playing Lady M in the Scottish play at the Ahmanson Theater here in Los Angeles?'

Meeting my grandfather's eyes in the rear-view mirror, I shook my head and tried not to panic. 'When does Eleanor arrive?' I asked.

'Next week,' he replied. 'In time for my birthday party.' Even though I'd been told that Grandpa had invited more than a hundred people, it had slipped my mind that my aunt might be coming. 'But don't worry about it,' he added. 'She and Roger have a house above the Strip now, so they won't interrupt our work.'

This did nothing to calm my nerves. Quite the opposite. A celebrated actress on both sides of the Atlantic, Aunt Eleanor had wed a New York producer some ten years previously. Widely considered to be a great beauty, my aunt had no children of her own, and a decade in Manhattan (years that had recently included her forty-seventh birthday) was unlikely to have mellowed her. If Grandpa had told her that my play was coming to Broadway, a single telephone call might be enough to undo me.

Craving nicotine, I noticed that many of our fellow motorists were smoking with grim fervour, sealed into their four-wheel killing jars. Even though the Bentley's interior was stifling on account of its primitive air-conditioning, Julie was perfectly at one with herself while I was at sixes and sevens, struggling to put the thought of Aunt Eleanor's impending arrival, and a cigarette, from my mind. According to a sign at the verge, this stretch of Ventura freeway had been 'adopted' by Margaux and John Lushing, and cracks in the road surface had been filled with tar, black dribbles that wiggled like the sutures of a cranium. Bruce was forced to swerve around a pothole just before the Topanga Canyon exit, and when I mentioned Scott Newton's call, Grandpa's neck jerked upright.

34

'Newton? That Australian they've hired? No idea about the creative process,' he said. 'What did you tell him?'

'Not a thing. I stalled him. I promised him three chapters when he gets out here in a fortnight. He asked if I'd come across the name Gene Bailey.'

Groaning, my grandfather explained that Jean (not Gene) Bailey was John Blumenthal's wife, the former starlet Grandpa was thought to have dishonoured in his autobiography.

'John must've put his lawyers on to Shaugnessy King,' he said. 'The bastard sends me an invitation to a charity bash one week and then does this to me the next. Can you believe it? The old goat used to be a close friend and now he's trying to give me a bloody coronary.'

The back of Grandpa's neck had flushed an unhealthy red and, worried that Blumenthal's wishes were about to come true, I suggested telling Newton that neither he nor Blumenthal had anything to worry about since I'd come across no mention of the name Bailey in the manuscript.

'Never,' Grandpa roared. 'Let the vermin stew. Someone's got to take a stand on a thing like this, and I absolutely refuse to be bullied by some blasted coat-hanger manufacturer. You hear me?'

As Grandpa went on to invoke his Constitutional right to free speech, his extraordinary vehemence upset Bruce, who drifted on to the shoulder and blew out a tyre. Motorists slowed to enjoy a moment of *schadenfreude* as my uncle and I laboured to change the wheel, sweat sluicing from every pore in the midday furnace. Pulling up on his motorcycle, a highway patrolman positively effervesced when he recognized Grandpa as the actor who'd portrayed Chief Brannigan, and the young man's eyelids fluttered with feeling as he confessed that my grandfather had inspired him to choose a career in law enforcement. It wasn't for me to point out that the officer was conflating the actor with the role he'd played. Watching each and every episode of the show as a

35

child in Britain, fascinated by the bright and very alien world it depicted, I'd done exactly the same thing, mixing up my grandfather and Brannigan, a happy paterfamilias and dispenser of wise counsel with a Boston-Irish brogue. Back then, I'd no idea that Grandpa had been married four times.

As the cop's knees buckled in an involuntary act of genuflection, I saw how hard it had been for my grandfather to retain even the slightest trace of humility. The whole world appeared to buttress his vanity, including the police force, and even though Grandpa had always dismissed his television work as mere bread and butter, the flattery went some way towards compensating him for the nuisance of the burst tyre. Without a second spare, Julie urged him to abandon the trip to Ojai, and when he finally agreed, the patrolman insisted on escorting us back to the San Diego freeway.

# Chapter Three

'Irving cannot resist seeking after the picturesque
even in his slightest movement. If he wishes to touch
his chin, he raises his arm and encircles it, his hand
makes the tour of his head, striking the audience as it
does so with a sense of its leanness, and never seizes
the point of his beard till after it has described a
complete circle.'

B. C. Coquelin, *Harper's New Monthly Magazine*,
May 1887

From the moment Aunt Eleanor arrived in Los Angeles the
following week, I was on tenterhooks. Having still not told
my grandfather the truth about Direct Debit, I'd decided that
my best option was to confess all to Eleanor at the first opportunity and to beg her to keep my secret. Grandpa had invited
her for dinner, and on her third day in the city, a car pulled
into the front drive at six-thirty, early even for Los Angeles.

Tall and stick thin, my aunt emerged wearing a Viet Cong-
style pyjama suit. With her enormous eyes and angular nose,
Eleanor's abundant, centre-parted white hair made her look
like a beautiful, if monochrome, Afghan hound. Watching
her from my bedroom window, my resolve wilted and I
fastened on to the hope that she'd be too embarrassed to
mention my theatre work over dinner. Despite the regular
mail-shots I'd sent her over the years, Eleanor had never once
attended a Direct Debit performance. Towards the end, I'd
taken to personalizing our flyers with increasingly desperate
marginalia, but my aunt's scribbled excuses had become ever
more threadbare before eventually drying up altogether.

Maddeningly, her own work had been harder for me to
avoid. Still inundated with offers, my aunt benefited from her

dual nationality, and her successful stage career had hardly been damaged by appearances in a number of mainstream motion pictures over the past twenty-five years. Notwithstanding her apparent lack of interest in Direct Debit, the world of the theatre is so small that it was quite possible that Eleanor had heard of our misfortunes, or more to the point, my misfortunes. I could only pray that my grandfather wouldn't repeat my lies about the play in front of her.

From the landing, I saw him make his way across the hall, accompanied by Julie, who, to my surprise, had put on a white uniform dress of the kind formerly worn by Mrs O'Connor. When Julie opened the front door, Eleanor made her entrance, throwing her arms wide.

'More happy love,' Grandpa boomed, stooped over his cane as if he'd become stuck taking a curtain call. 'More happy, happy love.'

'Daddy darling. How simply wonderful.' Eleanor cried.

Like her father, Eleanor had taken pains to preserve her English accent, and she stretched her vowel sounds into luxurious groans of pleasure. As Grandpa responded with a tinny whoop, she bent to kiss him on both cheeks, but stiffly, as if afraid of catching something.

'Dear boy,' Grandpa called to me. 'Your aunt's here.'

'Ralph,' Eleanor cried, going into a double air-kiss (repeat) manoeuvre. 'How lovely to see you.'

Grandpa found it difficult to negotiate the series of steps that led down into the living room, so he invited Eleanor and I to go on ahead. As he set off on his ramped route via the library, my aunt looked on, her eyes puddled with tears.

'I'm sorry, Ralph,' she whispered. 'I'd no idea how bad he'd got.'

'You mean Grandpa? It's only his knee,' I said, leading her down to the living room. 'Otherwise he's as healthy as can be.'

Eleanor was as tall as me in her flat shoes, strange rubberized moccasins that resembled black duck bills.

'It's so horrible to see him shrunken up like that,' she said.

'He's all right. Really. He's just getting on.'

I tried to comfort her but she broke away to snuffle into her crisp, white handkerchief. 'Look, Ralph, I owe you an apology. I feel awful that I haven't kept in touch with you,' she said. 'I should have –'

'It's OK. It doesn't matter.'

In retrospect, this would have been the ideal moment for me to tell Eleanor about my lies, but taken aback by her unexpected tenderness, I fixed myself a Dr Pepper instead. Drawn to the two dozen photographs ranked on the lid of the piano, my aunt's lips twitched to point out that I featured in more of them than any other family member. To my embarrassment, Grandpa had even framed a snap of me rehearsing Direct Debit in a community theatre in Rotterdam, yet only three pictures of Eleanor were on display, three publicity shots and one of her out of character. In this print, bleached to pale yellow and turquoise by the sun, Jerry Bauer had portrayed her with Bruce against the pool-house wall, and examining the photograph with the innocence of total narcissism, Eleanor murmured something I couldn't hear. Many times over the next few weeks, my aunt would drop her voice for no apparent reason, making me crane forward to pay her the very close attention she felt she deserved. I asked her to repeat herself.

'Do you know', she said, 'that I've only ever been to this house five times? How long are you planning to stay here?'

'A month or two I guess. I don't really know. I'm helping Grandpa with his memoirs.'

Replacing the photograph of herself and Bruce in a more prominent position, Eleanor obscured photographs of myself and of Pistol, her father's last, beloved labrador. 'It must be wonderful to write,' she said. 'If only one could find the time.'

Petrified that she was going to ask me about Direct Debit, I let slip that Grandpa's memoirs included an impassioned description of her début on the London stage. '*I went to the first night of* Kaleidoscope *with Binkie and darling Joyce,*' her father had written (or rather dictated). '*The play was forgettable fare, but Eleanor was tremendous, and when Trevor dried in the second act, she ad-libbed brilliantly. I was terribly proud of her. She curtsied to me at the curtain call, and then some idiot put a spotlight on me so I was forced to stand up and take a bow myself. There was a tear in my eye, I don't mind telling you. Like Banquo, I'd founded a dynasty, but unlike Banquo, I also got to wear the crown because over supper Peter asked me to play Richard the Third for him . . .*' Embellishing Grandpa's praise out of all recognition, I told Eleanor that he'd described her performance as the most auspicious début the London stage had seen in living memory, and wondered if I'd taken it too far. But it was impossible to take it too far. Eleanor's appetite for approval, especially approval from her father, knew no limit, and when I finally ran out of lies, she only just remembered to ask after my mother.

Eleanor and I had barely tilled the topsoil of my mother's marriage to her third husband, a Scots composer, when Bruce bounded into the room to hug his sister with real joy. Following their mother's nervous breakdown, Eleanor and Bruce had been raised from the ages of five and three, respectively, by their British grandparents, or rather by their grandparents' retainers. Bruce had begun to suffer fits a few years later, and he'd been brought over to the United States and cared for by Grandpa and his third wife, a French actress whose name was never mentioned, but Eleanor had remained in England.

As Bruce told Eleanor about the work he was doing at Ojai, she seemed to relax, but the moment Grandpa and Julie joined us, my aunt stiffened up again and embarked on a sweeping account of the problems she'd had refurbishing her house on Doheny Drive.

'And just when I thought the whole frightful saga was over, darling, there was a leak in one of the guest bathrooms,' she groaned. 'Can you believe it? Of course, they had to come back and repaint the entire kitchen. It's been a living nightmare, and I've hardly had a chance to sit down since I landed.'

Sipping a weak Scotch, Grandpa seemed bored, but his daughter didn't appear to notice and kept up her monologue as Julie served us grilled asparagus in the dining room. Having rehearsed the part of Lady Macbeth for three weeks in New York to fit around the commitments of a leading man who'd made his name playing a bald *mafioso* on television, Eleanor proceeded to regale us with the difficulties she faced in adapting her performance to the Ahmanson's stage.

'Now I'm meant to play half the banquet scene with my back to the audience,' she cried. 'I mean, it's preposterous.'

Eleanor's shrill tone finally got to Grandpa. 'I can't stand the Ahmanson,' he said. 'Ghastly theatre. I played there in '89. *Cat on a Hot Tin Roof.* And loathed every minute of it. Absolutely no atmosphere.'

Faltering, Eleanor moved on to question Grandpa about his health and his diet. 'I do wish you'd take selenium, Daddy. And there's this marvellous new mineral syrup they derive from kelp. I have two spoonfuls every morning. It'll work wonders on your knees. Julie can give it to you with your breakfast.'

'Over my dead body,' Grandpa said. 'I'm not slurping bloody algae at my age. Not for you or for anybody else for that matter.'

Eleanor gasped, and although Grandpa apologized for raising his voice, the taste of his temper lingered. It was a tense five minutes. As Bruce and I concentrated on keeping the food off our neckties, I recalled Lacan's definition of love as the giving of something you don't have to someone who doesn't exist, and felt for my aunt. After dinner we went through to the library, where she sat beside Grandpa on the sofa, facing a wall of framed playbills that charted his many triumphs on the stage.

'*Full Fathom Five*,' she said. 'I remember coming to see you in it. 1962?'

''64. On Broadway.'

Eleanor extended her hand towards her father, palm up on the cushion, but Grandpa's eyes had already misted over with memories in which she'd played at best a walk-on part. Bruce brought in a jug of decaffeinated coffee, and while he poured it into tiny china cups, I scanned the shelf above his head, intrigued by a number of books by the offspring of famous actors. One title, *I Couldn't Smoke the Grass on my Father's Lawn* by Michael (son of Charlie) Chaplin, struck a note of whimsical regret, while others, such as *PS I Love You* by Michael (son of Peter) Sellers, aimed for wry recrimination. A few went straight for the jugular, favouring the sledgehammer sarcasm of Christina Crawford's *Mommie Dearest* or the bitter punning of *Home Front* by Patricia Reagan. When Grandpa and Eleanor had exhausted the subject of his upcoming birthday celebrations, he asked, with a stage yawn, to be taken up to bed.

Left alone with me, Eleanor's face became drawn. 'Things certainly seem to have relaxed around here,' she said. 'Since Mrs O'Connor left.'

'You mean with Julie? Yes, Grandpa's very happy with her.'

'That's lucky. Of course, it helps that she's such a marvellous cook.' The words were drenched with irony. As a child, it had confused me that Aunt Eleanor often seemed to mean the exact opposite of what she said, and I'd assumed that she was getting away with her lies through some adult loophole. Later, of course, I'd learn the trick myself. Confiding to me that she was unable to drive, a real handicap in a city that revolved around a steering column, Eleanor asked me to run her home, and glad of another chance to come clean about Direct Debit, I was happy to comply.

As I slotted Grandpa's station wagon into the evening traffic on Sunset, Eleanor gave a little shudder, took a small brown medicine bottle from her bag and drew off some liquid with the glass dropper before dripping two globules on to her tongue.

'Bach Flower Remedy,' she said. 'I get so stressed seeing Daddy at the best of times. But it's my fault. I've left it all way too late. I blamed him for years, and now he's dying.'

'Oh, come on, he's not dying,' I said, convinced her words had been directed at the 'fourth wall'. 'He just gets a bit irritable when he's tired.'

My aunt sighed, and it occurred to me that unconsciously she wanted Grandpa dead so that she wouldn't have to worry about her relationship with him so much. It seemed quite possible that she would love him better buried.

'It's just that I get so worried that he doesn't approve of me. That he doesn't value my work. It's crazy,' she said. 'God, I need a massage.'

I braked involuntarily at the thought of Julie, and Eleanor shrieked. Accepting my apology, she rubbed at her temples and blamed her worsening headache on the visit to North Canon Drive. My aunt seemed far more unbuttoned than I remembered her, more emotional, and I liked her better for it. Grandpa had told me that her husband Roger Mooney had picked up a sinus infection on the flight from New York, so I asked how he was doing.

'Oh, Roger's absolutely fine. I just thought it best to see Daddy on my own,' Eleanor said. 'Do you know why I never had children? Because in this family we're too selfish to love them properly. At least with you it might be different. You're not so driven.'

'It's kind of you to say that,' I said.

'I'm sorry I never came to see your theatre company.' My fingers fastened on the wheel as if we were going to skid. Had she read my mind? 'You trained with Lecoq in Paris, didn't you, Ralph?'

'With Alain Knapp, at the Institut de la Personalité Créatrice,' I said. 'I was there for a summer, not the whole year. He wanted to make total theatrical creators. It was incredibly inspiring.'

Desperate to keep her off the subject of Direct Debit, I pontificated about clowns and described *commedia*'s recuperation by the bourgeoisie. Eleanor made encouraging noises, but too many of them, as if she was forcing herself to show an interest. And all the while I was scared I was going to crash the car. *I never came to see your theatre company.* Did my aunt's choice of tense mean that she knew that Direct Debit had disbanded?

'Daddy tells me you've won an award for most promising playwright,' she said. 'That's wonderful news.'

The air around my face went cold. 'Grandpa's got the wrong end of the stick. It was another prize we've won. A Fringe thing. You've never even heard of it. I mean, most people in the Fringe have never even heard of it. I shouldn't have mentioned it to him. I was showing off about nothing.'

'Hey, don't say that. Enjoy it, Ralph. Squeeze out every last drop. Daddy says there's even talk that Liz McCann's going to bring the play to Broadway.' Above Sunset, the road bent sharply, and I was on the point of blurting out the sad, painful truth when my aunt instructed me to turn up the curving drive of a Modernist glasshouse. 'I want you to come in and meet my stepdaughter,' she said. 'Park over there, would you?'

There was no arguing with Eleanor who, once inside the house, went straight upstairs, leaving me to roam around in a vast white, sparsely furnished living room. In a startling confusion of exterior and interior space, a corner of the swimming pool protruded into the room beneath a wall of glass the size of a cinema screen. Convinced that I was about to be exposed as a liar, I hiked over to look out at the carpet of lights that stretched all the way across the city to the horizon, giving a green glow to the darkening sky, and felt trapped.

Having changed into a white tunic, Eleanor returned holding her palm across the mouthpiece of a cordless phone.

'Here,' she said. 'It's your father.'

Cringing from the phone as if from a pinless grenade, I asked Eleanor why she'd called him.

'I didn't, darling,' she said. 'He happened to ring me, and I told him you were here. Why on earth wouldn't I? Talk to him, Ralph. He'd love to speak to you.'

Although I'd been trying to make contact with Larry for weeks, I was thrown. In retrospect, I was afraid that the deeper connection I wished for would be impossible to achieve. Taking the phone, I managed to ask Larry how he was doing.

'Well, I'm good, sonny,' he replied. 'It's so amazing you're here. Why don't you come over?'

'Now? To Laurel Canyon?'

'Sure. Why not?'

Since it was only nine o'clock, I felt I had to say yes, and when I returned the phone to Eleanor, she applauded my decision. 'Make things right with him, Ralph. I know how irritating he can be, but do try and give yourself a chance to stop being angry.'

This sounded like something she'd picked up from a shrink, but she meant well and I bit my lip, aware that a raised voice would only seem to corroborate her thesis.

'I understand what you're saying,' I said. 'But I'm not aware that I *feel* that angry with Larry.'

'Oh, but you are,' she intoned. 'And it's only by forgiving that you can be forgiven. See him for what he is, Ralph. A sad little boy who grew up trapped in his father's shadow.' Framed in the doorway wearing her white tunic, Eleanor might have been playing the Oracle at Delphi, reanimated for a guest appearance in *Star Wars*.

Many of the world's direst concept albums had been dreamt into being on the roads that curled up Laurel Canyon to Mulholland like plumes of marijuana smoke, and when I'd stayed with Larry as a child, the area had enjoyed none of Beverly Hills' respectability. Now, unsure exactly why I was doing so, I climbed Kirkwood Drive again, recognizing some of the overpriced shacks from previous visits. My father lived in a clapboard bungalow near the top of the canyon, and the closer I drew, the more apprehensive I became about seeing him again after so long. Just as I was beginning to fear that I'd overshot his house, Larry appeared in my main-beams wearing a white guayabera with his arms open Jesus-wide. Lacking the Saviour's omniscience, my father had presumably spied the station wagon winding its way up the road, but he held his pose as I parked beside his convertible with its Clinton campaign sticker sun-baked into the cracked cellophane of the rear window.

'Welcome,' Larry bellowed in a voice that would have carried all the way down to Sunset. 'I've been trying to call you in London,' he said, hugging me. 'I even tried your mother, but there was no reply.'

My mother was scrupulous about setting her answering machine, her umbilicus to her agent and the possibility of a part in a situation comedy, so, much as I wanted to, it was hard to believe him.

'Well, I've moved around a bit,' I said. 'I'm sorry. I should have given you my new number.'

Larry smiled. 'So you're staying with the old man?'

'Yes, he sent me a ticket. I thought I'd just get out here and surprise you. I called a couple of times.'

'I've been shooting in Mississippi. A pilot for a new show. God, it's so good to see you,' he shouted. While his sister was prone to whisper on occasion, Larry preferred life a little louder than most people, and in thirty years I doubt that I'd passed a single calm, peaceful hour in his company. 'Did your Grandpa tell you that he and I've been having some problems?' he asked.

'He didn't go into it,' I replied, paranoid that Larry had only invited me over to pick my brains on the matter.

Passing through the gate in the white wooden fence, we followed the illuminated path down through the trees, and Larry clapped me tentatively on the back. Reassured that he shared some of my own trepidation, I relaxed a fraction until I heard a buzz of voices coming from inside the house.

'It's OK,' Larry said, opening the French doors for me. 'Some neighbours dropped by to talk about Peter Brook. They're making a documentary. Just say hi, then we'll go out on the deck to talk.'

Entering the living room, the smell of marijuana brought back the time I'd come along the corridor aged six to find Larry playing Russian roulette with some fellow actors in the middle of the night. I'd screamed as my father put the pistol to his temple, failing to understand that he and his friends were simply fooling around with my toy cap gun, stoned. Cut up inside by the memory, I said hello to a bald man with a goatee beard and two skinny young women who were smoking the joint. Taking after his mother, Larry had been extremely handsome as a young man, with black hair, blue eyes and an unforced, reassuring smile. Perhaps because his working life had involved so much preening and little real labour, he looked much younger than his fifty-three years, and his female guests hung on his every word as he announced that I was a genius avant-garde playwright. I see now that nothing had changed; that, as always, everything in our lives had to be fantastic and wonderful, at least on the surface. But having endured some tired gossip concerning Brook's theatre work at the Bouffes du Nord, I was still hoping for something more from Larry when he finally led me out on to the deck and lit a candle in a glass wind-protector.

Several scripts lay by his chair, television scripts, and he kicked them aside as he sat down. At twenty-two, Larry had been possessed of sufficient passion for his craft to drag his tiny family to London (albeit in order to work with Peter Brook and divorce my mother), but like his own father, he'd ended up in Hollywood toiling in television. Best known for his work on *Galactic Patrolman*, the space series set at the precise point in the twenty-third century when shoulder pads and back-combed hairstyles were to enjoy a revival,

Larry hadn't done any work of artistic significance for more than a decade. *Patrolman* had run for eight seasons, resolving his alimony problems, but he'd come to see his acceptance of the role as a Faustian pact.

'Charly, the guy with the beard, is a producer,' Larry said. 'He came over to sound me out about doing an interview to camera on my work with Peter.'

As if rehearsing the interview, Larry proceeded to reminisce about his time with Brook, but I'd heard all the stories before so it was difficult to generate much interest. Success as a screen actor had come to Larry early, yet when he failed to win the Academy Award for which he'd been nominated as Best Supporting Actor, he felt the need to stretch himself artistically. Believing the British theatre to be the ultimate test of an actor's mettle, he traded our house in Topanga Canyon for a dismal terraced cottage off the King's Road in London shortly after my fourth birthday. My father had been encouraged in this decision by my mother Mary, a Coventry-born alumna of the Rank Charm School whose short-lived Hollywood career had fizzled to a halt shortly after I was born.

Once in Europe, Larry began work with Brook's company and soon found himself in Persepolis performing *Orghast*, a play written expressly for the group by Ted Hughes. 'The words', according to Brook in his memoir *Threads of Time*, '*were all* [Hughes's] *own, captured, he would say, in the strata of the brain where deep-rooted semantic forms arise, at the moment when they are becoming coated with shape and sonority but prior to the intervention of the higher levels of the cortex where concepts emerge.*' It's not hard to sympathize with the company's Iranian hosts, who, an outraged Brook informs us, '*watched every move with hostility and suspicion, constantly blocking the work they had seemed so anxious to encourage.*' Following a further mind-blowing odyssey through Niger, Nigeria, Dahomey and Mali, my father returned to London only to divorce my mother.

Leaving his crushed-velvet Herbert Johnson fedora to gather dust on the bent wood coat stand in the hall of our house in Chelsea, Larry went to live for a while with a Norwegian jewellery designer in Ibiza, but the relationship didn't last, and a year later he returned to the United States in a bid to reanimate his film career. The small groundbreaking films he'd made at this time were to my mind the best things he'd done, but if there are indeed seven ages of Man, my father always displayed a distinct preference for the third and the fourth, the one about 'bubble reputation'. Needless to say, he believed that his greatest work had been achieved with Peter Brook's company in the 1970s. As far as I knew, Larry was still married to his third wife Irene, a former widow who still had her own place up on Mulholland. Apparently she was in Europe, and Larry declared that he'd have gone with her if he hadn't been so busy on his film project.

'What's it about?' I asked.

Larry held up a copy of Ray Monk's biography of Wittgenstein, with the philosopher's face on the cover. 'What do you think, sonny? Spooky, no?'

Was this a joke? Give Wittgenstein another twenty pounds, a good tan, halve his IQ and, yes, on a dark street on a rainy night from a speeding car, you could just about mistake the man for my father. I didn't know quite how to react.

'Well?' he asked. 'What do you say?'

'Um, there is some physical resemblance I suppose, but a biopic of a philosopher?' I said, recollecting a Derek Jarman misfire on the same subject.

'I'm serious,' said Larry. 'I was thinking PBS. You could write the scripts. It'd be great for us to work on something worthwhile together.'

Perhaps so, but who would possibly want to watch a film about a man who'd sat motionless in a deck chair for hours on end? My father's self-delusion rendered me tongue-tied. Had he always been this far up his own backside?

'Hey, I almost forgot. Eleanor tells me you've won an Olivier award,' he said. 'And that the Schuberts are going in with Liz McCann to bring your play to New York. We've got to celebrate.'

'Hold on a second,' I said, appalled that the story was breaking so fast and getting inflated with every telling. 'There's a really, really faint, outside chance we might be going to Broadway but we only won a tiny prize. Sponsored by a new listings magazine. Grandpa and Eleanor have built it up out of all proportion. I'd forget about it if I was you.'

'Sure, sure. Now he's being modest. An Olivier Award,' Larry said, shaking his head. 'Remember that time we went to lunch at the old coot's place in Brighton?'

Named after my grandfather's good friend Laurence Olivier, my father had struggled to live up to the billing ever since, and the visit he and I had made to the Oliviers' home in Royal Crescent twenty years ago had been an awkward occasion. Even so, Larry Tait's ambivalence as to his own first name hadn't stopped him and my mother from christening me Ralph (long 'a', silent 'l'), a snobbish inflection that I'd struggled to live down ever since leaving boarding school (in radical theatre circles, I'd preferred my colleagues to employ the more commonplace short 'a' and to enunciate the 'l').

Lighting a fresh joint, Larry held the smoke in his lungs and squeezed his words out through clenched teeth as if trying to bench press five hundred pounds. Feeling the distance between us expand, I declined to smoke it with him.

'Good for you,' he said with a remote smile. 'They say cannabis can really mess with your sperm count.' My father's obsessive interest in such matters stemmed from a teenage motorcycle accident that had led a doctor to tell him he wouldn't be able to have children. Larry considered it a miracle that the persistent little sperm that was to become me had found a way to breach the impasse, and I'd been told that it was for this reason that I was an only child.

'Now,' Larry said, leaning forward to lay a hand on my arm. 'When are you going to give me some grandchildren?' This was the first personal question he'd asked me, but he still managed to turn it round to himself, and I asked myself if he'd always been this self-obsessed or if it had just got worse over the years. Shrugging uneasily, I turned to gaze at the lights of the Downtown district. 'I've got to mend fences with the old man before this birthday thing,' Larry continued. 'I guess there's a lot to do on his autobiography, huh?'

'It's a bigger job than Grandpa led me to expect,' I said.

'Hah. I knew Pa was full of shit, telling everybody it was nearly finished,' he said. 'Is there much about us in it? You and me?'

'Not a great deal,' I said. In fact there was next to nothing. 'It's mostly about his work.'

'Jesus, that's so typical.'

Walking me up to the road, Larry touched on his difficulties with my grandfather. 'It's about Bruce,' he said. 'What happens to Bruce after, you know . . . When the old man passes on.'

The thought was left hanging in the air as Larry stubbed out his joint, dug a hole in the earth, and buried it with a degree of pyrophobic overkill common among canyon-dwellers.

'I love you so much, sonny,' he said, wrapping his arms around me. 'You know that don't you?'

'Yes,' I said. 'And I love you too.'

Astonished as I was that this man was my father, I still thought I meant it. Driving away in the station wagon, I watched Larry wave me off in the rear-view mirror, knowing he wouldn't stop until I was out of sight.

Unwilling to go directly back to Grandpa's house, I drove up to Mulholland Drive. The road surface was in poor condition and few barriers protected the careless driver from the sheer drop on one side. On a perilous turn, some oncoming headlights almost blinded me, so I pulled over and climbed on foot to the top of a small promontory from where I could look down at the city while listening to the self-piteous whine of a Country singer on the car radio. Larry had seemed different to the way I remembered him, and I'd not felt close to him at all. Feeling drained and listless, I tracked a car's progress up Coldwater Canyon, just as Larry must have watched the station wagon, and recalled that to elucidate his 'alienation effect' Brecht had quoted the Eskimo definition of a car as 'a wingless aircraft that crawls along the ground'.

Driving back along the Strip, I opened my last pack of duty-free cigarettes beneath an illuminated billboard advertising an upcoming feature film. Contemplating its human stars, an ageing actor and a buxom newcomer, it struck me how tough it must have been for Larry when the good work dried up in a place that invites you to measure yourself against the gloating faces on the very billboards that he'd himself graced as a young man.

Five minutes later, my resolution not to drink evaporated and I found myself at the bar of the Chateau Marmont, ordering a vodka and tonic on auto-pilot, quite heedless of California's draconian drink-driving laws. The children of 'right-on' parents who went right on and on like mine often die young or end up as teetotal financial analysts, so I took my first two drinks slowly, but within an hour I'd made firm friends with three smashed Japanese, two men and a woman I'd come across smoking cigars and drinking neat malt whisky in the plastic-swathed patio area. We were doing fine until one of my companions tried to procure the services of the Goth waitress with the blue eye shadow. When he was ejected from the premises, I decided to make some even newer friends. After that, the evening became more than a little hazy.

The next thing I knew, I was lying flat out on a firm bed. Opening my eye, a shard of daylight stabbed in through the chink and a clothes hanger appeared to be hovering hookless against a window. Growing accustomed to the awful brightness, I saw that the hanger was part of an electric trouser press made out of fake red wood. The lush, sickening swirls of the photo-processed grain made me retract my poisoned head beneath the sheet. Every single cell in my body ached. With no idea as to how I'd ended up in this bedroom, my breathing sounded unnaturally heavy and laboured, but all too soon I realized that it wasn't my breathing at all. There was someone in bed beside me. Like a snake darting back into the brush, I recoiled. Her hair was a bundle of brass wire darkening at the root, and her deeply tanned shoulder had the texture of crepe paper. A full bottle of white wine stood on the bedside table, along with two empty glasses. Across the chair at the foot of the bed lay a pair of beige leather trousers that were covered in strange pimples. Ostrich skin. Some of it came back to me. Hadn't she said her name was Natalie?

A blue ceramic bowl on the dresser contained a handful of golf tees. In my hurry to get dressed, I tripped over her handbag and, stubbing my toe against a chair leg, hopped around on the carpet, screaming in silence while Natalie and her husband smiled at me from a photograph on the bureau. Hurtling down the curving staircase and out on to the porch, I closed the front door quietly behind me. It was 11 a.m. and it looked like Brentwood.

With my car back at the Chateau Marmont, I'd no option but to walk and in no time I was lost in a labyrinth of more or less identical curving roads. Each intersection opened up more vistas of large pale houses and over-tended front lawns, a sterile nightmare suburb that might have been planned by M. C. Escher. The sun beat down on my headache and I soon suffered a hideous floating sensation, as if my feet weren't quite connecting with the sidewalk. There was no sign of any other human being until, fighting off yet another tide of nausea, I came across an elderly woman watering her gardenias, but the moment she saw me, she scuttled inside her house. Well within what I rather fatuously took to be my rights, I went up to her front door and rang the bell. If I hadn't been so dehydrated, I'd have been hosed with sweat. A small window slid back in the door, and I glimpsed a solitary eye beyond the wrought iron grille before it snapped shut and failed to reopen. Feeling as if I was being cooked alive in a non-stick pan, I walked on until a Westec patrol car intercepted me at the corner.

Ever so courteously, the uniformed driver requested some ID and frowned at my almost useless charge card, but perhaps because I was white and English, he drove me back to North Canon Drive and waited at the kerb to watch me let myself into the house with my key. Luckily for me, Grandpa was busy declaiming Keats in the Valley, and Julie and Bruce weren't around, so I was able to take a taxi to the Chateau Marmont and collect the station wagon without anyone finding out.

Ostensibly suffering from a migraine, I spent the rest of the day in my room.

Early on the morning of my grandfather's seventy-sixth birthday, I was mud-wrestling with his manuscript in the pool house, painfully aware of how little progress we'd made in the light of Scott Newton's imminent arrival. Every evening, I'd read aloud my day's work to Grandpa while he sipped his Scotch in the den, and each page would ignite a dozen fresh memories in his mind, some of which he'd insist I incorporate into the text.

Going to the kitchen for some juice, I came across Eleanor giving a lecture on the benefits of raw food to Julie, who was gazing up at my aunt with wide-eyed adoration. Following the dinner party, Eleanor had sent her a huge bunch of flowers and, astonished by such kindness, Julie had failed to recognize this as part of a wider strategy by which my aunt sought to repair her relationship with her father. As I opened the fridge door, the soft sucking sound broke Eleanor's train of thought, and she asked me to drive her down to a vitamin store on Beverly Drive to get a particular herbal tea for Julie. Having still not told Eleanor the truth about Direct Debit (I'd long since decided to let the matter lie and hope for the best), I'd been trying to keep out of her way (the bankruptcy ticking like an unattended package in a departure lounge), but it was impossible for me to refuse her request without being rude.

Given Eleanor's hypochondria, sunlight meant cancer and, Los Angeles being a minefield of unexploded melanomas, she stepped out into the yard wearing a sun hat and a long-sleeved shirt. Even more alarmingly for her, we had no choice but to take the Bentley because the pick-up was being fixed and Bruce had taken the station wagon to Ojai.

'Is it safe? Do be careful, Ralph,' Eleanor said, applying some infant lip protector (SPF 25) to the backs of her hands as I turned the key in the ignition. 'I hope your father's going to behave tonight. How did you find him?'

Struggling to familiarize myself with the car's controls, I informed her of Larry's new interest in Wittgenstein.

'Dear, oh dear,' she said. 'When's he going to wake up? God knows what he's living on.'

'Well, his repeats from *Patrolman*, I'd imagine.'

'Still? With two ex-wives? Tell me, Ralph, do you think there's something between Julie and your grandfather?'

Recalling the shape and feel of Julie's naked body, I felt my throat tighten. 'I hardly think so,' I said. 'Grandpa's seventy-six years old.'

'I went upstairs with her when she took him his breakfast,' Eleanor said. 'They were very . . . physical.'

A wizened senior rode a custom motor-tricycle down his driveway on to North Beverly Drive.

'They're very fond of each other but they certainly don't sleep together,' I said. 'I'm in the room over the archway and I'd hear Julie go through.'

The interior walls appeared to be Mission-solid but were in

55

fact just board nailed to a wooden frame and covered with plaster. According to Grandpa, the house had been built by carpenters moonlighting from a studio.

'I'm sorry, Ralph, but I don't think you've quite got Daddy's measure,' Eleanor said. 'Have you ever stopped to think why the publishers are so keen to get the manuscript?'

'Greed, I'd imagine. Have you ever read *The Ragman's Son*?'

'Obviously not,' she said. 'But a lot of people are worrying about just how much dirt Daddy's planning to dish. After all, he used to change his girlfriends more often than most people change their bed linen. I doubt there's much mention of me in it, is there?'

Astoundingly, there were only three brief references to her in the entire piece, and I'd already inflated one of them into a full-blown eulogy, but my familiarity with Eleanor's career allowed me to fabricate a fresh account of her achievements so ridiculously bombastic that it pained her to tear herself away when we arrived at Great Earth vitamins.

As I waited at the kerb with the motor running, the Bentley's great age drew the attention of three girls laden with shopping bags, and I felt like a cretinous poseur. Two blocks from Rodeo Drive, this was the world capital of narcissistic self-obsession, one of the richest, most derided square miles on the surface of the planet, yet there was an anxiety in every passer-by that called to mind Brecht's observation that rich and poor alike fear destitution.

Great Earth was fresh out of Mu tea, so Eleanor asked me to take her to Bodhi Tree, another placebo-pusher on Melrose, and I bridled.

'Let's forget it,' I said. 'I ought to get back to work.'

'Look, do me just this one small favour, all right?'

'Why don't you just let it go? I'm sure Julie can live without the stuff.'

The good humour my aunt had been so keen to project at North Canon Drive melted away in an instant. 'It's not just for Julie,' she said. 'I've run out myself.'

Eleanor's thin skin flushed as we locked eyes, and my own buried tensions surfaced. 'Oh, now I get the picture,' I said. 'Well, if only you'd said so earlier.'

No longer in the least bit beautiful, my aunt's face looked as if it was being squeezed by a pair of elevator doors. 'You're not such a saint yourself, Ralph,' she said. 'Telling everyone that your play's coming to Broadway. I know your company's gone bankrupt.'

Stripped right down to my deceitful core, I wanted to disappear. To die. Without thinking, I aimed the car towards Melrose.

'It was all a misunderstanding,' I said. 'Grandpa got the wrong end of the stick. You know how he is, and then I couldn't let him down. God, I've been feeling such a fake.'

'In Beverly Hills? Please. It's a qualification for residency.' I was too mortified to laugh. 'Look, I'm sorry I snapped at you, Ralph, I've always had a  sharp tongue.'

'Well, I'd really appreciate it if you could keep this to yourself,' I said. 'At least until I've had the chance to tell Grandpa.'

'Why spoil his big day? I've no plans to tell him and I'm sure nobody else will. I mean, do you really think anybody out here gives a shit about the British theatre?'

'Maybe you're right,' I said. In the rear-view, a mirror-clad office building reflected its drunken twin.

'Don't worry, Ralph. I'm glad it's you ghosting Daddy's book rather than some horrid hack, and you have my sympathy. It must have been terribly hard on you when your company folded. Everybody's always telling me that you did marvellous work.'

Feeling Eleanor's hand pat my shoulder, I told myself that my secret would be safe so long as I didn't offend her, but it was scant consolation. By the time we arrived back at North Canon Drive to find the caterers unloading their van, I was aware that I'd placed myself in an obsessive-compulsive control freak's clutches.

Back-lit by agapantha, Grandpa was opening his birthday cards on the terrace with Julie, who was wearing his sun-faded golfing hat. The tableau struck me as perfectly innocuous, even touching, but it put Eleanor even more on edge.

'Good morning, Daddy,' she trilled. 'Are we interrupting you?'

'Darling girl, of course not.'

Julie vacated her seat for Eleanor, who took it without a qualm, all her attention on her father as he swallowed the dregs of his vitamin drink. 'Well done, Daddy,' she said. 'It's so good for you.'

In agreement, the automatic lawn sprinklers spurted to life with the sound of badly canned applause. Replacing his empty glass on the table, Grandpa belched, and to cover her embarrassment, Eleanor apologized to Julie for failing to obtain the Mu tea. As my aunt went on to describe our expedition in detail, her father's eyelids drooped and his body went lizard still, but as she enacted her final frustrated exchange with the hippie at Bodhi Tree, he jerked to attention, afraid he'd been caught napping.

'Have you seen the wonderful window Julie's given me?' he asked Eleanor. Making a spirited effort to show an interest, his daughter focused on a circular stained-glass window that lay on a sheet of bubble-wrap by his feet. 'Isn't it amazing?' he said. 'Seventy-six years' had been rendered in fragments of coloured glass, and some more words had been inscribed on the surround in Sanskrit. When I passed the gift to my aunt, she took it with reluctance. 'Hold it up to the light,' Grandpa commanded her.

'It's charming,' she said, making Julie blush. 'And so very beautifully made.' The strips of lead were joined together with messy blobs of solder, and if the maker (or artist's) signature hadn't comprised such a prominent feature of the overall design, I'd have guessed that Julie had assembled the window herself. Blindfolded. 'Where's the clock I gave you, darling?' Eleanor asked her father. 'Ralph would love to see it.'

This was the first I'd heard of a clock, but when Grandpa said that it was still in his bedroom, Eleanor went to fetch it.

'She's so darn wilful,' he whispered to me as his daughter disappeared into the living room. 'Just like her mother. I wish I could get along with her better, but she's always rubbing me up the wrong way, you know?' Julie glanced at her employer reprovingly, and I judged it a good time to give him the red necktie that I'd bought at the Beverly Center. Thanking me, he tied it on top of his sky blue turtleneck pullover, and took the opportunity to adjust the waistband of his trousers, which he wore high above his potbelly. 'You'll have to make an important decision some day, Ralph, if you live as long as me,' Grandpa said. 'About whether to wear your pants above or below your stomach. I suggest that you wear them high. It's more comfortable that way – so long as you can find a pair with a two-foot zipper.'

Watching my grandfather tear into his stack of birthday cards, I wondered how many I'd receive if I ever made it to his age. I was reading one from a former Vice-President when Eleanor called out to us from the living room.

'Hark, the gloom bird's hated screech,' Grandpa muttered as his daughter rejoined us, holding her clock and pointing out a second dial set into the face that marked Eastern Time.

'So Daddy will always know what time to ring me in New York.'

Ever the sycophant, I duly marvelled at the clock's elegance and Eleanor's munificence, but in doing so I suffered a sharp pain in my stomach. Was this an ulcer? Or more worrying still, had I been infected by my aunt's galloping hypochondria? Grandpa's good mood soon wilted in her company, and the more questions Eleanor asked about the catering arrangements for the party, the further he pulled back inside himself.

'It's going to be a splendid evening, Daddy,' she said with grim resolution. 'You'll see.' When she squeezed his freckled hand, he retracted it, and she stared longingly at his retreating figure as Julie took him inside. 'What am I doing wrong, Ralph?' she wailed. 'Can you please tell me?'

Comforting Eleanor did no good and, forgiving her the anguish she'd caused me in the car, I was angry with my grandfather for the first time in my life. Given his avowed professional skills, he might at least have disguised his feelings better, since it was hardly his daughter's fault that she reminded him of her mother.

Later that afternoon, I found my aunt in the living room, attacking a flower arrangement with cold fury and discarding the unwanted foliage across a double page of the *Los Angeles Times* Arts section.

'Julie's made it look like a gay funeral parlour in here,' Eleanor hissed. 'And does she usually flounce around the house dressed like that?'

'Like what?' I asked, mystified.

'Those shorts were so tight you could see her bloody vulva. And what about that horrid window she gave Daddy? Could you believe it? To see him mooning over a vulgar piece of trash. God, it makes me sick.'

A bluebottle made a series of unsuccessful attempts to smash its way out of the room through a windowpane.

# Chapter Four

'In ordinary life we know how to listen, because we
are interested in or need to know something. On the
stage, in most cases, all we do is make a pretence of
attentive listening. We do not feel any practical neces-
sity to penetrate the thoughts and words of our stage
partner. We have to oblige ourselves to do it.'

Konstantin Stanislavski, *Building a Character*

People are always telling me that I take after my father, but
my hair's paler and my eyes are set further apart. Up in my
room to change for the party, I checked my appearance in the
mirror and decided that I looked a lot more like my grandfather. Or rather, like a faint, criminally inclined version of his
younger self. Direct Debit's bankruptcy had reduced my
wardrobe to tracksuits and trainers, so, in need of a sober suit
for my new role as my grandfather's amanuensis, I'd bought
a lightweight navy blue one at a charity shop in east London
before flying out to California. For the sum of forty pounds, I
had hoped to side-step Thoreau's caveat concerning enter-
prises that require new clothes and to resemble a respectable,
if impoverished, academic. Instead, I looked like a convict on
day release.

Downstairs on the terrace, Grandpa awaited his guests
with Julie, who'd put a flower in her hair, and Merle, who'd
traded his habitual white uniform for a livid green blazer.
Grandpa's chair had been carried out from the den to serve
as his throne, and he was fretting over its optimum position
when Bruce joined us with his hair slicked down. Tables and
chairs had been arrayed on the lawn, and a caterer was laying
out ranks of champagne flutes in such an overly deliberate
manner that he might have been a Method actor researching

a new role. Expecting 150 guests for the buffet, Grandpa was worried that none of them would materialize (in England, such low-grade anxieties would have been focused on the vagaries of the weather). Eleanor was the first to show up, dressed to the nines, the tens even, in a shapeless white satin dress that shimmered in the late afternoon sun as if she was about to be teleported.

Rushing up to Grandpa, my aunt shrieked in delight. 'Darling, it's a festival.'

Any neutral observer would have received the news that she'd only left her father's side three hours earlier with outright disbelief. Eleanor's husband Roger was a willowy Samuel Beckett lookalike in his late fifties, with white hair and whiter teeth, and as he bent down to shake Grandpa's hand, the sleeves of the sweater he wore knotted around his bony shoulders dangled in the space between them. With minimum fuss, Roger introduced me to his daughter Lisa, an attractive pixie in her late twenties.

'So you're Ralph, right?' she asked. 'Like Ralph Fiennes?'

Though this made me blench, the oversensitive actor had at least served to popularize the pretentious pronunciation of our first name.

'Actually, I was named after Ralph Richardson,' I said, sounding even more of a prig than usual. Understandably, Lisa had never heard of him. 'Another British actor,' I said. 'My mother had a crush on him as a little girl.'

'Eleanor's told me all about you,' Lisa said. 'How you've been driving her around and everything.'

'I've seen you drop her off here yourself,' I said.

Lisa crossed one eye, then the other, and when I laughed, she glanced over at her stepmother and laughed along with me, as if we were sharing an unspoken joke at Eleanor's expense. Wondering if Lisa's purple shawl and floral print dress were a gibe at Eleanor's black and white aesthetic, I was curious as to how she'd learnt to move her eyeballs around independently of each other.

'It's not something I consciously studied,' she said. 'You're a playwright, right?'

'Sometimes,' I said, terrified that Eleanor had told her about my lies.

'How long have you been here?'

'In LA? Two weeks.'

'You like it?'

'I'm bored stiff,' I said. 'I've hardly left the house.'

'You're kidding. You've been to California before though, right?'

'Yes, I was born here. But I haven't been back for a long time. It seems very different,' I said. 'Los Angeles, I mean.'

'Really, Ralph? Maybe it's just you.'

Originally from New York, Lisa was a research biochemist at USC, where her work on the fruit fly was part of a major research project into the transmission of genes, co-ordinated from Berkley. Just as I was admiring the way her eyes slanted upward in her delicate, elfin face, a crowd of people arrived all at once and Lisa went over to join her father.

The average age of the guests was probably sixty-five, but the orange pink early evening light made them all look the picture of health, especially if you were prepared to squint. Several elderly actors and actresses were lionizing Grandpa on the terrace, intent on shoring up the febrile values by which they'd have liked to be judged themselves, and when an ancient film actor made an appearance in a wheelchair, Grandpa made a special point of walking over to welcome him. Avoiding direct sunlight, Eleanor spent the first hour of the party hopping from shadow to shadow. When her laugh rang out above the din, I saw her speaking to a man with a bouffant silver pompadour. Bruce was fooling around with some non-theatrical relations, and I chatted for a while with an American Tait from Boston, a voluble stockbroker in his fifties who happened to be in Los Angeles on business.

Following my recent misadventure in Brentwood, I tried to count my drinks, but the caterers seemed set on keeping my glass full and I was soon light-headed, lost in a forest of dyed and teased hair. A man walked past, the flesh on his face pulled back so tightly that he might have been standing in a wind tunnel, and he looked like a famous old actor because he *was* a famous old actor. Only the mottled, scrotal skin on his hands and throat had escaped cosmetic surgery. Trapped on the terrace by a mantis in a zebra-patterned pant suit, Roger was far too polite to break away, but when I caught Lisa's eye she leapt at the chance.

'There are way more Brits over here,' she said to me.

'Sorry?'

'You said it's changed here. Well, there are way more Brits now. 500,000 in LA.' This figure seemed incredible, but Lisa insisted that she'd heard it repeated many times; if true, it explained why my English accent no longer raised a flicker of interest from the shopkeepers of Beverly Hills. Lisa turned to survey the party. 'It sure looks like everybody's having a great time,' she said.

'Well, half of them are professional actors,' I said, watching Eleanor swoop down on a bejewelled crone wrapped in a purple kaftan. Mindful of my own non-existent relationship with my stepmother Irene, I was curious as to how Lisa got along with my aunt.

'Oh, Eleanor's just wonderful,' Lisa said in reply to my question. 'I adore her. And she and my dad are really devoted. I just wish he hadn't made such a huge song-and-dance about coming out.'

'Roger's gay?'

'Bisexual. It's why he left my mother. But then five years later, he broke up with Alfredo and went and married Eleanor.'

Somebody called my name, and when I turned round, a woman grasped me, pressing the entire length of her firm supple body against mine. Buzzed on the champagne and blinded by the sun, I responded with a sudden unwanted flood of blood to the groin. Noticing my undeniable reaction, the woman giggled in delight and I stepped back to find

64

myself face-to-face with Nonie, my father's godmother, who had to be in her seventies. It was all I could do to stop myself extending my compliments to her plastic surgeon – or upholsterer. Lisa had vanished, and as I strove manfully to retain the gas from my third or fourth glass of champagne, Nonie began, apropos of nothing at all, to tell me about an LSD trip she'd taken in the 1950s.

'I was off in this world of make-believe from the moment the doctor gave it to me,' she said. 'By injection, you understand, in Lausanne, a heckuva dose, and pretty soon I was fighting at a medieval battle in a suit of armour. Then I fell off my horse and I was lying in the mud and all the other horses were trampling on me . . .'

As Nonie and I queued for plates of poached salmon decorated with slivers of cucumber in a fish-scale motif, I poured the rest of my champagne into the herbaceous border. At a table by the fountain, Nonie picked at her food and reminisced about the time she'd taken Larry and me to a lake in a little high-sided car, driving it down a concrete ramp straight into the water. To my amazement, the car had transformed itself into a very slow motorboat with its own tiny propeller near the exhaust pipe, but when I'd told the story back at the boarding school on the south coast of England where I'd been sent at the age of eight after my mother had begun to smell of wine in the mornings, nobody had believed me.

Once Nonie had softened me up, she began to grill me about Grandpa's autobiography. 'Is it really as juicy as everyone thinks?' she asked. 'I've heard Jeannie Blumenthal's perfectly terrified. What does he say about her?'

Blocking Nonie's questions as best I could, it was a relief when she grabbed Roger Mooney's arm to tell him that she'd known his father. Indeed, she hinted that she'd once been on more intimate terms with Mooney Sr.

'Old Harry bought me the most fabulous blue chinchilla.' she cried.

Disentangling himself, Roger laughed politely and congrat-ulated me on my Olivier award. This knocked the champagne straight out of me, but when I tried to corrrect him, he asked me who was bringing the play to Broadway in the autumn.

'Really, Ralph. I wish you'd let me know about this earlier,' he continued. 'We could have kept it all in the family and made ourselves a pot of money.'

'Sorry, but there's no truth to any of it,' I said. 'Grandpa's exaggerated the whole thing.'

Roger looked genuinely disappointed. 'You don't say? Well, if he has, it's only because he's so happy that you've finally got some real recognition for your work, Ralph. It takes guts to stick to your guns the way you have, and your grandfather knows it. He's terrifically proud of you.'

With salmon leaping in my throat, I excused myself and edged my way through the crowd, half-expecting to find Grandpa bragging that I'd been knighted for my services to British theatre. Desperate to put him right before someone else did, I found him surrounded by an impenetrable cordon of guests, and suffering a slow-motion panic attack, I tried to take comfort from the fact that Eleanor hadn't yet told Roger the truth about Direct Debit.

A distinguished director was fawning over my second cousin once removed, the actor Daniel Tait, beneath the branches of the magnolia tree. Though I'm ashamed to admit it, my fears of exposure were quickly replaced by an all-consuming envy. I tried to tell myself that there was no rea-son for me to begrudge my cousin, who hardly warranted the fame and success that had recently been heaped upon him for his television work. After all it was I, not Danny, who'd picked up the baton dropped by my father and grand-father and gone in search of a meaningful new theatre. If Direct Debit had helped one single convict or disadvantaged schoolchild grow at all in confidence, our work had been of more lasting benefit than a hundred episodes of Danny's soap opera. Objectively, I should have accepted his easy success for what it was, but I despised him for it. Lisa appeared at my elbow, asking to be introduced to my cousin and, unable to hide my irritation, I asked her why on earth she'd want to meet him.

'Because he's cute. And talented, of course,' she said.

'How can you say that? Because of his TV rating?'

'It's a cool show,' she countered.

'A cool show? Danny plays a psychic telephone engineer, for God's sake,' I said. 'It's the worst kind of mass consumer culture. The rubbish Adorno called "unadorned make-up".'

'Theodor Adorno? He used to live in Brentwood.'

'No, no. The Frankfurt School philosopher. Listen, Lisa, that man over there licking Danny's boots made two of the epochal films of the 1970s. He shouldn't even know who Danny is, let alone be slobbering over him like that.'

'Hey, lighten up, Ralph. Who needs the lecture? And the guy's not slobbering. It's a party,' she said. 'We're meant to be mingling. Enjoying ourselves.'

When Roger Mooney joined Danny and the director, Lisa saw her chance and headed over to get her introduction. While I scowled at the edge of the terrace, my theatre company consigned to the dustbin of history and my new career as a biographer already imperilled, Danny basked in approval. With its small perfect nose, wide mouth and long eyelashes, his bland, handsome face seemed designed to illustrate a mindless magazine article, and the sight of it conspired with the champagne I'd guzzled to fuel my bitterness. Each week, thousands of journalists struggled to extract a worthwhile interview from actors like Danny who spent half their working lives pretending to be somebody else and the other half killing time in a Winnebago. Were these über-marionettes founts of original thought? Did they offer helpful suggestions as to how to be a better parent? Or lessen the unconscionable effects of Third World debt? I didn't think so, and it enraged me even more to see Lisa laughing at something my cousin had said.

Catching my eye, Danny called my name and punched the air. Although he'd not found the time to attend a Direct Debit workshop on his last promotional trip to Britain (where his TV show had already gained a following), my cousin had made a point of taking me out to dinner, so I felt I should at least say hello. As I made my way over, it delighted me that Danny turned his back on the Mooneys without a second glance.

'Ralph. I'm so glad to see you. Your dad told me you were going to be here. I flew in yesterday,' he said. 'And I'll be in town for a couple of weeks. You have to come and visit us at the beach.' For the next few minutes, my cousin gave me his full attention, asking a series of pertinent questions about my life and work before telling me how excited he was that my prize-winning play was coming to New York in the autumn. Was it true that the film rights had already been snapped up? Swallowing hard, I indicated that things weren't as well with Direct Debit as Grandpa might have led Danny to believe, and my cousin shook his winsome head at the unfairness of the world.

'Your work is real,' he said. 'God, if I wasn't tied up for the next ten months doing this junk, I'd jump on a plane tomorrow. If you could use me, that is.'

Danny was so engaging and self-deprecating that my rancour dissolved (indeed, for a moment I even forgot that he was an actor) and I wanted more than anything to be his friend. As we spoke, a flawless blonde beauty materialized at his side and, failing to catch her name when Danny introduced us, my English blood prevented me from asking him to repeat it.

'It's so good to meet you, Ralph,' she said. 'Daniel has told me so much about your work in the avant-garde theatre in Britain. So fascinating. You are familiar with Pina Bausch?' During the course of a wide-ranging discussion of contemporary European performance, I discovered that the young woman's name was Ingeborg, and that she was a German investment banker. Danny and Ingeborg glided off to get some food, and right then, yes, I would gladly have changed places with him. My cousin was immensely successful but behaved as if he knew that his success was undeserved; he had a beautiful girlfriend with an unpronounceable name, and he wasn't yet thirty. Furthermore, his parents were well adjusted and, as far as I knew, still happily married.

Hearing a peal of practised laughter, I turned to see my father heading in Grandpa's direction. Larry had donned a Hawaiian shirt in honour of the occasion, an original silk-screened collector's item, but its authenticity and his lack of punctuality were unlikely to find favour with Grandpa. Nevertheless, Larry marched up and wished him a happy birthday with such brio that no outsider would have guessed that a rift existed between them. Grandpa embraced Larry, whereupon Bruce came over and hugged them both.

At a signal from Julie, the caterers wheeled out the birthday cake, a gigantic pyramid of chocolate profiteroles, and the immediate family circle were invited to huddle around Grandpa for a group portrait. Being actors, Eleanor, Larry and Danny just happened to find themselves in the pole positions, as if they'd telepathically anticipated the photo opportunity and even intuited the best camera angles. Despite the fact that Grandpa had derided Danny's performance when we'd chanced upon an episode of his television show the previous week, he made no objection when one of the photographers suggested that Danny might stand next to him for the photograph. Knowing our place in the hierarchy of success, Bruce and I found space for ourselves at the end of the back row, and my neck itched as I imagined the scalpel of a magazine layout artist cropping our heads from the frame.

Once the shutterbugs' business was done, the guests formed a loose horseshoe to watch Grandpa blow out his candles. Julie helped him extinguish the last two, and as he cut the cake, we sang 'Happy Birthday'. Following a general cry for a speech, Grandpa cleared his throat with a show of reluctance, and his voice reverberated with emotion as he thanked his 'troop of friends and family' for coming. Then he proceeded to recite some lines from 'The Fall of Hyperion':

> *'When in mid-May the sickening East Wind*
> *Shifts sudden to the South, the small warm rain*
> *Melts out the frozen incense from all flowers,*
> *And fills the air with so much pleasant health*
> *That even the dying man forgets his shroud . . .'*

While her father declaimed the verse as if determined to extract a tear or two from his audience, Eleanor's smile looked increasingly fixed and Julie quivered at his elbow. Larry wiped the sweat from his upper lip and Lisa winked at me from over by the magnolia tree.

Grandpa finally laid the poetry aside. 'Wasn't that beautiful?' he asked us. At a soft murmur of assent, he paused for a moment to make sure of our attention, and even before he spoke I had a hunch that he was about to make a momentous announcement. 'I'm so very happy that you're all here today, my dear, dear friends,' he declared, 'because I have some wonderful news for you. Many of you already know how happy Julie Perrault has made my life here over the past year. She's an absolute angel, and it's with no small measure of delight that I'm able to tell you she's agreed to marry me.'

Kissing Julie full on the lips, Grandpa placed a diamond ring on her finger.

Before the shock wave hit, the frieze had all the frozen weight of a neoclassical masterpiece. Eleanor, Larry and Bruce looked on dumbstruck. I was devastated. It was only two weeks since I'd attempted *carezza* with the woman who was going to be my step-grandmother, and my mind reeled at the ramifications of what I'd just witnessed. The man beside me tweaked his hearing aid in disbelief, then someone's weak 'Hurrah' ignited a wave of applause all the more intense for its lack of spontaneity. The caterers came through the crowd dispensing glasses of champagne, and Nonie proposed a toast to the bride- and groom-to-be. Appalled, I stumbled among the horde of guests clamouring to offer their congratulations. Julie was in heaven, or Nirvana. The caterers lit the candles that Ernesto had placed in the herbaceous borders, and then Bruce dragged his carving across the terrace with all the indomitability of a straggler in an egg-and-spoon race intent on the winning-line. Guests stood back as he whipped the sheet away to reveal the fruit of six months' labour.

'Happy birthday, Pops,' Bruce cried.

'Good God,' Grandpa said. 'Who on earth's that meant to be?'

'It's you, Pops. I carved it myself.'

Stepping back to examine the wooden head, my grandfather frowned.

'It's your birthday present,' Bruce said. 'Don't you like it?'

Grandpa scowled at him, ignoring the question. The people standing near Bruce and me on the terrace didn't know where to look. Turning his back on his son without another word, Grandpa hailed the wheelchair-bound actor who was parting the crowd to bid him goodbye. Grandpa's cruelty sickened me. Larry, who'd witnessed the presentation from over by the makeshift bar, looked horrified. As the two elderly actors traded their well-rehearsed lines, only my father and I seemed to notice the tears shooting down Bruce's face.

Signalling to Larry that I could manage without his help, I led my uncle to the bottom of the garden and into the pool house, where he sobbed on to my shoulder, making a sound like a cat drowning. While I struggled in vain to excuse Grandpa's sadism, Bruce curled up in a ball on the floor, keening as he pulled at his hair, and scared that this might herald one of his breakdowns, I went to fetch Eleanor.

It was only nine o'clock, but cars were already queuing up on the driveway to collect the guests, and Grandpa stood propped on his cane by the front door to say his farewells.

'Isn't it wonderful?' Nonie cooed in my ear. 'There's hope for us all.'

As Larry's godmother climbed into her car, Eleanor headed towards me with the stiff gait of someone walking, not running, to the lifeboats. 'I need your help,' she whispered.

'Look,' I said. 'Bruce –'

'I know,' she replied. Gripping my arm as if intent on cutting off the circulation, my aunt led me quickly through the house and past some dawdlers who were milling on the terrace. In the deepening shadows, the wooden grin on Bruce's carving had become a salacious leer.

'Your father's talking to Bruce in the pool house, but I'm afraid he's drunk,' Eleanor said, employing the precise tone of solemn regret she'd used to deliver the line 'We've lost audio contact, sir' in a Cold War thriller twenty-five years previously. While it gladdened me to hear that Bruce wasn't alone, her words were all too depressingly familiar.

The sky was blue above the darkness of the trees, a disorienting effect that reminded me of Magritte's *The Empire of Light*, and I was in a daze as we stepped on to the lawn in search of more privacy.

'The whole thing's a catastrophe,' Eleanor continued. 'Roger's getting the car, and I want your father and Bruce to come with us. Larry's planning to have it out with Daddy, but this isn't the time. I can't get any sense out of him and he's making Bruce even more upset. Go and talk to him, will you?'

Larry and I hadn't spoken since my visit to Laurel Canyon, and I was the last person to persuade him of anything, but Eleanor made it impossible for me to refuse.

Making my way down to the pool house, the sweet reek of marijuana hit me as soon as I turned the corner of the hedge, the orange tip of a joint flaring before it described a loop in the gathering gloom. Bruce had stopped crying, and when Larry kissed me, there was sweat on his face.

'Can you believe the old man?' he asked me, grinning lopsidedly. 'I mean, marrying *Julie*? And he's been so shitty to Bruce. Did you see the carving, sonny? It's a goddam masterpiece.'

My uncle was staring into the middle distance with glassy eyes. 'You got him perfectly,' Larry slurred, putting an arm round his brother. 'Don't let any of this crap with Julie spoil your glow.'

What glow? Heartbroken, Bruce was too shut down to respond, not that Larry noticed. When I told my father that Eleanor wanted him and Bruce to go home with her, he opened his mouth and a wispy blue-white moustache floated across his upper lip as he sucked the smoke back inside through his nose.

'I'm sorry, but no way,' Larry said. 'Bruce is staying here with me. Aren't you, brother mine? And when everybody's gone I'm going to talk to the old man. Just me and him.'

'Eleanor doesn't think you should,' I said. 'She says he's too tired.'

'Who are you, her fucking errand boy now?' A hot hemp seed fell into Larry's lap and he brushed it off. 'Well, you run and tell her I'll do as I damn well please.'

Smarting inwardly, I watched Larry put the burning end of the joint into his mouth and blow a stream of smoke into his brother's lungs. It was little wonder Bruce had turned to stone, and I went up to the terrace and broke the bad news to Eleanor.

'Well, at least we've done all we can,' she said. 'Why don't you come back with us, Ralph? Get out of the way for a couple of hours?'

Keen to avoid the impending row, I accepted my aunt's invitation and we went to say goodbye to Grandpa, who was out on the driveway, waving off his guests with Julie at his side.

'Darling girl. I'm so glad you could come,' Grandpa said, dotting Eleanor's face with kisses. 'It's wonderful we're all together. I love you so much.'

Eleanor stifled a sob of what Grandpa mistook for joy: she'd been waiting all week to hear these words from her father but not in these circumstances. Flushed with euphoria, Julie was showing her engagement ring (a rock from Rodeo

Drive that Sri Rampa would have been hard pressed to create in his hand or anywhere else) to Ingeborg. When I kissed my step-grandmother-to-be goodbye, she barely registered me, but the touch of her skin on my lips brought back the full horror of what was happening, and I nearly tripped over my own feet in my hurry to get away.

Roger pulled up in his car. Seeing Lisa's bare knees in the passenger seat, Grandpa winked at me as I ducked to follow Eleanor into the back.

'Remember what I told you, Ralph dear boy,' he cried. 'Just do it.'

As Roger swept us out on to North Canon Drive, his wife trembled. 'Are all the windows up?' she asked her husband.

'Of course, darling,' he replied. 'We'll be home in no time. Hang on.'

Unable to wait a moment longer, Eleanor sat forward and howled a curse at the top of her voice (an instrument trained to fill the Theatre Royal, Haymarket, in the days before microphones). The noise was deafening.

'I'm so sorry,' she said. 'But I have to get rid of my negative energy and that's the best way for me to do it.' Roger remained unfazed, but the shriek had sobered Lisa, who turned round to cross her eyes at me the way she had when we'd been introduced. Eleanor took a paper handkerchief from the shelf behind us, blew her nose and faced me. 'You do realize, Ralph,' she said in her super-quiet voice, 'that your grandfather's taken complete leave of his senses? He knows himself but slenderly.'

Extracting a packet of herbal cigarettes from her shoulder bag, Eleanor ignited one with a platinum lighter. Following our pilgrimage to various health food shops that morning, I scarcely believed my eyes.

'Darling, are you sure you need to do that?' Roger said.

'Of course I bloody do,' Eleanor cried. 'They're for emergencies, aren't they? And what the fuck would you call this? My father's been nailed by a gold-digger from Iowa.'

74

'Julie's not that calculating,' I said.

'Are you blind, Ralph?' she said. 'You hear about this all the time. Some trailer-trash hussy marries a decrepit millionaire and fucks him to death. I mean, she's no better than a common prostitute. God, you can be so naïve. Just like your grandfather. You just let it all happen, didn't you? I told you this morning there was something between them.'

'At least Julie's giving him something to live for,' I said. 'If it all goes bad, so what? Grandpa might not have much time left.'

'Don't you dare say that,' Eleanor whispered, her fingers shooting to some wood veneer for luck. 'And what if Julie has a child? God, it's too disgusting to think about.'

Failing to reach her lawyer at home, Eleanor quizzed me about Julie's temple, convinced that Sri Rampa had set his minion on to her father in order to drain his bank account. After I'd described the anodyne content of the videotape Julie had shown me, my aunt was reduced to heaping invective on her gullible father and 'that scheming little bitch' for the remainder of the journey.

By the time we arrived at the house on Doheny Drive, I felt as if I'd been taken hostage by a lunatic, but thankfully Eleanor and Roger disappeared into the study, leaving Lisa and I alone in the gymnasium-space of the living room.

'Swim?' Lisa asked. Eager for the uncomplicated feel of the water, I asked to borrow some trunks. 'Hey, come on,' she said. 'We're all family here, right? Don't be so British.'

Lisa walked the length of the room, switched on the pool lights, shucked off her clothes and, egg-naked, descended the steps into the water. Did anybody in my extended family wear a swimsuit? Angry at being tricked but refusing to be shown up, I gave my cock a clandestine tug as I dropped my pants and ducked beneath the surface to swim under the glass wall. The water rippled over me as if I was shedding a layer of skin, and when I came up for air, the light from the pool played across Lisa's face, marbling it against the night sky. The far rim was invisible beneath the waterline. Swimming over to hang on the wet lip, Lisa told me that it was called an infinity pool. 'Which is pretty optimistic, I guess, being as we're on the wrong side of the San Andreas fault,' she said. 'Eleanor was pretty pissed at your grandfather, huh? But that thing in the car, it was too much.'

Though I felt some loyalty towards my aunt, I could hardly disagree. 'How does your father put up with her?' I asked.

'Oh, he doesn't seem to mind a bit. He's a serial carer. And Eleanor's a really great person underneath. She's been an amazing stepmother to me, just the best,' Lisa said, kicking her brown legs. 'But I don't see why she's so upset that your grandfather's getting married again. I mean, what's the harm?'

My own legs looked doubly white as they wobbled under the water. 'Well, it's the age gap, I'd imagine. Plus she's jealous of Julie. Eleanor wants to be close to her father, but he won't let her near him.'

Lisa began to tell me about her research at USC – the 'University for Spoilt Children' as she called it – where she was breeding 10,000 fruit flies in a bid to discover more about their genetic make-up. Lisa had her own apartment in Hollywood but she often stayed at her father's house, which was empty most of the time save for Ilena, the live-in maid, with whom Lisa had become friends. They threw parties together when Roger and Eleanor were in New York, and Lisa claimed that the best ones she'd ever attended in Los Angeles had been thrown by housesitters.

'Most rich people here are too uptight to enjoy what they've got,' she said, gazing down at the lights of the Strip.

Given that we were both naked, I found it surprisingly easy to be with Lisa, but when we swam back inside under the glass wall, I had a horror that Roger and Eleanor would walk into the living room just as we climbed out of the water. Happily, there was no sign of them. Once we'd got dressed, we found Lisa's father alone in the kitchen making a roast-beef sandwich.

'Hi there,' he said. 'Enjoy your swim?'

'Sure,' Lisa said. 'How's Eleanor?'

'Oh, she'll be better tomorrow. It's come as a shock, that's all. You know how concerned she is for her father.'

Eleanor had apparently gone to bed, but it was difficult to put her out of mind because the walls of the dining area were decorated with costume designs for roles that she'd played, camp and poorly executed watercolours tagged with swatches of fabric. Roger made sandwiches for us, and as we analyzed the current state of the London theatre, I took pains to steer him away from the subject of the fringe and the fortunes of Direct Debit. Lisa seemed close to her father, who was relaxed and affable. Still stung by Larry's harsh words by the pool, I was glad for her, and as she ran me back to North Canon Drive in her Jeep, I asked her for her opinion of the engagement.

'Well, I think your grandfather got a real kick out of surprising everybody like that,' she replied.

'But do you think Julie really loves him? Or has Eleanor got it right?'

'Who knows? It could be a bit of both. Or neither. Julie looks a little nuts to me, if you must know.'

There was no sign of Larry's convertible on the front drive and I was hoping he'd gone, but the moment Lisa drove off, his car barrelled out through the archway and he braked to a halt beside me.

Bright red in the face, Larry peered up from the open window. 'Where've you been?'

'Over at Eleanor's,' I said. 'What's happened?'

'The old man threw me out. Can you believe it?' Larry thumped his steering wheel. 'I told him he was making a big mistake with Julie, and he went crazy. Said he's going to disinherit me.'

Shuddering to picture the scene, I asked after Bruce.

'Oh, he just left for Ojai,' Larry said. 'I was up in his apartment with him. He'll be OK. He's been through worse than this, don't worry. Look, you want to come back to my place till this blows over?'

High on adrenaline and everything else besides, Larry's edgy, scared eyes drilled into me.

'I guess I'd better not,' I said. 'They'll be expecting me.'

'Do what you want,' he said. It should have been his motto. 'I'll call you, OK?'

The caterers had cleared up after the party, but a few stray champagne flutes remained half-hidden in the shadows of the sombre rooms. Julie was in the library, pale and dejected, doing the I-Ching in her jogging suit. Jumping at the sight of her, I knew that we needed to talk and told her that I'd just seen Larry.

My step-grandmother-to-be looked alarmed. 'He's still here?'

'He was leaving,' I said. 'He'd been speaking to Bruce, I think.'

Confirming that Larry and Grandpa had fought with each other after the last guests had left, Julie said that her fiancé had taken a sedative and gone to bed. 'Donald's taken it really badly,' she added, fiddling with her engagement ring. 'So's Bruce. He looked so wounded.'

'Larry says he's gone up to Ojai.'

'And I thought everyone was going to be so happy for us.'

It was hard to believe Julie was really that innocent, but she was in such low spirits that to raise them I asked her to describe for me the circumstances of Grandpa's proposal.

'Two days ago he asked me out of the blue, and it just seemed right,' she said. 'A young fawn had crossed the lawn that morning while I was doing my yoga. I told you about it, remember? And the moment I said yes, a hummingbird came and drank from the feeder outside Donald's window. It was all so magical.'

To my mind, Julie hadn't given a thought to Grandpa's money. Her love for him was true. 'Things will work out fine,' I told her. 'It's just hard for some people to accept at first.'

'Accept what exactly? That Donny and I love each other?'

Donny? 'People are bound to talk,' I said. 'I mean, Grandpa's old enough to be . . . Well, your grandpa.'

Julie snuffled at a polka-dot handkerchief. 'So what, Ralph? We have a spiritual bond.'

'Look, you have to understand –'

'Oh, I get it,' she cried. 'You think because you and I made love one time that this is all bullshit? Your ego's hurt, isn't it?' I wanted to object, but there was just enough truth in her allegation to give me pause. 'Just like your stupid father's,' Julie added. 'I don't suppose Larry told you how hard he used to hit on me when I first came to work here?'

Larry would have hit on a tree stump, and it was annoying to be grouped with him. 'I didn't hit on you, Julie,' I said. 'If you remember, it was you who hit on me.'

Her eyes tightened up another notch. 'Ralph, you were alone and in pain. I wanted to help you heal, but if you need to try and make something cheap and dirty out of it, that's your prerogative.'

'No. Listen, I . . . We have to talk, Julie. This is a terrible mess. You're planning to marry my grandfather, but you and I only slept together two weeks ago. How do you feel about that? How do you intend to handle it? I mean, are you going to tell him?'

Julie soughed. 'Why on earth should I? It hardly meant anything to us, so why on earth should it mean a thing to Donny? Jesus, Ralph. Don't make everything into such a big deal.'

'OK, OK. I'm sorry,' I said.

79

'Me too. I'm just so stressed out. I know Bruce hates me, and now your father does. And now you.'

As Julie began to sob, I patted her woodenly on the back and assured her that I didn't hate her.

Two tears raced each other down her cheeks. 'At least Eleanor's happy for us, isn't she?' she cried.

'Of course she is.'

Deeply hurt by the picture Larry had painted of him as a love-struck old fool, Grandpa was still seething when I joined him for breakfast the next morning.

'Your father's been nothing but trouble to me, Ralph,' he said, spearing his grapefruit segments with undue ferocity. 'Do you know, he's never once thought to give me a birthday present? How sharper than a serpent's tooth it is to have a thankless child.'

Ignoring the telephone that rang repeatedly as friends sought to congratulate him on his engagement, Grandpa had even postponed his recording session in the Valley half-way through *Endymion*. Scott Newton was due any day and we'd fallen way behind on the manuscript, but when I suggested that we might spend the morning working on it, Grandpa shook his head.

'I'm sorry, dear boy, but you'll just have to soldier on as best you can,' he said. 'I shall make dust my paper and with rainy eyes write sorrow on the bosom of the earth. Never have children, Ralph. They break your heart.'

Pondering this doleful advice, I polished up the pitifully few pages that we had actually managed to complete. Scott Newton was going to be very disappointed. By lunchtime, Grandpa was complaining of a throat infection, and Julie was doing her level best to stay calm in the hope that his symptoms and mood would pass of their own accord. Eating ham and potato salad in a state of nervous tension, none of us mentioned Larry or the party, and as Julie and I pretended to follow the ballgame on television, my feeble self-assurance thinned out even further. It was even unclear to me if I'd always held my fork like my grandfather, or if I was now aping his gestures. A soft rain had begun to fall. *La pluie pleut doucement sur la ville.* When Grandpa looked out of the window, Bruce's carving looked back at him.

'Would you kindly get that frightful thing off the terrace, Ralph? I can't stand to look at it while I'm eating.'

Given the vicious way he'd treated Bruce, I felt I should stick up for my uncle but didn't dare for fear that my grandfather might decide to turn on me. Agreeing to do as he asked, I was sick at heart.

Later that afternoon, the doctor came to the house and found nothing wrong with Grandpa save for a mild head cold, and Ernesto and I moved the carving to the back of the garage. When I told the pool man that Julie and my grandfather were getting married, he smiled and wished them happiness. Unable to reach Bruce in Ojai, I called Larry from the pool house to find out if he'd spoken to him.

'Bruce is working at the top of the pasture so he probably wouldn't hear the phone,' Larry said. It sounded to me as if he'd only just got out of bed. 'How's the old man, more to the point?' Learning of the doom-laden atmosphere at North Canon Drive, he groaned. 'I suppose he's blaming me for everything as usual. Jesus . . . Look, I'm sorry if I was mean to you after the party, but I had a lot on my mind. Do you want to go out for dinner with me tonight?'

Unmoved by his apology, I said I was busy and felt a familiar ache in the pit of my stomach as I said goodbye.

Grandpa spent the next day in bed, and when I came across Julie polishing the dining-room table, her face was pinched.

'I can't seem to get through to your grandfather,' she said. 'It's like he's put up a wall.' Recalling Eleanor saying much the same thing to me before the party, I tried to persuade Julie that it wasn't her fault and that Grandpa was just overtired, but she remained unconvinced. More worryingly, Scott Newton had arrived in Los Angeles, and when he rang to congratulate his author on his engagement, I had to break the news that my grandfather wasn't taking calls on account of his head cold.

'Well, that's a real pity,' Newton said in his reedy Australian accent. 'But why don't you come down here to the hotel yourself tomorrow?'

'I really think you should speak to my grandfather first,' I said.

'I don't agree. We need to talk, Ralph. I'll meet you in the bar of the Beverly Wilshire at eleven o'clock tomorrow morning. Bring what you've got and don't be late.'

Recalling Newton's query concerning Jean Bailey, I searched for John Blumenthal's name on the back-up disks later that afternoon and hit upon a reference to his new wife: *'I met a young actress in the studio commissary and got her a part in* Tiger's Heart. *We had a lot of fun together. Jean was a lovely girl, warm and open, and she used to make me recite Mr Shakespeare to her at her little condo in Malibu. I was going to take her to Italy with me, but it never happened. Jean had a pretty good career after that and ended up marrying my old friend John Blumenthal.'* For 'warm and open' read, 'Reader, I fucked her,' but at least it was something for me to give Newton.

That evening, Grandpa joked about the behaviour of various guests at his party, and it gratified the emotional Zelig in me that he'd cheered up a little. After dinner in the den, he mislaid his spectacles.

'I'm told they call something like this a "senior moment",' he said. 'I call it C.R.A.F.T.' Running my hand down the back of his armchair, I asked him to explain the acronym. 'Can't remember a fucking thing,' he replied. Locating his spectacles by the reading lamp, I told Grandpa that Scott Newton had insisted on a meeting. 'Be careful what you tell him,' he said. 'Just hand over what we've done and don't go promising him anything else. We're talking about men-slugs and human serpentry here, believe me. I've had it up to here with Shaugnessy King.'

For our evening's entertainment, I picked out a war film in which Grandpa had starred, and he stroked Julie's hair while he and his pals recreated the Battle of the Ardennes on the screen. Sitting at his feet, his fiancée had regained Nirvana.

When Grandpa's younger self stepped off the set for a moment, I said, 'My mother's uncle fought in the real Battle of the Ardennes as a corporal in the British army. Actually, he won the Distinguished Service Order.'

Grandpa shifted in his chair. 'Well, it's hardly the Victoria Cross, dear boy.'

Not for the first time, I regretted opening my mouth.

# Chapter Five

'Even if the lights go out; even if someone
tells me "That's all"; even if emptiness
floats towards me in a grey draft from the stage;
even if not one of my silent ancestors
stays seated with me, not one woman, not
the boy with the immovable brown eye –
I'll sit here anyway. One can always watch.'
                    Rainer Maria Rilke, *Duino Elegies*

The bar of the Beverly Wilshire hotel was deserted save for a middle-aged man in a neck brace who returned my gaze as if I was an insect crawling on the outside of his windshield. Jazz piano tinkled from concealed speakers, brightly dressed golfers swung their clubs in silence on the television screen, and the wood panelling that lined the room was inlaid with floral displays depicted in intricate marquetry. Sitting by the window, I ordered myself a juice and read over the seventeen pages of finished text; dull and poorly written, they made me feel even more like an impostor. Black limousines rolled past the window, depositing and collecting guests on the concourse, and at eleven o'clock, a Japanese man wearing a gold sword climbed into one of them. As I watched him, a burly Australian in a suit appeared at my shoulder.

'Ralph Tait? Scott Newton.' The publisher pumped my hand as if he was trying to extract water from the ground beneath my feet. 'Let me get you a fresh juice.' Beckoning the waiter, he ordered our drinks as if he'd hired the man personally. 'I used to do a lot of business here. It's changed,' he added. 'But then where hasn't?' Newton could have been anything between forty and fifty-five years old. 'I was such a fan of your grandfather when I was a boy,' he said. 'I loved his pictures. How's he doing, by the way?'

Reassured that, head cold notwithstanding, Grandpa's general health was excellent, Newton told me that he was looking forward to working with him on his autobiography. As a bellhop pushed a brass luggage trolley past the window, I asked him if it was his speciality.

'Excuse me?' Newton said, blinking.

'Your speciality as an editor,' I said. 'Autobiographies.'

'Not particularly.' His eyes met mine over the top of his glass of cranberry juice. 'I've been on a sabbatical for a year. Just travelling in Indonesia. I never knew my biological parents, you see, and I suppose I went there to find myself.'

Smiling just enough to reveal a row of little teeth that were yellow and crooked enough to be originals, Newton told me that he'd been friendly with my father in the 1980s, and I was able to tell him of Larry's marriage to Irene, but after that, our small talk shrank so drastically that I was almost glad to be asked for the finished material. Leafing through it, Newton's eyes ran over me as if adding everything up to reach a disappointing two-figure sum.

'Is this all you have?' he asked. 'You told me you'd have finished three chapters by now.'

'I know, and we're making progress. It's all down on paper so it's just a question of sorting it out. But my grandfather's an elderly man. We can only work on it together for two hours a day.'

'Maybe your grandfather can afford that luxury, but you're here to speed things along,' Newton said. 'This whole book's seriously out of whack. You've let me down.' Taking a closer look at the pages, his lips moved, silently mouthing certain words, and he asked what had happened to the 1960s and 70s material. 'I told you to start there and work back,' he said. 'That's the stuff that's going to sell this shit. Who cares about London in the 50s any more?'

'It's taking longer than I'd expected,' I said.

'Don't try and fuck with me, Ralph. You were flown out here to write the damn thing. I'm fast running out of patience.'

The man in the neck brace had turned to look at us, and it seemed to me that if Newton had succeeded in finding himself in Indonesia, the discovery must have come as a terrible disappointment. I disliked him intensely.

'By the way, I don't suppose you managed to locate any stuff on Jean Bailey?'

'I think I saw the name,' I said, reluctant to make the publisher's job any easier than I had to. 'Did Grandpa make a movie with her? Anyway, I tried to find the passage again, but it was like looking for a needle in a haystack.'

The muscles in Newton's jaw ground his teeth and he sat forward, forcing a smile. 'Level with me, Ralph. Tell me what's happening here. What kind of shape are we in?'

Bracing myself to tell the truth for once, I took a deep breath. 'My grandfather talked on to a lot of tapes and had them transcribed,' I said. 'We're working from the transcript, and it's not in particularly good order, so it's going to be a long process, I'm afraid. Months.'

I'd expected Newton to rail at me, but to my amazement, he let out a sigh of relief.

'Right,' he said. 'At least we know where we stand at last. You'll just have to do the best you can, Ralph, and I guess all that remains is your contract.' When Newton mentioned a figure, I said that it sounded more than reasonable. 'Good. I'll get it drawn up and have some copies sent round to you,' he continued. 'Oh, and I'd like the opportunity to look over the transcript while I'm here. The whole thing. I don't care what shape it's in.'

'That's impossible,' I said.

'Why? It's all on disks, isn't it?'

'No. Most of the earlier stuff's just in typescript form. I can't –'

Newton held up a milk-white palm. 'Just think it over. I'd only need it for a couple of hours, to take the general temperature. Your grandfather need never know.'

'Well, I'm not sure,' I said. 'But I'll give it some thought.'

'You do that, Ralph, you do that.' Signing for the juices, Newton's attention was drawn to a young woman at the bar wearing a pale blue body stocking and a purple stetson. 'Hey, you could do me one more favour,' he said. 'Jean Bailey. Check it out, would you?'

Saying goodbye, he patted my back as if he was working out the best place to bury a knife.

Grandpa came downstairs for lunch wearing a cravat, and learning of the terms Newton had offered me, proposed that Shaugnessy King should double my salary.

'You're doing a damn fine job of work, dear boy, so I won't let them exploit you like this. If my book means as much to them as they say, then they're going to have to pay you properly. After all, they're getting it for next to nothing.'

'Half a million dollars is hardly nothing,' I said.

Grandpa scoffed. 'D'you have any idea what they shelled out for Ronnie Reagan? And the man couldn't act his way out of a wet paper bag!'

Before I had a chance to remind him that Reagan had gone on to become the president of the Screen Actors Guild, the doorbell rang and Julie showed in a very tall septuagenarian whose bouffant silver pompadour I recalled from the birthday party. Grandpa introduced the visitor as his lawyer Bob Caswell.

'Bob married his secretary last year and completed the LA marathon in the same week,' Grandpa said. 'The man's three years older than me and he didn't even have a coronary.'

With Bob's cackle ringing in my ears, I went to help Julie prepare lunch, but she had no more idea as to the purpose of the lawyer's visit than I did. Ten minutes later, Grandpa

87

buzzed the intercom and asked us both to join him in the library: Bob had brought along some documents for Julie to sign and for me to witness.

Grandpa played it all so well that neither Julie nor I grasped what was happening at first. Having introduced his fiancée to his lawyer, Grandpa outlined the wedding plans to Bob (a simple service and reception at the golf club in Ojai), and Julie lapped up the details with spaniel fawning. Truly it seemed that the dark cloud of the past days could now be forgotten. Complaining of the need to complete some paper-work, Bob popped open the lid of his calfskin briefcase and, spreading his papers on the table, asked Julie for her date and place of birth, and her blood group. She answered with barely contained delight, but when Bob presented her with some 'insurance things', she looked bewildered and required a nod from Grandpa before she'd sign her name at the rele-vant places. Displaying an acre of whitened tooth enamel, Bob proffered a thicker document.

'The legal arrangements,' he said.

Julie looked at my grandfather and blinked twice.

'It's what we talked about last week,' Grandpa told her. 'So that you're looked after in case anything happens to me.'

Julie pouted. 'I hate it when you talk like that, Donny.'

'It's all right, darling,' said Grandpa. 'There's no need for us to go over it all again now. Everything's there. Just sign it.'

The room was silent save for the sound of the pages being turned. Concentrating hard, Julie nibbled her thumb, the same thumb she'd used to arrest my orgasm on the night we'd practised *carezza*. After a minute or so, she frowned at something in the document and looked to her fiancé for reassurance at the precise moment that he was shooting a nervous glance at Bob. If Grandpa had kept smiling at Julie all the while, she might well have done as he'd asked without a murmur, but instead she began to scrutinize the document even more carefully, tracking the print across the page with her forefinger, and flinched.

'What's this about "dissolution, separation, annulment"?' she asked Bob Caswell, and then began to read aloud. '"Except as otherwise provided for in this agreement, each party specifically agrees that neither shall make any claim for or be entitled to receive any money or property from the other as alimony, spousal support or maintenance." Is this what I think it is?'

As a relatively upstanding member of the California bar, Bob had no recourse but to outline the terms of the agreement, and hurt swelled in Julie's face.

'We never discussed this, Donny. You're trying to trick me,' she cried.

Squirming in his seat, Grandpa's lips had turned white. 'No, darling. No, I'm not.'

'Relax, Julie,' Bob said. 'Don explained –'

'He explained nothing,' Julie yelled. 'He just told me he was making a new will. That's all. He lied to me and I bet he lied to you too.' She flew at Grandpa and tried to batter him, but she was so slight that Bob and I managed to restrain her without difficulty. 'You think I'd ever take a penny from you, Donny?' she shrieked. 'You're worse than Larry. At least he had the guts to say it to my face.'

'Look, Miss Perrault,' said Bob, readjusting a hank of lacquered silver hair. 'I can promise you that this is really just a standard boilerplate document. In this state, most couples go this way.'

Bob leapt back as Julie tried to slug him, and Grandpa rose unsteadily to his feet. 'Bob, I think you'd better –'

The lawyer's livelihood depended upon his ability to take a hint. He amassed his various papers and promptly fled the house. His departure didn't help matters.

'If you'd told me what it was, Donny, I'd have signed it without a second thought,' Julie cried.

Grandpa swore that he believed her, but she kept on shouting at him until his face turned blotchy. Julie's genuine sense of outrage proved to me once and for all that she was no gold-digger, but I was terrified that Grandpa was about to blow a heart valve. Catching the alarm on my face, Julie sobbed that she'd never been so humiliated and ran out of the room.

'Go after her,' Grandpa said to me. 'Tell her I was too embarrassed to talk it over with her. Say I'll never mention it again. That Bob forced my hand. Go on, dear boy. I beg you.' He was breathing hard and trembling, and I could feel the raw fear in him, the terror of dying alone and unloved. 'Please, Ralph. Julie's everything to me.'

'I know, Grandpa, I know,' I said. 'But there's no point trying to reason with her until she's cooled off. I promise you. It's best to leave it for a few minutes. Just sit tight and I'll get you a Scotch.'

The drink evened out the colour in his face and when he'd calmed down, I crossed the yard to knock on Julie's door. There was no reply, so I pushed it open to find her kneeling by her bed, evidently listening to the recorded teachings of Sri Rampa on her Walkman. As I stepped into the room, she tore the plugs from her ears, and I saw that she'd been crying.

'You never thought I was after your grandfather's money, did you, Ralph?'

'It never crossed my mind,' I said, ashamed that it had.

'Did Eleanor?'

'I'm sure not.'

Julie had already thrown most of her few possessions into a nylon rucksack, and her posters of various Indian sub-deities had been rolled up inside her yoga mat. While the tape of Sri Rampa's honeyed voice spooled unheard through her Walkman, I asked her if she was planning to leave, and she shrugged.

'At least talk things over with Grandpa first,' I said. 'This is breaking his heart.'

Julie lowered her eyes. 'No, it isn't,' she said. 'It's better this way, believe me. Donny made a mistake. He knows it deep down, and that's why he's been so unhappy since the party. I thought it was because he'd been hurt by the mean things your father said about me, but it wasn't that at all.'

'Listen, Julie. Grandpa couldn't bring himself to discuss the agreement with you. And Bob Caswell insisted –'

'Please, Ralph,' she said, replacing the plugs. 'Let it rest. I need some time on my own.'

Ever the go-between, I went back to the library. Crouched in his chair by the fireplace, Grandpa clutched his cane and an empty glass. 'What did she say?'

'It's all going to be fine,' I replied. 'Julie loves you. She's hurt but she'll come round in time. You'll see.'

'How do you know, dear boy? How do you know? I've ruined everything.'

'Of course you haven't,' I said. 'Just let the dust settle. Then you can apologize to her all you like. Blame it all on Bob Caswell. Julie's bound to understand. Try and be patient.'

Misery and loneliness hollowed out his face. 'How can I be patient?' he wailed. 'I've lost my one chance of happiness. My Cordelia.'

Grandpa was working himself up again and there was no point reasoning with him (or reminding him that Julie was his fiancée, not his daughter), so I went to the den to recharge his Scotch.

When I returned to the library, my grandfather had disappeared. Hearing a sound, I raced along the corridor to find him collapsed on the floor in the hall, face down and motionless. I thought he was dead.

Time stretched as I stood there shaking.

Grandpa's groan broke the reverie. I space-walked over to the telephone and called 911, my voice hollow as I gave the address. The telephonist told me that the paramedics were already on their way, and I realized that Grandpa must have activated the alarm that he wore around his neck. Hanging up, I knelt down to comfort him, but he shouted at me like a terrorized animal.

'Don't touch me. I've twisted my fibula.'

My grandfather hadn't broken any bones, but the paramedics wanted to carry out various tests at the hospital. Despite their assurances, his pupils were black as spilled ink and his forehead felt icy.

Grandpa gripped my arm. 'Tell me,' he murmured. 'Am I dying?' His panic flowed into me, an electric current. 'I have to talk to Julie. Where is she?'

Playing for time, I promised him that he'd see her at the hospital.

The paramedics carried him out to the ambulance, and I followed them to Cedars-Sinai in the station wagon. At the Anita and Robert Silverstein Reception Center in the Ruth and Harry Roman Emergency Department, the receptionist gave me a nametag, directing me to the fifth floor of the Frances and Steve Broidy Tower, where Grandpa was propped up in bed, looking ancient and as vulnerable as a shelled turtle in his hospital gown. Even though the X-rays had confirmed that he'd suffered no more than a sprained ankle and a bruised hip, the doctor had decided to keep him in hospital overnight.

'Everybody's saying I've been very, very fortunate,' Grandpa said.

'Well, I don't know about that, but thank God you're still in one piece,' I said. 'How do you like your room?'

'It's a suite. Look.' The sliding door opened on to a second pale-green room, which contained two sofas and a complimentary bunch of flowers. Grandpa grinned weakly. 'Apparently the Sultan of Brunei's nephew's going into a smaller one down the hall, because they saved this for me when they heard I was coming. Nice of them, don't you think?'

The doctor had given him a mild sedative, and I could have used one myself as I dialled Eleanor's mobile on the telephone in the sitting room. My aunt said that she'd be there right away, and I tried to get hold of Julie at Grandpa's request, but the telephone just rang and rang at North Canon Drive.

Grandpa's brave face slipped. 'Do you think that means she's on her way here?'

Before I was forced to tell another lie, a curvaceous young nurse arrived to take his pulse. Holding Grandpa's wrist, she gushed that she'd seen all his films, and he smiled as she listed the ones she liked best.

'You're so pretty, Donna, you're welcome to give me a bed-bath any time you like,' he said, and his eyes lingered on her as she left the room. Grandpa's pride had taken more of a knock than any physical part of him, and Donna's attention had gone some way to restoring it, at least temporarily. I sat by his bed until Eleanor arrived, wearing dark glasses against the curiosity of her public and any newspaper photographers who might have staked out the Reception Center.

'Darling,' she cried, 'I'm so glad nothing's broken. But are you in terrible pain?'

Grandpa shook his head, and Eleanor held his hand as he explained that he'd been heading over to Julie's apartment when he fell. Faced for once with a genuine crisis, my aunt refrained from her usual histrionics and revealed hidden reserves. Speaking briefly with the doctor before calling Bruce in Ojai and Larry in Natchez (where he was apparently reshooting some scenes for his pilot), Eleanor's businesslike manner came as a surprise. While Grandpa dozed, she led me into the sitting room and asked me to describe for her in more detail the events that had led up to Grandpa's fall. Barely raising an eyebrow at Julie's reaction to the prenuptial agreement, my aunt reproved me gently for being wise after the event when I told her I was feeling guilty for having left her father on his own in the library. Grandpa was soon fast asleep, but we stayed with him so that he wouldn't wake alone in a hospital room, and it had grown dark outside by the time Bruce arrived in his work clothes, wide-eyed with alarm.

'Is Pops going to be OK, Elly?' he asked his sister. Considering the way Grandpa had treated Bruce at the party, the depth of my uncle's concern was doubly touching, and when the nurse brought us tea, he even insisted that she make up a bed for him so that he could spend the night at his father's side. Since Grandpa was in no danger, this was hardly necessary, but Eleanor agreed to it, and we left Bruce there watching television with the sound turned low while his father slept on.

There was no sign of Julie at North Canon Drive, not even a note, and her tiny apartment had been stripped of her personal possessions. Taking Julie's flight as proof of her opportunism, Eleanor was exultant, but I knew how badly my grandfather would react to the news.

'Grandpa's going to be heartbroken,' I said. 'Julie isn't in the least bit interested in his money.'

'Don't be ridiculous, Ralph,' Eleanor said. 'The minute she discovered she wasn't actually going to get anything, she fled. How much more evidence do you need?'

Brooking no argument, my aunt left me to spend an uneasy night alone in the empty house.

I slept badly, and when Eleanor called at ten the next morning to ask me to drive her to Cedars-Sinai, my mind was smudged. My grandfather was to be discharged at midday, and my aunt had prepared a fruit salad for his breakfast. Explaining that her presence wasn't required at rehearsals, Eleanor was in something of a holiday mood as I ferried her to the Medical Center.

'You can't imagine the impact Daddy had on Bruce and me as children,' she said. 'In those days he was so famous that the traffic stopped in the street when we stepped out of our hotel. Can you imagine that actually happening for anybody now? It was like he was covered in gold leaf.'

Grandpa had exchanged his hospital gown for a djellaba embroidered with silver thread ('a gift from the Sultan's nephew') and was sitting up in bed, enjoying bacon and eggs with Bruce. Wrinkling her nose, Eleanor asked her father how he was feeling.

'Too late for fruit, too soon for flowers,' he said. 'No, no, I feel marvellous. Is Julie with you?'

Glancing at me, Eleanor had no option but to tell Grandpa that Julie had gone, and the news destroyed his brittle good cheer.

'Really?' he said, a sliver of bacon tumbling from his lip. 'Do you have any idea where she is?'

'We don't know,' Eleanor said. 'She's taken all her things but there was no note, and she hasn't called.'

'I'm sure she will, though,' I said, fulfilling the conciliatory role I'd made my own.

Only the quavering wattle at Grandpa's throat betrayed his anguish. 'Well, I suppose what's done is done,' he said. 'Did they tell you they're sticking me in a damn wheelchair until my ankle goes down?'

Jumping at the chance to discuss his health, none of us mentioned Julie's name again.

My grandfather had never let it all hang out, and by the time we all returned to North Canon Drive, his mask had set harder than Bruce's carving. Installed in the den, Grandpa perked up a fraction when the phone rang, only to sink back in his wheelchair when he realized that the caller wasn't Julie. It was a brave act, but his smile seemed faked to me and his eyes were restless. Grandpa had been very badly hurt, and I said as much to Eleanor when she and Bruce returned from the store with a recycled cardboard box full of health food.

'Your father thinks he blew it, trying to pull that trick on her with Bob Caswell,' I said.

95

'Nonsense. Daddy's had a lucky escape and he knows it,' Eleanor said. 'You said yourself that it's mostly his pride that's been bruised.'

My aunt stared at me from the kitchen sink, daring me to disagree with her, and I decided to let it go.

Eleanor passed by North Canon Drive to interview some nurses and cooks on her way to rehearsals the next morning. That afternoon, she returned to play cards with her father, and this set a pattern for the next few days: for an hour each evening they played canasta and gin rummy, games he'd taught her as a child. I'd never known my aunt to be more carefree. Merle adored her. Carmelita, Julie's replacement and a trained nurse, was Eleanor's devoted fan and fulfilled her instructions to the letter. A cleaner came in every day from an agency, and a Japanese-born cook produced meals that were both satisfying and organically correct. Grandpa and I developed such a taste for this New Age cuisine that, after a couple of days, we even stopped missing the salt that Eleanor had banned from the house on account of her father's cholesterol levels.

Grandpa only dropped the pretence once.

Having taken a call from his lawyer, he found himself alone with me in the den. 'Bob Caswell's a fool in good clothes, Ralph. A fool in good clothes,' he said. 'I should never have listened to him. Howl, howl, howl, howl. Lear does say "howl" four times, doesn't he? You can't imagine how much I miss her, dear boy.'

When I tried to smoke out more of his feelings on the matter, my grandfather looked away and muttered something about that aching spot where beats the human heart. However badly Julie had wounded him, he was too proud to talk about it, preferring to airbrush her from his mind just as he'd done with his third wife, the French actress whose name we'd been enjoined to forget.

Our meals were taken in the dining room once more, and

Eleanor made sure that Bruce ate with us when he wasn't up at Ojai. Life at North Canon Drive was easier for my uncle now that Julie had left, but Grandpa's reaction to his gift was still a running sore.

'Why's my carving been moved into the garage?' Bruce asked me out of the blue early one morning.

'It rained last week and Ernesto and I thought we'd better put it somewhere dry,' I said.

'You needn't have,' Bruce said. 'I gave the wood seven coats of marine varnish, so the rain's no problem.'

Unable to rustle up an excuse to leave it where it was, I helped him carry the carving back up to the terrace. As lunchtime loomed, I feared the worst but Eleanor had foreseen the problem and had spoken to Grandpa on her way to rehearsals.

'Your carving's an extraordinary work of art, Bruce,' Grandpa said as we sat down to eat. 'Highly expressive. I've been meaning to tell you how much it's grown on me.'

Bruce blushed. 'You really mean that?'

'I most certainly do.'

At a loss for words, Bruce went over and kissed his father, whose own mood appeared to improve for the rest of the day. But by the end of the week, Grandpa was making less and less effort to hide his sadness and took to staring out of the window for minutes on end.

On Larry's return from Natchez, Eleanor persuaded my grandfather to ask his eldest son over for lunch, which, given her father's state of mind, struck me as an extremely bad idea. Lisa and Roger were bussed in to enforce our good behaviour, but Danny Tait and his girlfriend dropped out at the last minute. According to Eleanor, Danny had proposed marriage to Ingeborg that very morning, and our lunch party was consequently tinged with an air of anti-climax. Life, for once, appeared to be elsewhere.

My father arrived promptly, resplendent in fluorescent

trainers and a houndstooth jacket he'd worn on his last visit to London (I recognized it from the tiny hash burn on the lapel). Hugging me, he apologized again, *sotto voce*, for his harsh words down by the pool, and I was ready enough to forgive him. Grandpa felt differently. Perhaps he'd reached an age where the conventional social niceties seemed pointless, but it was still painful to watch him ignore his son's admittedly ham-fisted attempts at fence mending when we sat down to eat. Trying to retrieve the situation, Eleanor treated us to an anecdote from the New York rehearsals for *Macbeth* (her bald leading man had apparently propositioned one of the witches), which in turn inspired Larry to offer a vignette from his recent experiences in Mississippi. With its tenuous connection to truth, anecdote is tailor-made for actors, and while Eleanor and Larry traded an invisible microphone back and forth, Grandpa scratched his chin until he couldn't contain himself any longer.

'Speaking of put-downs, I was in Switzerland in 1968, staying with Charlie and Oona at the Manoir de Ban,' he said, 'when Noël Coward came over for lunch. The Master was at a low ebb, suffering from phlebitis I think, and though he couldn't possibly have been sweeter to me personally, he spent the whole meal saying beastly things about everyone under the sun. *2001: A Space Odyssey* had just come out, and he dismissed its star with one sentence: "Keir Dullea, gone tomorrow."'

Like Larry and Eleanor, Grandpa seemed to obtain an almost erogenous pleasure from the attention of others. Weaving a seamless web of reminiscence, he told us (as if we needed reminding) that when Vanessa Redgrave was born, he'd been in the audience watching her father Michael play Laertes in Olivier's *Hamlet* (the show having, all too predictably, gone on).

'At the final curtain, Larry stepped downstage to make an announcement. "Tonight",' Grandpa said, his imitation of Olivier's clipped, mannered speech making Eleanor smile, '"a great actress has been born. Laertes has a daughter." A shiver ran through me when I heard that, I don't mind telling you.'

As my grandfather spoke, a shiver ran through me – a shiver of embarrassment for all concerned. Compared to Vanessa Redgrave, I'd got away reasonably lightly, but Lisa's eyes glazed over as Grandpa told us how 'dear Larry' would rehearse a simple gesture on his own for hours, the hanging up of a raincoat, for example, or the opening of a window.

Roger and Lisa had barely spoken since they arrived, and seeing us through their eyes, I was ashamed to belong to such a monstrous family. Little wonder that as a child I'd believed myself to have been adopted, or had fantasized that a mix-up in the maternity ward would shortly be uncovered and that I'd be returned to my rightful parents, a faintly drawn suburban couple with a dog and regular meal-times. But being a child, such reservations had been at best cloudy and guilt-ridden: I'd known nothing else. Only now was I beginning to see, dimly, that my family were in fact grotesque egomaniacs.

Cutting a tiny slice of potato, Eleanor sprinkled it with pepper before pecking at it, and Lisa went into an eye-crossing routine that made me corpse. Having failed to pick up on the underlying tension, Bruce was the only one of us who seemed remotely at ease, but when he suggested that Grandpa and Larry might care to drive out to Ojai together, it took all Eleanor's social skills to steer the conversation on to safer ground. Larry had been reaching for his wineglass more frequently as the meal progressed, speed-drinking, and when the cook presented us with her organic fruit pudding, he chose precisely the wrong way to compliment her.

'This is the best food I've had round here for years.'

Grandpa looked up from his plate.

'Well, come on, Pa,' Larry said. 'Julie couldn't boil an egg and you know it.'

The silence pressed in, and my grandfather put his knife down. 'I won't have Julie disparaged in this house,' he said. 'Is that clear?'

Looking bewildered, Larry glanced over at Eleanor, whose lips had all but disappeared.

'Hey, I'm sorry, Pa. I thought you figured you got off lightly with Julie splitting the way she did. Eleanor said –'

Larry's sister cut him off with a glare.

Grandpa's irises went black. 'Don't you dare speak to me like that.'

My grandfather tried to raise himself up. Fearing that he might suffer another fall, Roger and I sprang from out seats.

'Hey, I'm sorry, Pa!' Larry cried. 'I got it wrong, OK? It's a misunderstanding. Eleanor, will you please tell him?' Grandpa's face purpled and I bustled Larry out of the dining room. 'What's going on?' he said. 'Eleanor told me the old man was cool about Julie. Christ sake, it was so tense in there, I was just trying to clear the air.'

Once outside, Larry kicked out at some shrubs. 'Fuck it,' he yelled. 'I've blown it again.' Alerted by the noise, Ernesto appeared in the archway holding a pair of shears. 'Hey, I'm sorry,' Larry said to him. 'I'm just pissed at my old man, OK?'

Puzzled, Ernesto retreated to the back yard and Larry caught my frown.

'Let's get out of here,' he said. 'You can drive if you like.'

## Chapter Six

'The actor was busy wiping face and neck with a
towel already stiff with rouge and grease-paint . . .
This then – such was the tenor of my thoughts – this
grease-smeared and pimply individual is the charmer
at whom the twilight crowd was just now gazing so
soulfully! This repulsive little worm is the reality of
the glorious butterfly in whom those deluded spectators believed they were beholding the realisation of
all their own secret dreams of beauty, grace, and
perfection!'
Thomas Mann, *The Confessions of Felix Krull,*
*Confidence Man*

Larry said he didn't care where we went, so I decided to take
us to Matador beach, but as we drove west on Sunset, my
father seemed an altogether different person to the one I'd
imagined him to be on our last trip there together thirteen
years previously. When I tried to lower the roof at some
lights, he told me that the catch had broken and lit a spindle-
shaped joint.

'I mean, how could Eleanor be so stupid?' he said. 'I just
*knew* the old man was still hung up about Julie.'

'If you thought that, why did you say the things you said?'

'To get at the truth for once. Nobody ever tells the truth in
that goddamn mausoleum and it just gets me down, you
know?'

At the Palisades, the reek of his reefer and the proximity of
an LAPD patrol car led me to mention the ongoing war on
drugs, but Larry just slumped down even lower in his seat,
as if Grandpa's new cook had de-boned him, and told me to
relax. On previous visits to California I'd felt like his sibling
but now I was assuming the role of his maiden aunt, and it

crossed my mind that Larry had encouraged me to call him by his first name as a child in order to make him feel younger and less accountable as a father.

'I think it was in 1963 when I was staying in Switzerland with Charlie and Oona,' Larry said, 'and Noël Coward invited us all for lunch at Les Avants . . .'

Larry's uncanny imitation of his father cracked me up, making me feel closer to him again, and the rain clouds massing beyond Malibu persuaded me to turn south on the crumbling coast highway towards Venice.

'Hey, you don't want to go there,' Larry said. 'It's turned into a really shitty place.'

Fascinated by the area's vibrant street-life as a child, I wouldn't be dissuaded. 'We're going,' I said.

A breeze carried the stink of a seafood restaurant into the car as we parked in a vacant lot near the Santa Monica pier, and I had a sudden impulse to tell Larry the truth about Direct Debit, but no sooner had I begun to confess than he closed me off.

'You're the smartest guy I know,' he said. 'There's nothing you couldn't do if you put your mind to it. So whatever troubles you've got, you'll sort them out. You were a golden child.'

'But –'

'No. Listen to me. I believe in you. Period,' he said, leading me on to the pathway that ran alongside the beach. 'Things will work out for you and you'll be fine. I just wish I felt the same way about Bruce.'

Stepping aside to allow a family of cyclists to pass, Larry complained that Bruce couldn't live alone and that he'd need to be set up in some kind of therapeutic community after Grandpa died. Annoyed, if not surprised, that Larry had once again redirected the conversation to his own concerns, I said that Bruce seemed to be doing very well out at Ojai for long periods of time.

'Sure, he's been pretty level just lately,' Larry said. 'But he gets these really heavy mood swings. The thing with the carving sent him way down. Couldn't you tell?'

'Maybe so, but it didn't last long,' I said.

'You're only seeing about a quarter of the picture, sonny. In a way Bruce is a better actor than any of us. He has to be.' An intrepid gull landed at the edge of the path to inspect a spent nicotine patch. 'You're so lucky to be an only child,' Larry went on. 'Every time I did anything good it made Bruce look bad. It was even a problem for me when I won a swimming cup. Can you believe that? And Bruce was such a sweet kid. All he ever did was to try and get by, but the old man was ashamed of him back then because he wasn't perfect. So I had to excel at everything, to let everybody know that Bruce's problems weren't down to Donald Tait but to my brother's crazy English mother. Can you imagine what that was like for me?'

Of course I could, because Larry had already described his childhood to me twenty times in microscopic detail, but I was still waiting for something from him, some missing piece that might explain everything to me once and for all. Even then, I was unaware that Larry had even fewer answers than I did.

'I was always kind of torn in two,' he said. 'Because to please my father was to hurt my brother. It's why I've never really followed through on anything.'

Like being a father yourself, I wanted to say, but despite my irritation, I was enjoying being there with him, breathing the sea air and dodging the flailing arms of less experienced roller-bladers. When I'd misbehaved as a child, Larry had seldom told me off but he'd played the part of a normal father if the need had arisen, on school sports days, for example, if he'd happened to be in England. Naturally, it had been understood between us that he'd only be faking it, just as he'd sometimes taken me along as a prop when he went for auditions, to help make him look respectable if the part demanded it. Instead of feeling cheated by this, I'd felt privileged to be let into the secret that adults pretended too, and it had bound me to my father more tightly. But as we neared the boardwalk at Venice, I couldn't escape the feeling that we were rehearsing our stories to convince some notional bureaucrat that we were a *bona fide* father and son.

An old woman on the boardwalk recognized Larry, and her face opened as she mistook him for someone she knew in real life. Realizing that he was an actor, she coughed to hide her embarrassment, yet Larry barely reacted, because wherever he went in the world, the faces of old friends and perfect strangers smiled in precisely the same way whenever they saw him.

Young black men were smoking grass beneath the palms, a white rasta with leg tattoos was jabbering into a mobile phone, and a homeless man was stitching a patch on to his decaying jeans with bright pink fingers. Larry began to look troubled, but it was only a matter of minutes before a couple with the pear-shaped physiques of career television viewers came up to tell him how fantastic they considered him to be. The man claimed that he always caught reruns of *Patrolman*, but the woman seemed (to my mind, if not my father's) unsure as to exactly which part Larry had played in the show.

Moving on, Larry smoothed his hair for the benefit of the imaginary film crew who attended his every waking moment, but the effects of the flattery were short-lived, and soon he began to ruminate once more about Grandpa's lack of provision for Bruce in the event of his death.

Choking in the acrid fog of scorched fat that billowed from a hot-dog stand on the boardwalk, I began to share Larry's opinion of Venice. The spontaneous street theatre had vanished, leaving fake swamis to practise massage on the unwary, and burnt-out hippies offering to paint your name on a grain of rice. The area's integrity had been swept aside by a tide of homogeneous tourist shops which sold the same unfunny T-shirts and cheap sunglasses that I'd seen in Tel Aviv with Direct Debit when we toured our mime version of *The Importance of Being Earnest* as part of the British Council's cultural exchange programme.

Sightseers wandered the boardwalk in search of something that wasn't there, the fatter men keeping their torsos covered while those who'd worked out bared their chests to show off the peculiar results of their labours. The body was a site of terrible anxiety for everyone, and Larry checked out the tourist girls with a wolfish leer that sat uncomfortably on the face of a man old enough to be their father.

Passing a bookshop, he asked me about my work on the manuscript without sounding remotely interested. Indeed it seemed likely that if Grandpa's autobiography were eventually to be published, Larry would simply check his name in the index, read the relevant sections and leave it at that – just like the other fifty people who might actually pick it up. When I mentioned that Scott Newton had asked after him, Larry shrugged and said that the name was unfamiliar.

'An Australian. He says he knew you in the 80s,' I said.

'Everybody knew me in the 80s,' Larry said. 'Tell me, have you figured out the real reason the old man's so desperate to finish this book?' I shook my head. 'It's a spoiling exercise,' he said. 'He's trying to get his story in first to stop me writing about what really happened. You hadn't thought of that, had you? About what story he's trying to suppress here?'

This was absurd, and I was glad when Larry suggested that we might sit on the bleachers to watch a paddle-tennis match between a stringy fifty-five-year-old man wearing a bandanna and a much younger opponent. Possessed of an awesome will to win, the younger man looked to be the stronger player, but when Larry began rooting for him, it astonished me that my father identified with someone my age rather than with his peer. The youngster won the match, and as Larry rose from his seat, his mobile rang. It was Lisa, calling to say that Danny Tait had invited me to an impromptu engagement party, and suggesting that I might meet her at a café near her apartment.

Picking up on this, Larry grabbed the phone from me. 'I want to take you and Ralph for dinner at the Truffola in

Hollywood before we head over to Danny's,' he said to Lisa. 'You're with a girlfriend? Great. Bring her too.'

Annoyed with Larry for gate-crashing the evening, I got my revenge when we drove past a hundred banners suspended from the streetlights on Santa Monica Boulevard advertising Eleanor's *Macbeth*. Having avoided the stage since the lynching of his Mark Anthony by the New York critics in the early 1990s, Larry's mood deflated at the repeated vision of his sister acting her heart out in a long black wig.

The Truffola was owned by a fat Lothario of fifty who wore his grey hair long enough to cover his collar, and when my father introduced me as 'my son, the playwright', Michael confessed to an obsession with the theatre, having himself originated a television series in the 1980s. Extolling a recent production of the short plays of Frank O'Hara, he led us back into the large open-air dining area that accounted for his restaurant's popularity. On our way to our table, a dozen diners gave Larry 'that Hollywood look, that always seems thrown over one shoulder'. My father grinned when two young female fans called his name, and I had the feeling he'd have taken their telephone numbers in a flash if not for the lurking possibility that a gossip columnist or a divorce lawyer might have been within earshot. Having partied together regularly for twenty years, Larry and Michael traded increasingly pungent reminiscences, and I endured their banter with a faint heart until Michael went off to glad-hand another dear friend. Scanning the oversize menu, Larry again talked up his Wittgenstein project for my benefit (and that of the diners at nearby tables) with all the zeal of the autodidact. There was even something showy about the way my father held the menu, as if he'd conditioned himself to follow Goethe's suggestion, in *Rules for Actors*, that '*since the eye of the spectator wishes to be charmed by pleasing groupings and positions, the actor must strive to preserve these even when off the stage; he should always imagine before him a group of spectators*'.

106

'The most amazing thing is that Wittgenstein ate the same meal every day,' Larry said, snapping a bread stick. 'Didn't care what it was as long as it was the same as the day before. Can you believe that?'

'And how would you convey that on film?' I asked, envisaging a procession of lamb cutlets in a mind-numbing montage sequence.

Larry frowned. 'I'm not sure. Maybe some kind of dispute with the cook? We'd shoot the whole thing in Eton College. They used it for *Chariots of Fire*, remember, that time they ran round the quadrangle.'

Our waiter came to refresh our drinks, and when Larry referred to me as 'my son' five times in less than a minute, I had to wonder why he was trying to impress his paternity on a twenty-five-year-old stranger interested only in finding out what wine we wanted to quaff. Italian restaurants had long been Larry's natural habitat, and the words *Barolo*, *vongole* and *osso bucco* were familiar to me by the age of six. I'd known my father to arm-wrestle with a Hungarian director on another table following a lengthy meal, or order sambuccas for all his fellow diners before treating them to some *a cappella* karaoke. On one occasion, he'd slipped a disc while trying to lift a waitress above his head; on another, he'd started a small fire attempting to ignite an amaretti wrapper behind his back. Amazingly, such antics had been tolerated by moustachioed *maître d*'s the world over, men who'd have kicked Larry into the street before he'd even punctured his *pollo sorpresa* if he hadn't been famous. Instead they often requested (and received from Larry's agent) black-and-white publicity stills. According to a friend of mine, a trattoria in Worthing, Sussex, still has a snap of my father framed above the till, inscribed 'To Luigi, Fly me to the Moon! Larry Tait', the damage he'd inflicted on the loggia long forgotten. During such escapades as I'd witnessed personally, my quiet groans had invariably gone unheard.

While we waited for Lisa, Larry trotted out another dozen anecdotes that I almost knew by heart, and tension and sadness tied knots in my stomach. For the umpteenth time, my father mock-complained about my response to his Hamlet at the age of nine ('Why was it so long, Daddy?' I'd apparently asked when brought round to his dressing room following the matinée), and I longed to tell him to change the record. Feeling the effects of the wine, a tooth blackening Chianti, anger and a sense of helplessness boiled over inside me, and I went to the men's room to try and regain some composure. Larry's self-centredness knew no bounds. Was I really of his flesh and blood? And if so, could it be that I was blind to a similar vein of self-obsession in myself? Appalled by this possibility, I took my crinkled plane ticket from the pocket of my tweed jacket and stuck it to my forehead. When I bowed my neck, it fell off and I just managed to catch it against my chest before it glided into the urinal.

Still agitated, I returned to the table to find that Lisa had arrived with her girlfriend, a long-legged flirt called Mitzi who worked as a location manager. Lisa's presence soothed me, even as Larry reheated his new anecdote about the job he'd just completed in Natchez. Befuddled like me by the Chianti, it must have slipped his mind that he'd told two thirds of his audience a variant of the same story at lunch that very day. But while Lisa and I struggled to listen politely, Mitzi acted as if it was the funniest thing she'd ever heard, squealing 'You're *kidding*' as Larry delivered his new, improved punchline.

Perfect in themselves, Mitzi's features didn't sit easily together, and although she was highly attractive at first glance, her face's composite quality led me to wonder if she'd already undergone cosmetic surgery. While she and Larry exchanged double entendres, Lisa told me that Grandpa had retreated upstairs directly after lunch, blaming Eleanor for inviting Larry to his house. Apparently my aunt had cried all the way back to Doheny Drive, releasing her negative energy again by cursing my father at the top of her voice.

'Is she all right now?' I asked Lisa.

'Don't worry,' she replied. 'The minute Eleanor got home, she called her masseuse and her aromatherapist.'

In the soft light, Lisa looked to be make-up free, but on closer inspection, I noticed that she'd applied a layer of paint with a high degree of artifice. As the meal dragged on, Mitzi's flirtation with Larry made Lisa more and more uncomfortable, and it puzzled me why good-natured single women like Lisa so often picked a girlfriend with bigger problems, blonder hair and less of an appetite for food, since the net result is usually only a lowering of their self-esteem. When we'd finished eating, Larry insisted on covering the check, the fin on his back rising at the prospect of the party. Crammed into the back of Mitzi's sports car with Lisa, I buzzed the window down to try to clear my head, and Larry screamed as twenty bucks' worth of grass formed a tiny twister in his lap before disappearing into thin air.

Lined with mangled fenders, the Pacific Coast Highway glittered with chips of broken tail-light, and rain began to hose the windshield as we neared the ocean. Facing the possibility of a truck jack-knifing into their living room at any minute, the people who'd chosen to live in the glorified shacks perched precariously on the thin strip of land between the highway and the beach had taken the injunction to live on the edge quite literally. Having been to a dinner at Danny's new house the previous week, Mitzi knew the way once we reached Malibu, and turning on to a road that bordered the beach, she pulled up behind a magenta dune buggy just as a thickset man with the tapering, trapezoidal head of an Easter Island statue climbed out of a limousine.

Protected from the rain by his chauffeur's umbrella, he squelched through the downpour to an open door in a high fence. Following him, we found ourselves on a walkway that led to the top floor of a large two-storey wooden house. By the front door, a woman in a tie-dye dress was muttering into a mobile phone, getting drenched in the interests of privacy or better reception, and her cold, scared glance sobered me as we entered the house.

Groups of guests were clustered at one end of a cavernous room, shying away from the massive picture window that faced the ocean as if they were afraid that the rainstorm might shatter the glass. Film and television people in their thirties and forties, their socializing seemed constrained by a knowledge of their respective places in the pecking order. Goatees abounded on the men, some of whom felt confident enough to actually smile at us, but the majority were careful not to be seen to be trying too hard.

Danny came over to hug Larry and hailed him, improbably, as his mentor. 'I'm sorry we couldn't make lunch, but it's been really last minute,' our host said. 'When I woke up today, I just knew I had to propose to Ingeborg, and after that we needed to tell our parents and it took for ever. Then we decided we'd better throw a party.' Clapping my father on the back, Danny told the man with the trapezoidal head that Larry had inspired him to become an actor. 'His performances have this abrasive quality,' Danny said. 'I've never got enough of it.'

As Larry and Danny sprayed each other with mutual affirmation, I was desperate to feel that close and relaxed with my father. My cousin could accept Larry as he was, failings and all, so why couldn't I? My frustration would have driven me to drink if I hadn't already been there, and when Ingeborg offered Lisa a tour of the house, I staggered along behind them.

Speakers set into the walls of a series of barely furnished rooms emitted Willie Colon as background music, and Ingeborg outlined her ideas about redecoration for us in a voice that had the tonal range of a dripping tap. In the master bedroom, piles of screenplays teetered against the wall, supporting ashtrays, paperbacks and Ingeborg's cosmetics.

'This morning we woke up and a pelican landed on the deck,' she said. 'And then Danny asked me to marry him. Romantic, no?'

While Ingeborg showed Lisa the contents of her wardrobe, I stumbled across a group of surfer types, one of whom had stepped out on to the deck to dance in the rain, naked to the waist. Another smiled at me as he sucked on an air-roach, dragging the imaginary smoke deep into his lungs. Was he asking me if I had any marijuana, or simply plumbing new depths of idiocy? In search of a bathroom, I wandered into one of the spare bedrooms, surprising a woman who was try-ing to get through to someone in Milan on the bedside tele-phone. At the end of the corridor, a young English actor was sitting by himself playing on a Gameboy, and his eyes flicked up to make sure that I'd noticed his insouciance. Half-drunk, I recognized my own alienation in his glance.

The rain had stopped, so I went down the steps to the beach and urinated against the pilings that supported the house, lulled by the black crash of the ocean at my back. Meanwhile, more guests were arriving, and I found Lisa with Danny and Ingeborg in the big room upstairs, talking to the man with the Easter Island head. Possessed of mobile, untrustworthy features, he turned out to be Danny's manag-er, and when we were introduced, I mentioned that I'd seen him outside with his chauffeur.

'I told you, Carl's my manager, so of course he's got a chauffeur,' cried Danny, managing both to flatter Carl and affirm his own status simultaneously.

Danny's got it too, I thought. Egomania. Although he does a superb job of covering it most of the time, he has the virus. This was both reassuring and infinitely dispiriting, in that it made me face seriously for the first time the unlikelihood that I'd escaped my family's raging self-obsession. But Carl had already begun to disparage a famous actor, and the man-ager's grandiosity made it all too easy for me to suppress my

111

troubling insight. Although Carl's complaint (that the actor in question was a psychopath) may well have been valid, he was making one of the name-dropper's fundamental errors: in denigrating somebody famous, he was only pointing up the improbability that (chauffeur-driven limousines notwithstanding) the celebrity in question would be wasting his own breath bad-mouthing Carl.

Roger Mooney was talking to Danny in the corner, and I asked Lisa if she realized that her father had arrived.

'Sure,' she said. 'Some actor passed on his Elizabeth Bowen thing, so he's thinking about Danny as a replacement.'

'What Elizabeth Bowen thing?' I asked.

'*The Heat of the Heart* or whatever.'

It seemed inconceivable that Roger could cast my cousin, charming though he no doubt was, in a serious film, and I could only imagine that, like me, Lisa was slightly drunk. An original psychedelic projector cast oily patterns on to the wall, recreating the 1960s with neither the hallucinogenic drugs nor the requisite innocence, and an actor who'd quite literally broken a leg was hobbling around on crutches. With his arm around an enraptured Mitzi, Larry seemed over-energized as he introduced himself to a man with a pointed grey beard, pressing his victim back against the wall with the force of his deadly personality. When an over-tanned couple in their mid-thirties arrived, my father zoomed across the room to greet them.

'It's funny,' I said to Lisa. 'Have you noticed that Larry walks exactly like me?'

'Are you serious?' she said. 'You sort of lope and he waddles. From the look of you, I'd never have guessed that you were even related.'

'You think some night-tripping fairy exchanged me with another child? Hah. You haven't seen our ears. They're identical.'

'That's not true. They're a totally different shape,' Lisa said. I gulped. Was she putting me on? 'Why are you always so weird about your father, Ralph?' she asked. 'He's really proud of you, you know.'

'Oh yeah?'

'The first time I met him, he couldn't stop talking about the plays you'd written and all the great work you were doing in the UK.'

It was all too easy to picture Larry boasting about my achievements, but he'd rarely asked to read my work and, on reflection, had only ever attended three of Direct Debit's fifty or so productions. 'Larry's proud of me only so far as he can take credit for being my dad,' I said. 'Face to face, my work threatens his fragile ego.'

'Oh, that's nonsense,' Lisa said. 'Negative, pompous bull-shit.'

'It's the truth,' I said, 'and I'd rather live with that than the sentimental fantasies Larry peddles.'

Shrugging, Lisa asked me how long I was planning to be in California, and as I explained the open-ended nature of my work on the autobiography, it struck me with a deep sense of unease that there was nothing for me back in England. At a professional dead-end, my basement flat in Hackney was sub-let to a South African Business Studies student, and most of my personal effects were stored in cardboard boxes in a friend's garage.

Two models wandered into the room, strange big-eyed gazelles, and wandered out again just as a stand-up comedi-an sat down on a cowhide floor cushion. The over-tanned couple made a beeline for the comic, crouching down to talk to him, star (or asteroid) fuckers reduced to gibbering servil-ity by his mere presence. At eleven o'clock, half the guests went home and the real party started. I remember very little of it.

The next thing I knew, I was sprawled naked on an unfamil-iar bed in a sunlit room, smelling fresh coffee. My own clothes were strewn across the floor along with a collection of cuddly toys, and it was an enormous relief to see Lisa's floral print dress draped over the back of a chair. Such memories as I had of the second half of the party were as sharp and fractured as broken glass: an argument over the merits of *A Propos de Nice* with one of the goatees; Larry and Mitzi's departure; falling over on the beach while dancing with Lisa; Danny and Ingeborg going to bed. At dawn, only five of us had been left sitting on the wet sand around the long-dead fire, and I dimly recalled pouring my heart out to Lisa while a Dane pissed into the sea ten feet from us.

Hearing a toaster pop, I figured I'd have time to retrieve my shorts before Lisa came back into the room, so I stepped away from the bed and was standing, giddy and poisoned, my erection serving as an auxiliary bladder, when she appeared in the doorway carrying a tray. Grinning, she hooked my shorts with her foot, kicking them over to me as I clambered back beneath the sheets, and asked me how I was feeling.

'Marvellous,' I said.

'Liar.'

To my horror, Lisa had prepared breakfast for me, complete with French toast. Having also showered and washed her hair, she smelt pleasantly fresh, unlike me, but as I attempted to complete the previous night's jigsaw of remorse, Lisa promised that I hadn't disgraced myself at the party but rather had been its very life and soul. The more insistent she became, the more I wondered how much of the evening she actually remembered herself.

'Relax, Ralph. People here either go home at nine-thirty or they stay up until eleven the next day on coke and go insane,' she said. 'There's not a lot of middle ground.' Neither one of us had a clue as to the identity of the man with the ponytail who'd ferried us back to West Hollywood as dawn broke, nor did we allude to what had happened when we'd climbed into bed and attempted, with limited success, to make love. Lisa was in reasonably good spirits despite my fumbling incompetence as a lover, but worries multiplied in my mind like bacteria on a microscope slide as I munched the French toast. Did her good humour mean that she thought we were now involved, or did a slightly shrill tone indicate some measure of regret as to the sexual slapstick? Sitting there in Lisa's bed with my head hammering, I was in no state to try and second-guess her feelings. It was enough that my new friend was kind, and the pain behind my eyes diminished as she drove me back to North Canon Drive on her way to (or rather out of her way to) college.

Ernesto was leaving as I let myself in through the side door, and the house was oddly silent. Hoping to make it upstairs to my bed without being seen, I was half-way across the hall when Eleanor came running out of the library, wild-eyed.

'Ralph! Where've you been? Daddy's gone missing.'

Steadying myself against the wall, I asked her what she meant.

'He's not here. He's left the house. Vanished.'

Trembling, my aunt told me that Grandpa hadn't been in his room when Carmelita had arrived earlier, and that his bed didn't appear to have been slept in. The wall beside me seemed to billow out like the sail on a galleon.

'Bruce says the phone rang at six yesterday evening,' Eleanor said. 'They were watching baseball in the den and Daddy wanted to take the call in private, so Bruce left the room, and when he went back, he says Daddy seemed a lot more cheerful. In any case, Bruce took him up in the lift at around nine o'clock last night and that's the last anyone saw of him.' Swallowing hard, she told me that my grandfather had been left on his own in the house because I was at the party (I told Eleanor that I'd stayed the night at Danny's house) and the staff had long gone home. This wouldn't nor-mally have presented a problem since Grandpa had a panic button by the bed in addition to the one he wore around his neck. The intruder alarm had still been primed when

Carmelita opened the front door at 7 a.m., and as soon as my aunt arrived an hour later, she and the nurse made an extensive search of the property to no avail. It looked as if, at some point in the night and for reasons best known to himself, Grandpa had left the house.

'This doesn't make sense,' I said.

'I'm pretty sure the call was from Julie,' Eleanor said. 'Carmelita says a young woman rang up after lunch asking to speak to Daddy. When Carmelita told her he was asleep, whoever it was said that she'd try later.'

Dazed, I followed my aunt through to the kitchen where Carmelita was busy making tea for Bruce.

'We can't tell how many clothes he took with him,' Eleanor told me. 'But his cane's definitely gone. We checked, didn't we, Carmelita?'

The nurse nodded, and Eleanor asked Bruce if he was sure that he hadn't heard a car pull up during the night.

'You asked me that before,' he said.

Eleanor peered directly into his eyes. 'That's right. And now I'm asking you again. This is terribly important.'

Bruce looked hunted. 'Well, no. No, I didn't, OK?'

'Grandpa probably just went to meet Julie,' I said.

'And what if he's been abducted by her cult?' Eleanor cried.

My aunt called some local hotels to see if Grandpa had checked in, bidding us to be silent as she interrogated the receptionists. Unlike Eleanor, I'd never believed for one minute that Grandpa was glad to be rid of Julie, and even through the mist of my hangover, it crossed my mind that the unhappy couple might have eloped. By the time Larry arrived, his eyes as ringed as a redwood tree and wearing the same clothes that he'd worn the previous day, his sister had only succeeded in working herself up even further.

'Has there been any news?' my father asked, flushed from the exertion of his fifteen-pace shuffle from car to kitchen.

'Not a word,' Eleanor said.

As she ran through the chain of events for him, Larry tried to comfort her. 'Sounds to me like the old man and Julie are probably shacked up somewhere,' he said.

My aunt regarded him with contempt. 'Don't be so disgusting.'

'Hey, I'm being serious here,' Larry said. 'It's not as if he hasn't done this kind of thing before.'

'Daddy's in danger. I'm going to call the police.'

'No way,' Larry said, his upper lip slick with sweat. 'In the old man's absence, I'm the head of this family and no one's bringing the police into this until I say so.'

'Don't you dare tell me what to do,' Eleanor cried. 'Who do you think you are?'

'Your elder brother for one thing.'

Bruce banged the table. 'Please will you two stop fighting?'

'Fighting?' said Larry. 'This isn't fighting, is it, sister mine?'

Bruce began to sob, Eleanor skewered Larry with an arctic glare, and then the doorbell rang. Electrified, we rushed through the house to find Roger on the threshold.

Eleanor fell into his arms and began to cry. 'I did everything I could for him,' she said. 'I got him his food, I tried to make things nice . . . Christ, I only took this bloody part to be near him.'

As she sobbed into her husband's pocket-handkerchief, he stroked her hair.

'We think the old man took a call from Julie last night, Roger,' Larry said. 'It looks as if he went off to make up with her.'

'You don't know that,' Eleanor said. 'Something's happened to him. I just know it.'

'Has anyone called the car service?' asked Roger.

'That's a point,' Larry said, popping his fingers as he moved towards the telephone.

'And what about the cars in the garage?' cried Eleanor, dismayed that she'd forgotten to look.

But when Bruce and I went to check, all three vehicles were in their usual places. Glad of a moment's respite from the commotion, I went to the pool house for a Dr Pepper and found that the sliding door was open. It seemed as if Eleanor and Carmelita had unlocked it when they were searching for Grandpa.

The various piles of manuscript were missing from the ping-pong table.

Reeling, I searched the shelves for my back-up disks, pulling down a dozen books before finding them on top of a copy of *I'm OK, You're OK*, a self-help manual that my mother had used to read and re-read at times when she hadn't been OK at all. Confounded by the manuscript's theft, I ran back up to the kitchen to break the news.

'It's a burglary,' said Eleanor, stepping into the pool house.

'Kids probably. Look,' Larry said, indicating the pile of books on the floor. 'They've ransacked the place.'

'That was me,' I said. 'Searching for the disks.'

My father grunted. 'So what's actually missing?' he asked.

'Well, the manuscript itself,' I replied. 'With all Grandpa's notes in the margins. Only a quarter of it's backed up.'

'That settles things,' said Eleanor. 'We have to call the police. There's no question now.'

Swishing an imaginary petticoat, she scurried back up to the house, but Larry caught her at the kitchen door.

'Let's just talk this through first,' he said, wheezing. 'What if the old man took his book with him? I mean, it's more than possible, isn't it? Well, think of all the publicity you're going to kick up. Seems to me he might not be too happy to see his face flashed on the early evening news while he and Julie sip champagne in their honeymoon suite.'

'Don't be so ridiculous,' Eleanor said, entering the kitchen and reaching into her handbag for a herbal cigarette. 'This is a police matter now.'

'It's you who's being ridiculous,' Larry said. 'You're just feeling guilty because your damn meddling drove him away.'

Eleanor's lips went thin, and she and Larry scowled at each other like two kids in the back of a car.

'It might be a good idea to call Bob Caswell first, darling,' Roger said. 'Before you speak to the police.'

'Nobody's calling the police,' Larry said. 'You got that, Roger?'

When I tried to take my father aside, he wrenched his arm away, on the point of losing control.

'But what if the manuscript's been stolen?' I said. 'Surely that in itself –'

'From what I hear, sonny, it'd be very convenient for you if it *had* been,' said Larry. 'Maybe you were so scared about everybody knowing what a fuck-up you've made of the book that you staged this burglary business yourself.' Everyone's eyes were on me. I laughed and shook my head in a futile attempt to cover my distress. 'Maybe you're just making all this up,' he added. 'Like all that stuff about the prize and your play coming to New York.'

Something splintered inside me, and before I knew it, I was running at Larry and shoving him against the sideboard. His coffee cup fell from his hand, causing me to slip on the wet floor and, throwing out an arm to regain my balance, hit him accidentally on the side of his head. Howling in pain, Larry fell to his knees. As Eleanor screamed, my father looked up at me in abject terror.

'Get away from me, you maniac!' he yelped, beetling back across the kitchen floor. 'You've burst my eardrum.'

# Chapter Seven

'Some of the greatest love affairs I have known have
involved one actor, unassisted.'
                                        Wilson Mizner

The eardrum had survived the fracas intact, but the crown on
one of Larry's teeth had come loose, so Roger offered to run
him to his dentist in Century City. Once Larry had checked his
face in the mirror and applied an ice pack to his eye, he cursed
me as they left the house, refusing to accept that the blow
hadn't been intended. While I sat numb-faced at the kitchen
table watching the cleaner from the agency (whose name I'd
never thought to ask) mop up the spilt coffee, Eleanor followed Roger's advice and called Bob Caswell, who said he'd
come over immediately. Appalled at what I'd done, my
behaviour struck me as completely out of character, but my
aunt, a veteran of countless psychodramas at the Esalen
Institute throughout the 1970s, remained unruffled.

'Don't worry about it, Ralph. It was just your American
side coming out,' she said, kneading my shoulders with her
long thin fingers. 'You needed to kick out at Daddy.'

'I don't understand how it happened,' I said. 'I never lose
my temper. Never.'

'Maybe that was the problem,' she said. 'Larry's been a terrible father to you, and this has been boiling up for years.'
Her words struck like a match in a dark cave but my heart
shrank as I recalled Larry's accusation, and I asked Eleanor if
she'd told him that I'd lied to Grandpa about Direct Debit.
'Of course not,' she said. 'It was Larry who told *me*.'

My stomach turned upside down. 'How did he find out?'
I asked her. 'Not from Grandpa?'

'God, no. I think he'd been talking to a friend of his in London. In any case, Larry was only too happy that you'd put one over on Daddy. Actually, he thought it was hilarious.' I was speechless. 'I honestly remember him saying he was glad you were taking after him.' Eleanor laughed. 'You've never really understood that your father's a fake, have you, Ralph? He's a complete fake in absolutely everything he does.'

A Japanese saloon pulled up on the driveway, and when Bob Caswell had unravelled himself from its grey leather bowels, my aunt led him through to the shuttered living room. As I followed them on empty legs, she outlined the events leading up to the discovery of Grandpa's disappearance, concentrating on the telephone calls she believed Julie had made the previous day. Surprisingly, Eleanor barely mentioned the missing manuscript, and it compounded my hurt to think that she might share Larry's suspicion that I'd staged the burglary in the pool house.

'I've called the Sri Rampa temple here in Los Angeles,' said Bob, arranging himself on a long patterned sofa. 'But they refused to discuss the personal affairs of individual worshippers.' Before Eleanor could interpret this as proof of a conspiracy, Bob added that the temple was a legitimate enterprise boasting two prominent Beverly Hills lawyers as members of its congregation. Unimpressed, my aunt flared her nostrils as if to say that only a fellow Beverly Hills lawyer could take this as evidence of the temple's integrity.

Bob's suit gleamed as he uncrossed his legs. 'Remember that time your father disappeared to Ireland for a month, Eleanor? On a spree with a group of fellow actors?'

'Yes, but that was nearly nine years ago,' she said.

'Sure, but only three years ago Don went fishing in Mexico. Gone for two whole weeks without telling a soul, remember? Not even Mrs O. I've no wish to be disrespectful, Eleanor, but I believe you wanted me to alert the FBI over that one.'

My aunt pursed her lips. 'Daddy hardly leaves the house these days except to go to Ojai.'

'And you're sure he's not up there now?'

'Quite sure. The woman who looks after the place went up to check for me. No, I'm certain he's in the clutches of that bloody cult.'

Eleanor's theory was laughable because Grandpa was still in love with Julie, or at least he thought he was (which amounted to the same thing), and the most likely explanation for his absence was elopement, not abduction. Although a suitcase full of manuscript pages was no aphrodisiac, I tried to raise the matter of its disappearance with Bob Caswell, but my aunt shot me a scornful look.

'For God's sake, Ralph,' she said. 'Let's not cloud the issue here.' Bob Caswell was intrigued nonetheless, and Eleanor turned to him with some weariness. 'Daddy's manuscript's gone missing,' she said. 'But the door to the pool house was left open overnight. Anybody could have got in there. A vagrant. Or some kids.'

That gave me pause, because it wouldn't have been the first time I'd forgotten to lock the pool-house door, but no kid (or adult) in their right mind would think to steal a manuscript of theatrical memoirs. Eleanor's explanation didn't hold up. Before I had a chance to put my case, Bob asked Eleanor if she thought it possible that Grandpa had heard a prowler in the yard and gone to investigate.

'If Daddy heard anything, he'd just call security,' she said. 'Seventy-six-year-old men don't go chasing burglars.'

'Perhaps not,' said the seventy-nine-year-old marathon runner. Given the superhuman effort Grandpa had made to disguise his knee problem both at his birthday party and on Bob's subsequent visit, I suspected that the lawyer had little idea of its gravity. 'Of course, it's possible that Don could have taken the book with him,' Bob added. 'To work on it on his own for a few days.'

Grandpa deign to labour on the manuscript himself? Highly unlikely. In any case, the sheer weight of the paper would have taxed Bruce or myself, so he couldn't possibly have lifted it unaided. I was about to say as much when my uncle wandered into the room with wet hair plastered to his forehead. Distressed by the affray in the kitchen, Bruce had fled to his apartment. Now, asked how he was doing by Bob, he fought for words that refused to come and became so agitated that Eleanor and I took him through to the kitchen and helped him to take a tranquillizer.

'I'm so sorry, Elly,' he said.

'It's going to be all right, darling. Daddy'll be coming back. It's all going to be all right, I promise.'

I wondered whom she was really trying to convince.

Back in the living room, Bob's neck made a series of measured oil-pump nods as Eleanor explained how badly Bruce had been thrown by Grandpa's disappearance, but it surprised me when the lawyer advised Eleanor against making a Missing Persons report for the time being. In all probability he believed himself to be protecting his client's interests, but it seemed possible that he'd smelt profit in delaying official involvement. As hard as Eleanor tried to persuade Bob to reconsider, he stood his ground, reminding her that Grandpa was a free agent and of sound mind. Checking his manicure, Bob added that if the police posted Donald Tait's name on the Missing and Unidentified Persons system, his disappearance would be all over the news within twenty-four hours.

'But that's exactly what we want,' Eleanor said.

Bob shook his head. 'I disagree. It's most likely that Don's perfectly safe and well. After all, seniors can be as impulsive as the rest of us,' said the recently remarried septuagenarian. 'And it's quite possible that your father's visiting with a friend, perhaps even with Miss Perrault. There's really nothing the police can do that we can't do ourselves at this stage, and if Don gets into any kind of trouble, he won't be able to get half a block without being recognized. That can be a big plus in a situation like this.'

Writing his home number on his business card, Bob asked

Eleanor to keep him informed as to any developments, and left.

'Smug prick,' Eleanor hissed as she waved him off. 'If only I'd come by yesterday evening, this would never have happened. Daddy felt lonely, that's what it was, and Julie heard it in his voice and seized her moment.'

To escape the treadmill of self-recrimination, Eleanor called her own lawyer, insisting on a meeting at his office in an hour's time, and then three of Grandpa's friends to find out if they'd heard from him. Sounding so relaxed that none of his cronies could have guessed anything was wrong, Eleanor fiddled with a lump of quartz as if in the hope that some of its unfeeling qualities might rub off on her. My grandfather's whereabouts concerned me less than the manuscript's disappearance. While I was fairly confident that Grandpa would show up in a day or so with his new bride on his arm, it seemed unimaginable that he'd have taken the manuscript with him. And if it had been stolen, I was in deep trouble: I'd left the pool-house door unlocked.

Having drawn a blank with her father's friends, Eleanor called her husband, who told her that Larry was planning to make his way back to North Canon Drive following his visit to the dentist.

'I know it's painful for you right now, Ralph,' my aunt said, 'but actually this is a brilliant opportunity. You and Larry need to have a good long talk together, and it seems to me that a broken tooth's a modest price to pay for so much potential renewal.'

Her words startled me. 'You expect me to have a heart-to-heart with Larry when he gets here?'

'Oh God, no. You're coming to spend the rest of the day at my house,' Eleanor said. 'Leave things with your father for now and try not to worry about it. But I've a feeling this could turn out to be a very healing experience for both of you.'

Even though it had come cloaked in hackneyed self-improvement jargon, Eleanor's concern touched me.

Convinced that I was too overwrought to drive, she called for a taxi and led me down to the pool to say goodbye to Bruce, who was staring into one of Julie's alternative dimensions and barely noticed us. No sooner had we said farewell than Eleanor began to flagellate herself for abandoning him.

'Don't be so hard on yourself,' I said, sliding across the taxi's vinyl backseat to make room for her. 'You've done everything you could. In any case, Grandpa's sure to turn up tonight or tomorrow morning and then Bruce will be right as rain.'

Putting a warning finger to her lips, Eleanor pointed to the driver beyond the security window and called Grandpa's house to check that Carmelita was answering the phone as instructed.

When Roger had collected Eleanor from Doheny Drive for her meeting with her lawyer, I found a pair of swimming trunks, ducked beneath the bottom of the glass picture window and swam out into the main pool. Having decided to let matters lie with Larry for a day or two, I began to brood, unable to see our altercation in any positive light. Instead of serving as a catharsis, it felt like another disappointment, and floating at the wet lip, the hazy Cyclorama of the cityscape looked to me like a painted backdrop that might at any second curl up faster than a broken roller-blind to reveal only grey hideous space.

Apprised of my tussle with my father by Roger, Lisa stopped by Eleanor's house on her way back from college and sat herself beside me on the sofa in the television room, eager for the details of Grandpa's disappearance and my clash with Larry. As I laid it all out for her, Lisa suffered a fit of giggles, and to my surprise, I found myself laughing along with her, relieved that she considered the 'fight' with my father to be little more than a spat that owed more to late nights than to any underlying tensions in our relationship, and that Roger had come to share my view that Grandpa had most likely eloped with Julie.

'Relax, Ralph,' Lisa said. 'Today was always going to be something of a battle, you know? I'm probably meant to play it a little detached, not call you for a couple of days, but the truth is that I just don't care. Is that crazy?'

I shook my head, and in what soon began to feel like a misconceived attempt to re-establish the honesty we'd shared on the beach the previous night, tried to explain why I'd lied about the play to my grandfather.

'What's the issue here?' Lisa said. 'Your presentational skills? I thought you told me you were in showbusiness?'

Unwilling to discuss the matter further, she reached for the television remote. At Danny's party, Lisa had shown little reluctance to discuss her own doubts and fears, admitting to being unhappy at USC and feeling lonely in a strange city with few if any true friends. Now she tuned me out in favour of a PBS costume drama portraying the events leading up to the War of Independence, and it grated.

An extra appeared at the top left corner of the screen dressed as a redcoat, gulped as he received his cue, and started off across the set gripping his musket. Struggling to mask his excitement that this short walk was going to be recorded for posterity, repeated endlessly on satellite channels and ultimately dubbed into Ukrainian, he gave an electrifyingly bad performance, but all too soon a close-up of a principal broke the spell. Suspension of disbelief is always a problem for me when it comes to films because I spent so much time on sets as a child. Since I was eleven or twelve, I've been unable to sit through a feature without checking the frame for a glimpse of the boom microphone or imagining the second assistant director just out of shot, stepping over a cable with exaggerated caution.

Having watched the English die for five minutes, Lisa was as bored as I was and, changing channels, chanced upon a group of actors being reverenced at yet another televised awards ceremony. This was hardly surprising: according to *Variety*, there were 252 entertainment industry awards in the

United States in 1997; in 2000, there were 332 – almost one a day. To the bemusement of the live audience, an actor declaimed a poem by e. e. cummings and then a child actor venerated the co-star of a film he'd worked on. As these people were showered with more praise than a Nobel Laureate might hope to receive, I longed to cry out: 'But they're only actors! Can't you see?'

As backs were slapped and prizes dispensed, I began to see these popinjays in a colder light. They hadn't been thrust into the public eye by accident, the way athletes sometimes are. They'd pushed themselves forward, inch by inch. As a child I'd heard an actor, a household name, call a television network to praise his own performance in a phoney Southern accent, simply in order to effect an infinitesimal improvement to his TV rating. And, of course, being an actor, he'd got away with it. If Lisa hadn't already accused me of pomposity at Danny's party, I'd have suggested that we needed to see the actor through Rilke's eyes: *'However lightly he moves,/ he's costumed, made up – an ordinary man/ who hurries home and walks in through the kitchen'* – then proceeds to talk about himself until the rest of the family falls asleep around the table.

Members of Direct Debit had never become puffed with themselves like the preening jackasses on the television, but then, of course, they'd never been invited to an awards ceremony. Zooming in on a nominee, the cameraman provided Lisa and me with a glimpse of a friend of my grandfather sitting at a nearby table, an actor in his eighties caught sharing a joke with his young wife, his auburn wig horribly at odds with his trademark silver beard. Truly there seemed to be life after death, and I begged Lisa to change the channel.

'Why?' she asked. 'I can see you're fascinated.'

'Disgusted, more like.'

'How come, Ralph? I mean, you grew up surrounded by these people.'

'Exactly.'

Laughing, Lisa reverted to the PBS drama and placed her hand on mine. Having squeezed it dutifully, I let my own go slack, unsure if she'd been inviting me to kiss her or making no more than a sisterly expression of affection. Feeling about ten years old, I shifted my weight on the sofa, and Lisa interpreted (or chose to interpret) this as my move, turning to me with her eyes closed for a kiss. As if by design, Aunt Eleanor picked that moment to call upstairs and we broke apart, smiling nervously.

Standing in the middle of their sound-stage of a living room, Eleanor and Roger looked worried. There'd been no word from Grandpa, and anxiety had drawn my aunt's face into sharp points. She'd been crying again, and Roger was trying his best to comfort her.

'Your father's being an absolute nightmare,' Eleanor said to me. 'He's driving me mad.' To her intense irritation, her own lawyer had taken Bob Caswell's line over the police, and she'd returned to North Canon Drive to find Larry awaiting news of Grandpa with a heavily tranquillized Bruce. Told of Eleanor's intention to ignore the lawyers' advice and call the police anyway, Larry had lost his temper, threatening to phone in his own reading of events.

'He went absolutely berserk,' Eleanor cried. Neither Roger's tenderness nor a bucketful of Bach Flower Remedy had done much to settle Eleanor's nerves, and by the time Ilena called us through for dinner, she was so uptight that a screamed release of negative energy would have been almost welcome. Instead, my aunt tinkered distractedly with the chicken on her plate and rearranged the vitamin pills she'd assembled in front of it. Flustered, I kept my head down, but Lisa was enviably relaxed as she fed Roger carefully edited highlights of Danny's party and listed some other young actors she thought might be right for the part he was still trying to cast. After our early dinner, Roger took Eleanor up to bed, and when Lisa suggested that we might take a drive together, I proposed a visit to Julie's temple.

Half an hour later, Lisa parked her Jeep opposite a large glass-fronted building in a nondescript residential neighbourhood south of Pico. Passing through the revolving door, we crossed a reception area decorated with enlarged colour photographs of an irrepressible Sri Rampa surrounded by enchanted acolytes to a desk where a young man put a bundle of literature into our hands and invited us to take a look around. A photo-realist mural of the temple in India lined the corridor that led to the cafeteria, and we followed it into a brightly lit hall in which a hundred young people were eating vegetarian food.

In contrast to the cold appraising glances we'd received from our fellow guests at Danny's party, these diners smiled at us with real warmth, but not one of the dozen people I spoke to knew of Julie Perrault or her whereabouts. Making space for us at a refectory table, a man with a shaved head told us of the inner peace available at the temple and suggested that we might care to attend a lecture on breathing in the main hall. Declining his invitation, we left him there, and even though we'd discovered no news of Julie, I found myself smiling as we climbed back into the Jeep. Eleanor's suspicion that this bustling spiritual Youth Hostel might be the front for a kidnapping and extortion racket was a joke, and I said as much to Lisa.

'Maybe, but don't let the soft sell fool you,' Lisa said. 'I bet there's someone in a Brink's Mat van round the corner, counting up all the money.'

'That's so cynical,' I said. 'They're just at ease with themselves, that's all.'

'There's something creepy going on in that place, believe me,' Lisa said. 'A bunch of lost souls, desperate for some kind of fix. That guy you were talking to had been brainwashed.'

Keen to show me one of her favourite hangouts in Hollywood, Lisa turned on to La Cienega and accelerated. The bar was close to her apartment, and I tried to divine from her expression whether she planned for us to spend the night there again, but it was dark and I couldn't catch more than the odd glimpse of her face in the light of passing cars. In truth, I was so tired that I didn't mind much either way.

Mitzi was at the bar on Franklin with some friends, and when she'd kissed Lisa hello, she came over to tell me what a really amazing guy my father was. Tempted to ask her if she'd acquired her little ski-jump of a nose through rhino-plasty, I went to order some drinks and entered into a dreary conversation with a dreadlocked French Canadian documentary filmmaker.

After an hour or so, our party moved on to The Whiskey, a bar on the ground floor of the Sunset Marquis hotel. The relocation seemed pointless since both establishments were patronized by the same clientele: people in their late twenties and early thirties trying to drink away their fear, smiling while their guts roiled, lost in that no-man's-land between work and sociability, disfigured by the twin imperatives of greed and career. Exactly like me. Although it was scary to see my own anxieties and self-interest reflected so clearly in their strained faces, I was comforted to know that others were suffering too.

Wearing casual clothes that weren't casual at all, a young man with a pierced eyebrow broke away from a herd of goatees to say that he'd met me at Danny's party. Having no memory of him, I was none the wiser when he mentioned some remarks I'd made about questions of perception raised by Robert Wilson's *Einstein on the Beach*.

'You were wrong about the violinist,' he said. 'I checked. He's dressed as Einstein, just like the performers on the stage. But he's a character in the opera too, not just a soloist.'

His eyes bored into me and their pupils grew as he went on to describe for me a film he'd made for television about a

130

telekinetic airline pilot. I wriggled free of him with some difficulty. Some months later I happened to see the film this person claimed to have directed, and when the end credits rolled, his name wasn't among them. A drunk woman asked me to sell her my tweed jacket, and I jumped at the chance to raise some cash, but negotiations foundered, at which point the Canadian wanted to smoke some grass, so the two of us went outside.

Reaching the corner, he lit a joint, and I took two big hits in the vain hope that it might balance out the booze. I hadn't smoked in a while and the drug went to work straightaway, a pleasant airy rush that telescoped me back inside myself, but as we returned to the hotel, the pavement began to twist and buckle beneath my feet, and by the time I reached the bar, people's faces were beginning to look evil. Feeling faint, I headed for the restroom where I dry-heaved and sat on the lid of the lavatory for a few minutes before sliding off on to the floor. Wave after wave of nausea washed over me until, miraculously, the cool porcelain wall tiles seemed to soften and conform to the contours of my cheek. My breathing became light, fast and regular. Quite happy to stay curled up there for ever, a knock on the door of the stall disturbed my trance.

'Is everything all right, sir?' I stifled a groan: a hotel official, no doubt suspecting that I was breaking, or had broken, the law. 'Will you please open the door?'

'I'm so sorry,' I said, trying to sound like John Gielgud. The words came out like Donald Duck on short-wave radio. 'Would you mind giving me a minute, please?'

'Sir, if you don't open the door, I'll have to force entry.'

I needed to stand up and flush the cistern; convince the flunkey that I was *compos mentis*; wash my hands; make it back to the bar; tell Lisa I was going home; leave the hotel; find a cab; pay the driver; get upstairs to bed at North Canon Drive without running into Larry . . . Lying motionless on the floor of the stall until the door was unlatched from the outside, I was thrown without ceremony on to the sidewalk by the hotel staff. Although I've no idea how Lisa and I made it back to her apartment, I do recall crawling into her spinning bed before I passed out.

The next day, Lisa took me for breakfast in a West Hollywood café, where a body-built midget wearing a fishnet T-shirt and lederhosen sat at the next table, wiping droplets of soya milk from his handlebar moustache as he ate a bowl of muesli. All things considered, I was surprisingly clear-headed as I sipped my black coffee, if unhappily aware that my burgeoning friendship with Lisa was the only thing I had going for me. Relieved that she hadn't censured me too harshly over my behaviour at the Sunset Marquis, I was equally glad that our second attempt at coupling had been more successful than the first. Just before dawn, I'd woken to find Lisa tugging at my thickening penis, and we'd made love in the grey light. Afterwards, I'd enjoyed some rare peace of mind as she fell back to sleep with her head on my shoulder.

When we'd finished breakfast I called Eleanor, who told me that there'd still been no word from Grandpa and asked Lisa and me to come straight over. Lisa had a day off from USC and we'd already made vague plans for a trip to the beach, but when I told her that the Thin Controller had requested an audience, she knew well enough to comply.

'I'm so glad you're both safe and sound, Ralph,' Eleanor said, opening the door to us. 'To lose more family members at this point might look like *carelessness*.'

With a bitter laugh, my aunt led Lisa and I across her living room to where an athletic-looking middle-aged woman sat wearing a business suit beneath an Ed Ruscha stencil print of the word 'avocado'. Eleanor introduced her as Sandra Simmons, an investigator who worked for her lawyer's firm.

Frustrated in her desire to call the police, my aunt had hired the sleuth to see what she could find out, and from the way that Sandra's head bobbed up and down as Eleanor spoke, it looked as if she was quite taken by her celebrated client. Apparently the telephone-company records showed that the first call had been made from a payphone in Century City, and the second from an unlisted Los Angeles number. Sandra was having difficulty tracing the second call but her primary aim was to find Julie, and she assured us that her secretary was making every effort to locate her through her charge-card transactions. Sandra had made discreet inquiries via certain members of the Sri Rampa temple, but so far Julie appeared to be exactly who she said she was: a young woman from Iowa who'd gone to India as a junior nurse and stayed for two years. There were no criminal convictions in her past, and the temple was apparently reputable. The only noteworthy detail to emerge from Sandra's preliminary investigation had been Julie's recent enrolment at an acting school on Melrose.

'Poor little thing,' said Eleanor, heading off towards the kitchen.

When Lisa asked Sandra how she'd become an investigator, she explained that some five years previously she'd begun to supplement her income as a stunt double by making videotapes of weddings and bar mitzvahs.

'Through my work, I met a lawyer who employed me to tape his clients while he coached them for court appearances,' Sandra said. 'And from there, it was a simple step to conducting various interviews myself on the firm's behalf. The work's really varied and it brings me into contact with lots of fascinating people.'

Evincing all the enthusiasm of a television chat-show interviewee, Sandra adored her job, and I asked her if there were any openings. The investigator shook her head. 'But since you're here, Ralph,' she said, 'perhaps you wouldn't mind if we talked over what happened from your point of view?' Flattered, I followed Sandra through to the dining room to conduct the interview. 'Can we move the chairs?' she asked.

All the chairs in the room, indeed all the furniture and even the *objets d'art* on the sideboard, had been aligned at precise ninety-degree angles. With some trepidation, I repositioned two chairs as Sandra popped the latches on a steel case.

'What have you got in there?' I asked. 'A polygraph machine?'

'There'd be little point with so many of you being actors. No, this is just a camcorder. I prefer it to sound tape because it helps me remember who was talking when I play it back.'

Joking with Sandra about my 'best side', I enjoyed a mild adrenaline buzz as she set up her equipment, but the moment the red light went on, performance anxiety crippled me. Acute cramps, the wooden terror of the marionette, summoned up gruesome memories of my audition for *Yerma* at Oxford: standing alone on the dusty stage, the deep darkness of the auditorium broken only by the reflection of the director's John Lennon spectacles, I'd stumbled clumsily through Hamlet's third soliloquy. Guilty of what Stanislavski once called 'the thoughtless parrot-like pronunciation of lines', I'd wished all the while that my too, too solid flesh would melt, thaw and resolve itself into a dew.

Now, hung over and painfully aware of the camcorder's unblinking eye, the interview began to feel like a hellish screen test. Focusing on Grandpa's state of mind and the atmosphere in the house prior to his departure, Sandra asked me the same questions again and again in a slightly different way, and the fifteen-minute interrogation seemed to last hours. Bashful almost to the point of paralysis, I tried to stress the importance of the missing manuscript, and as Sandra finally put her camera away, advised her not to ignore the possibility of a break-in.

'Ralph, I hear you. Believe me,' she said, tightening the clasp on her Rolex. 'I'm not in the business of discounting anything.'

Out on the deck, Eleanor was sitting in the shade of an umbrella, wearing a sun hat for extra protection. 'Quite an ordeal, isn't it?' she said. 'Did you resort to the branding irons, Sandra?'

'No need. Ralph sang like a canary.'

'You were lucky,' Eleanor said to me. 'I had to go through an hour of it. Hair and make-up was a little thin on the ground . . .'

'But we got the whole scene in one take,' said Sandra.

Lisa slipped into the pool and floated there with sunlight bouncing off the water. From where I sat, semi-dazzled, she might have been buried up to her neck in mercury.

'Maybe you should speak to Ernesto,' I said to Sandra. 'The gardener. He usually starts work around six o'clock.'

'I met with him earlier this morning,' Sandra replied. 'He didn't see a thing.' When the investigator made to leave, Eleanor sprinkled her with thanks and asked me to see her out. 'Oh, there's just one other thing, Ralph,' Sandra said as we stepped on to the driveway. 'I spoke to your father on the phone, and he said he was with you most of the night. Is that right?'

'Sure,' I said. 'We went out to dinner and then to a party at my cousin's house in Malibu.'

Sandra stowed her camcorder in her spotless hatchback. 'What time did you leave Malibu?'

'I don't know. Maybe three? I don't know.'

It was a lie, of course. Lisa and I had stayed there until around six, but I'd no wish to reveal the scale of our debauchery.

'And was your father still at the house when you left?' Sandra asked, shading her eyes with the flat of her hand the better to see me.

Remembering him leaving with Mitzi, I said I wasn't sure. 'The party was really spread out by then. In different rooms. Some people were on the beach.'

'Try and think, Ralph. This is really important.'

This was preposterous, an out-take from *Cagney and Lacey*. 'Why?' I asked. 'What's happened?'

'Your father's refusing to speak to me,' Sandra said. 'And your grandfather's neighbour says she saw him on North Canon Drive at around seven o'clock yesterday morning. Driving a light-coloured convertible.' Larry and Mitzi had left Danny's party together at around two in the morning, long after Larry had abandoned his car in Hollywood. It made no sense. 'Your father became angry when I asked him where he'd been at that time,' Sandra added. 'He told me he'd stayed the night in Malibu and driven home at nine the next morning. Your cousin can't remember him leaving, but I thought you might be able to fill me in on that.'

Sandra's beady eyes twinkled, and I looked beyond her to the Downtown district where the skyscrapers were flocked by smog the colour of French mustard. 'Ah yes. It's coming back to me,' I said. 'My father was there when I left. Definitely. He went to sleep in one of the spare rooms and that was the last anybody saw of him.'

No sooner had I lied to Sandra than I regretted it, but she drove off before I had a chance to correct myself. Back out on the deck, I asked Eleanor if she thought Larry was involved in Grandpa's disappearance.

'Obviously not,' she said. 'Sandra asked those questions because it's her job, but Larry had nothing to do with it. He's just being difficult to spite me.'

'So what do you suppose he was doing in Beverly Hills yesterday morning?' I asked her.

'Who can tell what your father gets up to while Irene's away? I wouldn't pay it any mind if I were you,' she replied. Soon afterwards, a car arrived to take my aunt to rehearsals.

From the top of the cliff, El Matador was just as I remembered it: two colossal jagged rocks piercing a swathe of smooth pale sand. The sun was high, but a breeze cooled our limbs as Lisa and I went down the wooden steps and ran into the ocean, swimming out until we could no longer touch the bottom with our toes. Pausing to catch her breath, Lisa reached out to me, and saltwater mixed with our saliva as we kissed. Afterwards, we headed back to the shore and lay drying side by side. I was still shaken by my final exchange with Sandra.

'Where does Mitzi live?' I asked Lisa.

'In a condo in Beachwood Canyon,' she replied. 'Why do you ask?'

Lisa had no idea that I'd lied to Sandra about Larry. 'Nothing really. I just wondered,' I said.

But Lisa had just given me another reason to wish that I'd told Sandra the truth, because Beachwood Canyon was to the east of Larry's house and nowhere near Beverly Hills. Given the way my father had humiliated me in the kitchen, I couldn't understand what had led me to lie to Sandra. A sense of loyalty, or a desire to have something over him? In either event, I'd protected him. And protected him from what? The consequences of his own actions? Try as I might to put the matter aside and enjoy the day, I began to see Larry's attack on me in a new, more alarming light – even as a desperate attempt at misdirection. Trapped in my own head and losing my grip on events, it was easy for me to picture him fighting drunkenly with Grandpa at North Canon Drive; lying on the beach in the sunshine, a chill passed through me, forcing me to open my eyes. Beads of seawater had evaporated to leave traces of salt on Lisa's shoulder blade, and when she wanted to know what was on my mind, I asked her if Mitzi had slept with my father after Danny's party.

'That's funny,' she said, pulling a strand of hair from her mouth. 'Eleanor put that same question to me when you were talking to Sandra.'

'And what did you tell her?'

Lisa grinned. 'Mitzi's a bad girl but she can keep a secret. Especially if it's about herself.'

The breeze caught a stream of sand as I released it from

my fist. Eating our overstuffed sandwiches, Lisa and I swapped stories about ourselves, only stopping to watch two brown pelicans fly the length of the beach. Was Lisa hoping (and scared) that this might just be the real thing, or was it just me?

'Your mother's an actress, right?' Lisa asked. 'Is she a lot like Eleanor?'

'Not at all,' I replied. The two women had seen a great deal of each other at the time of my mother's divorce, and for a year or so I'd been dragged along on a series of best-behaviour visits to Eleanor's pristine apartment in Kensington, but they hadn't remained close. 'They're really different,' I continued. 'My mother's very relaxed. Maybe too relaxed. But not about everything. I mean, Eleanor was able to let her hair go white in her thirties, but my mother leapt into a vat of henna at the very first strand of grey and she's fought a running gun-battle with nature ever since.'

I didn't mention that my mother's go-to-bed eyes had made an ill-advised visit to a cosmetic surgeon in the 1980s and were now very wide-awake, set in an expression of permanent astonishment. A slip of the scalpel had also left her with a slight tremor in her right eye that, combined with her heavy reliance on eye shadow, gave her a murderous aspect.

'Is she still acting?' asked Lisa.

'Mum keeps pretty busy,' I replied. It was far from the truth. Unfortunately British Equity overflows with actresses of a certain age who are more than capable of playing psychopaths, and my mother's career had ebbed as a result. In contrast to Eleanor's enduring success, a speaking part in a 'telly' or the odd radio play were now occasions for lengthy celebration in the decaying house in Wandsworth that mum shared with Rory, the Scottish composer.

'Your mother sounds like a fun person,' Lisa said. 'I'd like to have the chance to meet her. Tell me, Ralph, are you still upset with Larry because of what happened yesterday?'

'What do you think?'

It was on the tip of my tongue to tell her that my father had only turned on me in the kitchen to divert attention from his own complicity in Grandpa's disappearance and to stop Eleanor calling the police. But Lisa would almost certainly have dismissed this as paranoia, much as her stepmother had done, and I was just wise enough to check myself. 'I'm sorry,' I said. 'I guess I'm feeling anxious about my grandfather.'

A big bird wheeled above us in the sky and Lisa told me that it was an eagle, explaining that a hawk has a fork in its tail. Following a second swim, she gave me a more comprehensive account of her work on the fruit fly *drosophila* and the transitional gene, complaining that the financial imperatives of the corporations funding genome research were in fact impeding its progress. Fixated on what might have occurred at North Canon Drive on the night of Danny's party, I nodded unconvincingly taking in little of what she said. Fully aware that I was ruining the day and hurting Lisa, I still couldn't derail my train of thought, and once she'd finished describing the problems she was having with her project coordinator, she went ominously quiet.

Heading back, sun-blasted, past the old Getty museum, we barely spoke, and Lisa smiled at me in the vaguest way as we parted outside her father's house. When she drove off without a backward glance, I found myself regretting my behaviour yet again.

Pecking my cheeks in a lightning one-two at the door, Aunt Eleanor informed me that there'd still been no word from Grandpa and that Sandra had been unable to locate Julie. The bloodhound had also failed to secure details of the unlisted number from the telephone company, and it sounded to me as if Eleanor was already losing confidence in her.

'I'm so worried about Daddy that I couldn't concentrate at rehearsals,' she said. 'And to cap it all, Macbeth tried to stick his tongue half-way down my throat again in Act Two. Look,

Ralph, I know it's a chore, but would you hear my lines? I really need to refocus.'

Such requests had chilled me to the marrow since childhood, but there was still no escape. Bound in a pigskin folder, Eleanor's script was marked up in her tiny, hem-stitch handwriting, and her notes detailed the often conflicting emotions she wished to convey in a particular scene. Pink and yellow highlighter ink stressed individual words in a bright blizzard of notation that made it harder for me to give her the correct cues and to check the words off one by one as she delivered them. In *Leaving a Doll's House: A Memoir*, Claire Bloom mentions a fax that Philip Roth sent her during their divorce proceedings. Roth apparently claimed $150 an hour for the 'five or six hundred hours' he'd spent hearing his wife's lines over the course of their marriage. Naturally enough, Bloom cites the fax as evidence of Roth's parsimony, but after half an hour working with Eleanor on her script, my sympathies were divided.

Having already rehearsed the role for three weeks in New York, my aunt's Lady Macbeth was virtually word-perfect, but when she muddled a sentence in the 'Out, damned spot!' speech, she insisted on going over it seven times for good luck. Once we were done, I sought to compliment her and (aware that it was impossible to overdo such things) alluded to Coleridge's famous remark that a performance by Edmund Kean had been like 'reading Shakespeare by flashes of lightning'.

'Ah well, of course, you're absolutely right. That's what it's all about,' Eleanor said. 'Reading Shakespeare by lightning. It's a wonderful image, isn't it?'

I agreed with her. Indeed, sceptical as Coleridge was of the manner in which Kean 'took over' Shakespeare, his metaphor wasn't altogether complimentary, implying to me at least that a Kean performance ('all passion, all energy, all relentless will', according to Hazlitt) might leave a large section of the audience with little more than a blinding headache.

Roger was attending a conference in New York and it was Ilena's night off, so my aunt and I were on our own in the house. At seven o'clock precisely, Eleanor began to cook spaghetti, fretting about her father as she stirred in the yellow sticks while keeping an unnecessarily safe distance from the boiling water. *Fire burn and cauldron bubble.* Convinced of her own abduction theory, Eleanor groaned when I suggested that Larry might have had something to do with Grandpa's disappearance.

'You're barking up the wrong tree, Ralph,' she said. 'Listen to yourself. Bow, wow, wow.'

There was plenty of pasta for both of us, but Eleanor spooned all of it on to my plate and munched some celery as she observed me eat the steaming heap at the breakfast bar. As ever, the smell of food seemed to drive my aunt slightly mad, and feeling as if I was taking part in a laboratory test, I wolfed the spaghetti down while listening to her complaints about the backstage arrangements at the Ahmanson. As she moved on to bemoan the vocal range of the bald actor playing the part of Macbeth, I suffered the first proprietary stab of indigestion.

After dinner, Eleanor seemed even more preoccupied as we watched a new release on DVD that featured a good performance by an actress of her own age, and my aunt's mouth tightened slightly each time her peer enjoyed a close-up. Having sat through half the film without speaking a word, I felt acutely self-conscious when (at a suitable break in the action) I was obliged to get up from the armchair.

'Would you mind terribly fluffing up the cushions before you go?' Eleanor asked me.

'Um, sure,' I replied. 'If you like. But I was planning to come straight back. I was just going to get myself a drink of water, if that's all right. I think I'm a bit sunburnt.'

'Oh, of course. I'm sorry,' she said in a shrill, tortured voice. 'It's just that I thought you were going upstairs to bed.'

My aunt was in pain, but there was no way to cheer her up because she'd already shut me out, just as Grandpa had done to Julie following his birthday party and just as I'd done to Lisa at Matador beach. This dose of my own medicine tasted distinctly sour, and on my return from the kitchen, neither of us said another word. As soon as the film ended, I felt I had to deal with the cushions before wishing Eleanor a good night's sleep.

Waking to the machine-made warble of the bedside telephone the next morning, I learned from Eleanor that Larry had taken Bruce to a clinic in Anaheim.

'Your uncle climbed over the wall into the next-door-neighbours' garden during the night,' she said. 'And Mrs Knudsen found him wandering around naked on her tennis court at six o'clock this morning.'

Apparently two Westec patrolmen had escorted Bruce home ('wrapped in a blanket, thank God. We must remember to return it'), and the thought of this procession made me truly miserable. The calamity had a galvanizing effect on Eleanor, however, and breezily confident that Larry was already heading back to North Canon Drive, she asked me to drive her to Bruce's clinic.

Having dispatched Ilena on a mission to Whole Foods, Eleanor went through the house shutting the doors. In the kitchen, she pressed the refrigerator door twice to make sure that it was properly closed and tapped the controls on the cooker to make certain that they were in the 'off' position. *I have known her continue in this a quarter of an hour.* Still not satisfied, Eleanor unplugged the kettle and moved the radio another six inches from the threat presumably posed by the empty double sink. Setting the intruder alarm, she checked the red light three times. Only then was it safe for us to leave, but even as I wheeled Roger's car on to Doheny Drive, she jiggled the fastening of her seatbelt to make sure it couldn't spring free. Rubbing sleep from my eyes, I thought I was hallucinating.

'You should have turned left,' she said to me as I crossed Sunset. 'Take Santa Monica and just keep on until you hit the freeway.'

Eleanor used her mobile phone to check in with Sandra and then called Carmelita. Once she'd satisfied herself that the nurse hadn't gone deaf or expired, for the next few blocks my aunt lectured me on the imbalance in Bruce's brain chemistry, and the difficulties the doctors faced in prescribing correct medication for him. Eleanor was becoming a little manic herself, but as we joined the Hollywood freeway, she finally relented and lit a herbal cigarette, releasing me to smoke a Marlboro Light right down to the stub. As I drove, my aunt catalogued the murderous intentions of our fellow road-users, anticipating collisions that somehow never happened and then, in an unexpected change of tack, revealed that she'd been suffering from insomnia ever since Grandpa's disappearance. Had I ever heard of *Xeroderma pigmentosum*? Shaking my head, I asked her if it was a new sleeping pill.

'It's a disease, Ralph,' Eleanor said. 'If the sun's rays hit your skin, you develop cancer within seconds.'

'I assume it's pretty rare then?'

'Obviously,' she replied, inspecting various moles and blemishes on her arms for evidence of cellular disturbance. Her white shoe tapped annoyingly in her foot well. Eleanor's compulsions were only symptoms of stress, but she hadn't stopped talking since we got into the car and her behaviour was driving me slowly insane. 'Careful,' she shrieked.

*Unfix my hair and make my seated heart knock at my ribs.* Braking hard, terror washed down my legs as an eighteen-wheeler changed lanes half a mile ahead of us. Furious, I asked Eleanor if she'd prefer to drive the car herself.

My aunt rubbed the side of her neck. 'I'm sorry,' she said. 'I know I can be a nightmare, but I can't help it. I'm just so worried about Daddy and the play and now Bruce.'

This was the first time she'd acknowledged the way her obsessive nature controlled her (and now, increasingly, my own) life. The admission broke down my anger, but it was soon replaced by a fresh anxiety: although I'd heard about Bruce's crack-ups, I'd never witnessed one at first hand.

During the summer of my first year at Oxford I'd come close. Larry had been working on a horror film in Italy at the time, and he'd taken a house in a village on the coast near Rome for the duration of the location work. My father invited me to bring some friends down and Bruce was visiting from the States so, including Larry's girlfriend, there were seven of us staying in the rambling, dusty villa that overlooked the sea. Every morning a car would take Larry to the location, and the rest of us would either accompany him to hang around the set – as ever an experience of brainwithering ennui – or sprawl by the pool at the villa. Possessed of a limitless supply of patience, Bruce had been an ideal playmate for me when I was a child, but on that holiday I began, for the first time, to find him something of a liability: a bovine, if good-natured, presence whom I (in my arrogance) judged myself to have outgrown.

One day, Bruce announced that there was going to be a lunar eclipse that night, claiming that he'd read a headline to this effect at the newsstand in the village, and the more my friends and I tried to disabuse him of this notion, the more insistently he defended it. Even though none of us believed him, after dinner we all lay on our backs in the garden, staring a little drunkenly at the moon as it wobbled in a cloudless sky.

Bruce had told us that the eclipse would occur at midnight, and when nothing happened, he went very quiet. Larry and his girlfriend went to bed, but my friends and I teased my uncle, lying around in the moonlight drinking more wine, smoking hash and laughing until after two o'clock. When we got up to clear the dishes, Bruce was nowhere to be found. Fearing the worst, I woke Larry, who went to look for him down on the rocks, and as soon as he called up to us that he'd found his brother and that Bruce was safe, the rest of us turned in for the night. The next morning Larry had a bruise on his cheek that would test the make-up artist's skills for a week, and Bruce spent the whole day in his room. When I asked Larry what had happened, he wouldn't give me a straight answer, but his sharp tone left me in no doubt that he blamed me and my friends for encouraging Bruce in his fantasy, and then making fun of him when it failed to come true. The memory's still fresh because this was one of the few times in my life that Larry had ever come close to reprimanding me. When Bruce did finally emerge from his room, I tried to apologize, but he laughed it off. The incident was never alluded to again.

When I told Eleanor this story and confessed that I was nervous about visiting my uncle in a mental hospital, all her sharp angles seemed to soften.

'I'm tense too,' she said, watching a big-haired throwback in a Cadillac use her rear-view mirror to apply yet another layer of make-up. 'Thank you so much for coming with me, Ralph. I don't think I could face this on my own. I feel things so acutely where Bruce is concerned. You can't imagine how awful it was for us to be separated when we were children. He had nobody.'

# Chapter Eight

'And this new mask, glued shrinking to our faces, compressed our skulls, bruised and deformed our brains.'

Blaise Cendrars, *Moravagine*

Set on a rise, the clinic was cut off from the rest of the world by a sea of slow-moving cars, and once we'd given our names at a gatehouse, we drove up to a red-roofed building that looked like a run-down country club. A nurse led us through a series of candy-coloured recreation rooms decorated with large paintings (seemingly culled from occupational art classes) in which abstraction fought an indecisive battle with figuration. A dozen patients were sunning themselves and smoking cigarettes on a veranda, and we found Bruce by the steps, looking out across the lawn towards the trees that masked the high perimeter fence. My uncle appeared surprisingly at ease, but when Eleanor called his name, he looked round with double-glazed eyes. Several seconds passed before his mouth widened in a rubbery smile.

'Elly,' he said. 'Thanks for coming.'

In contrast to Eleanor's pin-sharp RADA contralto, Bruce's voice sounded like the message on a worn-out answering machine. Asked how he was feeling by his sister, his pale, dry lips opened and closed as if he was blowing an imaginary smoke ring. It was excruciating to watch. No more words came, and the lobotomizing effect of the drugs appalled me. *Throw physic to the dogs – I'll none of it.* Eleanor repeated her question, but Bruce was distracted by a flash of light that penetrated the trees from the road beyond, so she asked it a third time, and he mumbled that he was doing fine. Encouraged, Eleanor squeezed her brother's hand, and my respect for her grew as she went all out to connect with him, describing some of the happier times they'd shared together as children. While Eleanor couldn't even leave her house without performing a series of compulsive rituals, in Anaheim her composure put me to shame: Bruce's mental suffering and diminished capacities were such a stark reminder of human limitations that I ached with pity.

Sensing that my presence might be a hindrance, I wandered on to the lawn and came across a young woman down by the trees who appeared to be talking into a hands-free mobile phone. As I drew closer, I saw that there was no wire leading from her ear, no phone and nobody else involved in the conversation. A second patient was stooped over as if searching for a lost contact lens, or his marbles, in the grass. Smoking a cigarette to try and quell my growing unease, I waited until Eleanor beckoned me back.

On his feet to say goodbye, Bruce moved ponderously, as if through treacle, and I wondered if he had the slightest idea who I was. When Eleanor and I made to leave, a young man with a reddish goatee beard intercepted us, introduced himself as Dr Hendricks and asked Eleanor how she'd found her brother.

'Bruce is always having these episodes,' she said. 'It doesn't seem any more or less severe than usual.'

Hendricks nodded. 'Judging by his records, I'd tend to agree with you. We'd like to keep him here for another day or so while we adjust his medication. Then, with any luck, he'll be able to come home. One more thing, Ms Tait. Your brother was very anxious about his father when he was first admitted. Is there anything we should know about that might be worrying him?'

'Father's been ill,' my aunt said, giving me a meaningful look. 'No, it's nothing serious. A mild virus.'

Eleanor and I were leaving the clinic when a door opened

147

on the far side of the hall. Larry stepped through it, vexed, followed by an older doctor.

Sweat beaded my forehead like bubble wrap.

Embracing Eleanor, Larry introduced her to the doctor but chose to blank me, his face a mask as our eyes met. Clearly frozen out, I blurted that I'd wait for Eleanor by the car and rushed down the steps. Hurt and confused, Larry's cold gaze stayed with me as I wandered the parking lot counting up all his sins of omission.

When my aunt finally came out to join me, I accused her of lying to me.

'I told you the truth, Ralph. Larry said he was on his way back to Daddy's house when we spoke on the phone. But since he's still here, why don't you give him five minutes? He feels awful about what happened and he's desperate to make things right with you.'

'Really?'

'I promise you. Your father was as shocked to see you as you were to see him. It really upset him when you ran off like that.'

My indignation drained away as quickly as it had risen.

Larry was on the veranda, whispering into Bruce's ear, and I was summoning my courage to call his name when he looked round, stood up and came over to me, putting on a smile as he removed his sunglasses. His eye was dark pink and swollen.

'I'm sorry about your eye,' I said. 'I'd no idea –'

'That's OK,' Larry said. 'I asked for it. I was hung over and I overstepped the line.'

Was there nothing I could do to win my father's enduring disapproval? Staggered, I watched him wipe his palms on his jeans as he told me that his tooth was fine and that his eye was improving. To my amazement, he even apologized for not greeting me in the hallway, claiming to have been 'freaked out' by the sight of his sister following their own clash at North Canon Drive. This magnanimity was strangely disappointing. How could I ever have an Oedipal struggle with a man who loved the play, but declined the role of his father Creon because it was a little underwritten?

'Christ, Eleanor can be a real fucking dragon,' Larry said. 'Did she try and make you talk to that snooper of hers?' On learning that Sandra had interviewed me the previous day, he sucked his teeth and glanced back at Bruce, who hadn't moved an inch. 'She thinks I'm mixed up in all this, doesn't she?'

'Who?' I said. 'Eleanor or Sandra?'

'Whoever.' Sensing an underlying agenda, I kept my mouth shut in the hope that he'd tell me more. 'They think that's why I don't want to get the police involved,' he added. 'Am I right?'

'Mixed up in all what?' I asked him, as coolly as possible.

Larry ran a hand through his hair. 'I don't know. Maybe they believe I helped the old man run off with Julie or some-thing,' he said. 'To spite Eleanor.'

I knew to tread carefully. 'Sandra thinks you might have gone round to North Canon Drive the night Grandpa left,' I said. 'The night of the party at Danny's place.'

The words bit, and Larry shook his head slowly, exactly as he'd done following rows with my mother at Godfrey Street, when he'd climb the stairs to kiss me goodnight and hug me as if it was the two of us against the world.

'Eleanor just doesn't get it,' Larry said. 'I mean, the old man's only been gone for two days, you know, and he's snuck off like this plenty of times before without telling a soul. Christ, he's never given a thought to anybody else in his life, so why's he going to start now? He's probably fishing, I don't know. Or trying to get Julie back, more likely. And if he is, he's not making a song and dance about it, in case it doesn't work out.'

Part of me thought Larry was probably right, but I could-n't resist pushing the knife in a little deeper. 'A neighbour told Sandra that they saw you driving away from North

Canon Drive early yesterday morning,' I said. 'She probably just wants to know what you were doing there.'

The fear and guilt in his face hardened my suspicions. It was a look I remembered seeing when I'd suggested postponing my flight back to London and getting a job in Los Angeles for a couple of months in the spring of my gap year. But my three-week visit had been more than enough time for Larry to show me around to his friends as 'my son, the scholar'. His sentimental kind of love operated better at a distance of several thousand miles, and needless to say, I'd flown home as arranged.

My anger returning, I asked Larry why he'd told Eleanor that he'd fallen asleep at Malibu.

'Excuse me?' he said

'Come on, Larry. I saw you leave the party, remember?'

Watching him ransack his mind for a credible explanation, I became convinced that he'd been over to Grandpa's house and was involved in his disappearance. In a crazy way I was glad. I wanted Larry to have to pay for whatever he'd done.

'Did you say this to Sandra?' he asked, putting a hand to his forehead. The gesture was so ham that a tortured 'Woe is me' seemed a very real possibility.

'No,' I said. 'I don't know why, but I said you'd been telling her the truth.'

Larry tried to hug me but I pulled back. 'I left the party for a couple of hours or so,' he said. 'To go and do some blow, OK? As a special treat. Then I went back.'

'I thought you were meant to have quit all that. I'm really sick of your lies, you know? And the way I always play along with them.' Larry's eyes went this way and that, looking for a loophole. 'Tell me the bloody truth for once, just once.'

My volume level surprised us both, and several patients turned to stare at us, including Bruce. Fingering his stubble, Larry looked to the trees by the perimeter fence. 'I spent the night with Mitzi, all right?' he said. 'And I picked up my car on the way over there.'

'Rubbish. Your car was in Hollywood and she lives in Beachwood Canyon. So how come you were seen driving around Beverly Hills?'

Larry's smug grin made me want to take him over to the hydrotherapy unit and hold him under the water till the bubbles stopped.

'You're right, sonny,' he said. 'Mitzi does live in Beachwood Canyon. With her boyfriend. But she has the keys to her parents' place in Benedict Canyon, so we ended up there. I didn't want you to tell Eleanor or Sandra because it might, you know, make things difficult with Irene later on.'

This duplicity rang hideously true. Larry had been chasing young women ever since I could remember, cheating on my mother and the rest besides. Because it was all I could do to stop myself knocking him cold, I turned on my heel and left him there. The Tait family was sick, ravaged by a streak of pathological selfishness that ran back a hundred years or more. Julie had been wise to get away.

Retracing my steps through the clinic, I thought back to the journey my parents and I had made to my new boarding school when I was thirteen. Larry had been in England at the time so he'd driven my mother and me out of London through the rain, but the charade of my parents' reunion and my terror at the prospect of a new school made me despondent. My mother tried to console me but it didn't help, and Larry began to rail against the barbarities of the English public school system, invoking the film *If . . .* as evidence. Since he'd taken no part in the debate as to which school I should attend, his posturing maddened my mother, who no doubt saw it as a cheap shot in their secret battle for my allegiance.

We'd covered sixty wet miles before I asked my father to pull over by a wooden gate where, shivering in the wind, I struggled with the zip on my new grey trousers and peed against the hedge and then, unwilling to get straight back into the car, stared out across the muddy field to where a bar of dark cloud weighed on the horizon. My mother called my name, and when I turned, Larry was looking at me across the roof of the car.

'Run for it, sonny. Go on,' he cried. 'I'll be right behind you.'

Looking over the field and then back to my father, for one glorious moment I believed that he'd meant what he'd said, but seeing his smile crumble, I climbed back into the car and we drove in silence until we reached the school gates. Two decades on, my father's empty words came back to me.

'Run for it, sonny.'

There was nobody behind me.

Sitting in the car with her arms folded, Aunt Eleanor chided me for not making peace with Larry.

'That's funny,' I said. 'Because he just told me that he thinks you're, quote, a fucking dragon, unquote.'

Eleanor retaliated by laying down a napalm mood, so I turned on the radio to annoy her even more. When Howard Stern's personality filled the car, sudden and unwelcome as a faulty air-bag, my aunt stabbed the power button as if she wanted to push it right through into the engine block.

'You know something, Eleanor? You're a real control freak.'

Jolted by my newfound rage, she drew herself back in her seat. 'Maybe I am, Ralph. Maybe I am,' she said. 'But let me give you some free advice. You can't go around blaming everything on your father for the rest of your life, so this might be a good time to do some growing up.'

'Oh, fuck off.'

Sighing, Eleanor shook her head. 'Just drive, will you? I'd quite like to get home in one piece.'

'I'll drive the car if you'll stop telling me how to behave, OK?'

Sinking into an uneasy truce, my aunt lit a herbal cigarette, and by the time we left the freeway, my loathing had boomeranged on me. Though I'd never have admitted it, there'd been something in what Eleanor had said about growing up, something that was going to require painful consideration.

Two hours later, Eleanor was resting in her room and I was sitting by her pool, wondering if my aunt was keeping anything from me and asking myself if I'd been too quick to believe Larry when he'd said he'd spent the night taking cocaine with Mitzi. The hydrangeas bordering the deck looked as if they'd been made out of paper, and my mind ached. When the telephone rang, I answered it without thinking, and Lisa was far from delighted to hear my voice.

'Why did you get so weird at the beach, Ralph? I felt you didn't want to be with me.'

'That's not true,' I said. 'I was just preoccupied. Tell me, do Mitzi's parents live in Benedict Canyon?'

'No,' she said. 'They live in Florida. Why do you ask?'

'They don't have a house in Benedict Canyon? Larry says he spent the night there.'

'They've never even been to California as far as I know,' she said. 'And I don't think all this curiosity about your father's sex life is particularly appropriate.'

I let her know that 'appropriate' was one of my least favourite words and put her call through to Eleanor. Larry was guilty of something, that much I knew, but I'd only the cloudiest idea as to what he might have done. In my mind's eye, I could see Grandpa and Larry having another row, in an empty house this time, and things getting out of hand. But was this simply a fantasy, the kind I'd dwelt in as a child, or was it real? Recalling the look on Larry's face at the clinic, I was certain that he'd been back to North Canon Drive that night.

My misgivings were reinforced when Eleanor came downstairs to phone Bob Caswell. 'Did Daddy talk to you about anything, Bob, anything at all, in the days before he disappeared?' she said into the handset. Leaning in the

153

doorway, I listened to my aunt's end of the conversation. Despite the disrespect I'd shown her in the car, she was glad of an audience. 'You have to tell me the truth, Bob' she continued. 'This may well be a matter of life and death.' I could tell Eleanor really enjoyed saying that line, but she was in a pugnacious mood and wouldn't let up until she'd forced the lawyer to admit that Grandpa had indeed called him. 'What did Daddy want? Tell me, Bob. I have to know.' Nodding as she heard Caswell out, Eleanor looked disappointed.

Hanging up, she frowned at me. 'Daddy did talk to his lawyer the day before he left, apparently,' she said. 'But only because he wanted to alter something in his will.'

I remembered Larry saying that my grandfather had threatened to disinherit him. 'What did Grandpa want to change exactly?'

'Bob wouldn't give me any details,' she said. 'But I'd imagine Daddy simply wished to strike Julie's name from the list of beneficiaries.'

'Or Larry's.'

Irritated and more than a little bored, my aunt squeezed a dollop of moisturizer on to her forefinger. 'I doubt it.'

'Think how hurt Larry'd be,' I said. 'The money aside, he lives for Grandpa's approval, even more than Bruce does. Larry just covers it better. There's no saying how he'd react. Listen, Eleanor, I know he had something to do with Grandpa going missing.'

Turning her back to me, she removed a speck of lint from the sleeve of her white tunic. 'That's ridiculous. You sound like Hercule Poirot. Or Tintin,' she said.

'Hear me out. Larry admits he was drunk that night. What if he went over there to confront Grandpa? Maybe he hit him or pushed him over. You know how frail your father is. Don't tell me you haven't been thinking the same thing.'

'For God's sake, Ralph. It hasn't even crossed my mind. In any case, Sandra says you told her that Larry spent the night at Danny's house.'

'Maybe, but then what was he doing around North Canon Drive yesterday morning?'

'That's enough, Ralph. Go for a run or something. You're driving me mad.'

Glowering at her, I left the room and drove Roger's car up to Griffith Park.

Watching joggers pound the pathway hell-bent on self-improvement, it was impossible for me to escape the fact that any relationship I'd enjoyed with my father was now destroyed, and that I'd estranged both my aunt and her stepdaughter. The common denominator was me, and my obstinate conviction that Larry had played a part in his father's disappearance. And I couldn't let it go.

On my return to Doheny Drive, Roger came out of the house to greet me.

'Your aunt's very stressed, Ralph, which is why I had to fly back early. This business with her father and Bruce aside, the rehearsal schedule's incredibly demanding.' Unable to look me in the eye, Roger tied the sleeves of his jumper more tightly round his neck. 'The thing is,' he continued, 'since Larry's moved back to Laurel Canyon, Eleanor would really appreciate it if you'd hold the fort for us at Canon Drive. I could run you over there now, if you'd like.'

This was the brush-off I'd been expecting. Steeling myself, I told Roger that I'd get my things and say goodbye to his wife, but as I turned towards the front door, he stopped me. 'Eleanor's resting,' he said. 'She really needs peace and quiet. I hope you won't be too upset, but she took the liberty of asking Ilena to pack your things.'

Watching us climb into Roger's car, my aunt made an odd little wave with her hand, like a window-cleaner wiping at a persistent, possibly invisible, spot.

Shaugnessy King's contract lay on my bed at North Canon Drive, along with a covering note asking me to call Scott

Newton. The contract seemed in order, but when I re-read the material that I'd shown the publisher at his hotel, it was difficult to believe that he was prepared to pay me for more of the same. The pages were so poorly written that I threw all seventeen of them into the wastebasket. If not for my privileged background, I'd have been just another tormented indigent pushing a trolley in the Downtown district.

Still smarting from Eleanor's rejection, I drifted along the hall to my grandfather's room where a fine layer of dust on his dressing table was being turned into gold by the late afternoon sun. The art deco initials on the back of an ivory-backed hairbrush had all but worn away, but the brass locket lying beside it contained a swatch of somebody's fine blonde baby hair that shone as if it had been newly cut. On my grandfather's bedside table stood a black-and-white photograph of myself at twenty-four, directing a play for Direct Debit in a room above a pub in Bloomsbury. Sepia prints in silver frames were ranked on top of a bureau, portraits of forebears whose names I might never learn if Grandpa didn't come back.

Flinching at this thought, I noticed a slight depression on the right side of the emperor-sized bed and laid myself down on top of the covers to find that the shape of Grandpa's body had registered in the springs of the mattress. I could smell his hair oil on the wooden headboard, and the pinstripe suit hanging by the wardrobe was the same one he'd worn on a trip he'd made to England when I was eight or nine. Because my grandfather lived abroad and because he was a famous actor, he'd been given permission to take me out from my boarding school in Sussex on a weekday afternoon, an extraordinary event that provoked equal measures of contempt and envy in my fellow pupils.

The day my grandfather came to visit, the Headmaster, a cologne-soaked sadist named Seaward, fetched me from my double maths lesson and, escorting me out to the car, actually ruffled my hair with a pretence at affection. I took my seat beside Grandpa in the back of the car, and as we were driven off across the empty playing fields, he introduced me to a woman who wasn't his wife, a widow named Diane with stiff black hair like a helmet made of liquorice. The gold charms on her bracelet tinkled as she pinched my cheek. Wearing a hat and a raincoat, Grandpa asked me questions about football and school food, and gave me a big duck-egg blue box of chocolates from Fortnum & Mason. The chocolates were dark with soft rich centres, and Grandpa smiled as I tucked into them.

'Eat as many as you want,' he said. 'There's no charge.'

Diane and the driver laughed at this, and Grandpa seemed to enjoy watching me gorge myself, so I kept eating them all the way to Eastbourne, where we were to enjoy a tea of crumpets, sandwiches and cakes at the Grand Hotel. When I'd finished being sick, Grandpa described the play he was rehearsing in London, and although I didn't understand much of what he said, I was thrilled to be given five fake bullet holes, latex volcanoes an inch across with glossy red craters, that he'd obtained from the props department. For the next year, they were my most treasured possessions.

On North Canon Drive, a city employee in a cherry picker was using a chainsaw to cut back a palm tree, and the dead brown fronds fell sixty feet to the roadway with a soft husking sound. The walls of my grandfather's bedroom pressed in. When I roused myself to ring Scott Newton, he was unavailable, so I left a message for him. Lonely and feeling guilty, I called Lisa's mobile, but it was switched off and her landline was permanently engaged. Assuming that she'd taken her telephone off the hook, I drove over to Hollywood only to find that the lights were off in her apartment. There was no reply when I rang her buzzer.

With no wish to return to North Canon Drive, I drove around Hollywood. Rudderless, I read the illuminated signs that glowed against the orange-violet sky, and when I felt hungry, parked behind a Boston Market franchise at the intersection of Sunset and La Brea, where motorized javelins revolved above a billboard to prevent birds from shitting on the towering face of a film actor. Across La Brea, a twenty-foot-tall inflated plastic hen sat atop an El Pollo Loco outlet, grimy and askew, so I crossed the road and ordered a chicken enchilada in the strip-lit restaurant.

The faces of my fellow customers were either bright with guilt or faded with exhaustion, every crack in each façade shown up by the merciless lighting. Winners didn't dine alone at El Pollo Loco, and as I chewed my enchilada surrounded by other solitary men, the quality of our loneliness astonished me. You could catch another man's eye without danger there, because even a gunshot could only mean an end to despair.

Reaching a terrible place in my own head, I was compelled to go to buy a pen and paper from a drugstore and begin to write down everything that had happened since my arrival in California. When I ran out of paper, I went back to North Canon Drive and typed up another thirty foolscap pages of fact and conjecture. Everything poured out of me, no matter how far-fetched, but by the time I finally went upstairs to bed I was still no wiser as to what was really going on.

The next day I woke at noon and stayed in my room, brooding on my family, my mental emptiness deepening. *Heavily hangs the hollyhock, Heavily hangs the tiger-lily.* In my heart, I knew that I'd only insulted Eleanor because I was angry with Larry. My mother had borne the brunt of my hurt as a kid for much the same reason, and I had a nasty suspicion that this was something my aunt might well have called a pattern, but although I owed Eleanor an apology, I couldn't bring myself to pick up the phone.

By the time Carmelita came up to my room that evening to say that my aunt wished to speak to me, my anger and sorrow had turned into bitterness, and I'd decided that it was for Eleanor to make an apology to me. My aunt had thrown me out of her house after all, so I told Carmelita that I had a headache. When she left my room, I crept to the door to hear her whispering to Eleanor on the hall telephone. Neither Lisa nor Scott Newton returned my calls, so I left another message for Newton at the hotel and afterwards lay like a fly trapped in the hardening amber of my bed.

Reading over the notes I'd begun at El Pollo Loco the following day, inspiration released me from my torpor. Abandoned by my family once again, I decided to write about them, and from the outset my own memoir was to be an act of retribution. Of vengeance. *Reckless what I do to spite the world.* No mere cry for attention, my work would lay bare the clinical degree of self-involvement that infected the Taits and serve as an act of decontamination. Humming to myself, I fetched the computer from the pool house and set it up in my room.

For three solid days I typed out my invective, and then Eleanor brought Bruce back to North Canon Drive. From my bedroom window, I watched him cross the yard with the shaky gait of a yachtsman re-experiencing dry land after months at sea. Eleanor led Bruce up the wooden staircase to his apartment and my heart heaved into my mouth when he slipped on the sixth step, but I decided to finish the paragraph I was working on before joining them. Five minutes later, I turned round to find my aunt standing by my bed, reading the first page of my memoir.

'What's this, Ralph?' she asked. '"*For Artaud, an actor is a heretic being burnt at the stake, signalling madly through the flames. Let this book serve as a can of petrol hurled on to the pyre.*" Charming. Daddy didn't write that, did he?'

My cheeks burnt. 'Er, it's something I've been working on myself,' I said.

Frowning as she laid the page aside, Eleanor told me there was still no news of Grandpa, and that Bruce was resting. Pale at the best of times, my aunt's face now looked green.

'According to Dr Hendricks, Bruce is going to sleep a great deal,' she said. 'But he's still very medicated, so it's a battle to reach him. I've told him that Daddy's gone on vacation, but I'm not sure the message has got through.' My aunt's face relaxed when I apologized for my behaviour following the trip to Anaheim. 'Well, you had to lash out at somebody,' she said. 'We've all been under tremendous pressure, and I'm sorry I sent you packing, but it's been almost a week now since Daddy went and I really think I'm beginning to fall apart. I haven't slept properly for days and we've got the tech run tomorrow. I'm absolutely exhausted.' Eleanor paused to examine her teeth in the ornamental mirror by the door. 'How are you feeling, by the way?' she asked. 'Carmelita tells me you've been shut up in here for days.'

Eleanor sidled over to inspect the computer screen, and scrabbling to shut it down, I felt her eyes dart over the paragraph I'd just written. She pulled my hand from the keyboard and began to read aloud: '"*I am sick of their narcissism, their exhibitionism, their hypocrisy. I am sick of their selfishness. According to Edward Gordon Craig, Ellen Terry's son, it is conceit that drives the actor to become the object of universal attention . . .*" I think you're missing an apostrophe, Ralph.' With a sigh, my aunt stripped some dead petals from the begonia on the windowsill. 'It must have been so terribly hard for you,' she continued. I had no idea what she was talking about. 'Your childhood,' she whispered, making it sound as if I'd been orphaned in a war zone.

Swallowing this cant as best I could, I asked if Sandra had turned up any new information.

'Not a thing,' Eleanor replied. 'She called the police yesterday evening, and they say they'll be on the lookout. I don't hold out much hope, but at least the fact that Daddy's missing will be public information some time today. My agent's preparing a press release.'

Galled that our unfolding misfortunes were now subject to the exigencies of public relations, I left her in the kitchen with

Carmelita and went to find Bruce, who was slumped on a lounger by the pool. The sallow flesh on his face had gone slack as if the medication had penetrated his very cells. Arrowheads of dried spit had formed at the corners of his mouth and his hair was flat and greasy, but he smiled at me, said my name and told me that he was feeling better. I asked about the pills he'd been prescribed, but Bruce only knew that Carmelita was going to be giving them to him as required.

'I don't like taking them but I have to,' he said. Far more present than at Anaheim, my uncle appeared to have no difficulty following me as I reminded him of the huge sandcastles we'd once built together at Matador beach, and avoiding the subject of Grandpa's disappearance for fear of upsetting him, I suggested that we might make another journey to Ojai when he felt better. It was as if I'd tripped a hidden wire. Bruce stood up, kicked over the lounger and stormed about on the flagstones.

'What are you saying? What are you saying?' Screeching like a seagull trapped in an oilspill, he jumped back when I tried to get close to him.

I ran to fetch Eleanor and Carmelita, but by the time they reached the pool, my uncle was sitting on the lounger once more, staring at his foot and smoking a cigarette. Sensing that the women suspected me of crying wolf, I went up to check the battery in the smoke detector in Bruce's apartment where, tacked to the wall below his Dodgers pennant, I recognized a portrait that I'd drawn of him when I was three. The Abe Lincoln beard he'd sported at the time had been rendered as an extended Slinky-toy running around the bottom half of the egg-shaped face, and my thick felt-tip strokes had almost faded away in places, but it moved me that he'd kept the picture.

An overnight thunderstorm had washed the city clean, and when I woke in my bed over the archway, the air smelt freshly made (or even imported). There'd still been no word from Scott Newton, but Lisa called offering to take me out for breakfast, and she sounded so upbeat that I guessed Eleanor had asked her to lift my spirits.

Sliding into one of Nate 'n Al's button-back booths, Lisa pointed to a small news item buried in the middle of the *Los Angeles Times*. A photograph of my grandfather from the *Brannigan* period showed him wearing a tuxedo and a crooked smile, but the story itself was little more than a pretext for running the picture. Bob Caswell was quoted as saying that while Donald Tait had been out of contact with his family for almost a week, there was as yet no cause for alarm. Eleanor Tait was about to open in *Macbeth* at the Ahmanson Theater and had been unavailable for comment, but there was no mention of Larry in the piece, an oversight that would undoubtedly spoil his morning. According to Lisa, my aunt had been on the telephone to her therapist in New York every few hours, and was taking Prozac again to ease herself through the get-in at the Ahmanson. Lisa added that Roger had begun to share his wife's (and my own) concerns for my grandfather's wellbeing. Mustering my courage, I replied that I believed Larry knew more than he was saying about Grandpa's disappearance.

Lisa stared at me, goggle-eyed. 'Come on, Ralph. That's crazy. You're trying to say Larry kidnapped his own father or something?'

As I listed my evidence – the lie that Larry had told Sandra, the sighting of his car on North Canon Drive, his guilt when I'd confronted him at the clinic – Lisa wiped some juice from her lower lip and shook her head.

'It doesn't add up to a thing,' she said. Her reaction devastated me. How could she be so blind to the truth? 'I had dinner with your father over at Danny's place two nights ago, and he told me he's really stressed about Donald,' she continued. 'We talked a lot about your grandfather. And about you. Maybe Larry just lied because he doesn't want you or Sandra to know he slept with Mitzi.'

Self-centred to the last, I wondered why Danny and Ingeborg hadn't thought to invite me. 'Was Mitzi at this dinner?' I asked.

'Yeah, she was. What of it?'

Something in Lisa's tone told me not to push it, and I endured her fervent description of the meal she'd eaten at Danny's house until my smile grew so fixed that my upper lip became stuck to my teeth. But as Lisa heated herself up over the way my cousin had barbecued all the food himself, I could hold back no longer.

'Wow,' I said. 'With no help? Amazing.'

I sounded all too like Eleanor, but luckily Lisa missed the inflection, and when she mentioned Mitzi's name again, I asked her why her friend had been there.

'Why shouldn't she be?' Lisa replied. 'You're only pissed at Mitzi because you think she might have slept with your father.'

'Well, did she?'

'I wouldn't know.'

'You as good as told me she did just now,' I said.

'Well, why shouldn't she? Larry's an attractive guy and a lot of fun.'

'Hah! Unlike me, I suppose.'

'You said it.'

Lisa and I glared at each other, and only just managed to pull back before we had a proper row. Asking for the check, she offered to drop me back at Grandpa's house out of common courtesy, and as we drove there in silence, my future looked gloomier than ever. Given the volume of traffic on Canon Drive, it seemed almost inconceivable that I'd bicycled up and down this road as a child counting the palms as I dodged the odd scything fender; water hadn't just passed under the bridge since then, it had swept the thing off its pilings and carried it out to sea. At the five-way intersection south of Sunset, a teenage Chicano held a hand-lettered sign advertising Star Maps, unofficial guides to various celebrity-owned homes in Los Angeles, but the only human beings the gullible tourist or stalker was likely to glimpse at these addresses would be gardeners or service personnel. Sometimes cars would slow down opposite my grandfather's house, pause as if experiencing a moment of existential doubt, then move on. Stopped at the lights, I regretted ever coming back to California, and then Grandpa's Bentley hurtled towards us.

As it flew past, I saw Bruce at the wheel. Feeling the first prickles of panic, I begged Lisa to follow him.

'But I'll be late for my lecture.'

'So what? He's not supposed to be driving. Eleanor even hid the keys to his pick-up.'

To her credit, Lisa made a sickening loop in pursuit, tailing my uncle as he headed east on Sunset, a hundred yards ahead of us. Although we were trapped in the traffic flow and couldn't catch up with him, the Jeep's height allowed us to keep the Bentley in view as we lurched along the Strip, its coachwork appearing to wobble in the heat rising from the road surface. By the time we reached Greenblatt's, Lisa had narrowed the gap to thirty yards, but just as I opened the door to make my dash, the lights changed, and Bruce swung across the path of three oncoming cars before accelerating up Laurel Canyon Drive, one of the busiest roads in the city.

Overslept commuters were streaming down Laurel Canyon from the Valley, but the traffic thinned on its way up the gradient and Lisa spotted the Bentley, quite empty, in the parking lot of the Canyon country store. Delighted to have found it, I went to look for Bruce, but heading down the slope towards the store, I recalled his tantrum the previous afternoon and became anxious as to how he might react when he saw me.

Two dozen people were sitting around drinking coffee and reading newspapers on the front terrace, screened from the road by a bamboo fence, and I picked out Bruce at a table in the shade of an awning at the far end.

Talking to my father.

Larry was gripping Bruce's arm. The magma seemed to move beneath the crust. Terrified of being seen, I darted sideways into the store itself. Halfway down an aisle, I pretended to look at the various fruit juices in the chiller cabinets. Convincing myself that Larry and Bruce were meeting at the store to elude observation by Carmelita or Sandra, I dawdled for a moment by the doorway before risking another glimpse. As I edged out on to the terrace, my heart pressed up into my throat.

The brothers appeared to be in some kind of dispute, and I ordered myself a coffee from the terrace counter for cover. Paying with shaking fingers, the hot liquid slopped over the rim of my cup, scalding my hand, and I almost dropped it. Luckily Larry and Bruce were still caught up in their conversation. My father looked as tense and blinkered as a man backing a milk float down a narrow mountain road, so I slid over towards the payphone some fifteen feet from them and pretended to make a call. All too aware that Larry would know I was spying on them if he saw me, I kept my face averted and pricked my ears to eavesdrop, but given the noise of the traffic, I was just too far away. At my elbow, a thin woman guzzled an overweight sandwich, and I obeyed a mad urge to look again, just as my father banged on the table to make a point.

Bruce turned to face me.

My uncle was looking straight at me. Petrified, I expected him to get up and say hello, but even as I tried my best to smile, he looked away again.

'Are you using that phone or just fondling it?'

Grating, nasal and right in my ear, the voice belonged to a hirsute Munchkin whose overpowering male fragrance got a fleeting stranglehold on my respiratory system. When Larry stood up and led Bruce down some steps to the lower parking lot, I gulped some fresher air, handed the Munchkin the phone and walked along the side of the building to see my father drag his brother across a patch of open ground beneath the branches of a massive tree. Bracing Bruce against the side of his convertible, Larry shook him by the shoulders. The two men scuffled briefly, pushing at each other mostly, and when Bruce started crying, Larry bundled him into the car. Hurrying back along the length of the terrace, I sprinted across the upper parking lot.

'Where's Bruce? You've been ages,' Lisa said.

'He and Larry had a fight. Larry forced him into his car. We've got to follow them.'

'Cool it, Ralph. *We* haven't got to do anything. Tell me what happened first.'

'I think Larry killed Grandpa, and Bruce knows it. He's trying to make him keep his mouth shut.'

'Drop the bone,' Lisa said. 'Bruce is safe. He's with Larry, right? Who's probably taking him home to Beverly Hills. End of story. Nobody's killed anybody. Jesus. I'm already late for college as it is.'

'Look, you have to drive me up to Larry's house.'

Lisa refused, and it took my best efforts to get her to take me back to North Canon Drive.

'You know, you've got a real hang-up about your dad,' she said, driving us down to Sunset. 'Maybe you just like to think he killed or kidnapped his father because that's what you want to do yourself. Maybe it's just one great big projection?'

'Where'd you get that one from? Your psychology class?'

'No. But I think you're wrong about Larry, that's all.'

And that was all either of us said until we reached North Canon Drive to discover, just as I'd suspected, no sign of Larry's convertible. Still angry with Lisa, I kissed her coldly on the cheek, and to my lasting shame, it gratified me when she looked hurt.

'You know, you're a great guy, Ralph. It's fun being with you most of the time. But I just think you'd be a lot happier if you could drop this stupid stuff with your dad.'

'Really?' I said. 'Any more advice?'

166

'Sure, since you ask. Larry's a playboy and a Peter Pan, but so what? You think you drew the short straw getting him for a father, but I'd choose Larry over Donald any day. Can you for one second imagine what it must have been like for Larry, trying to live up to your grandfather's expectations? Having him put you down the whole time you were trying to grow up?'

It was true that Larry had never bad-mouthed me in public until the day of Grandpa's disappearance, but it upset me that Lisa couldn't see that his careless cruelties had proved equally hurtful. 'Anything else you'd like to add while you're at it?' I asked her.

'You like to think you're a sensitive artistic type, Ralph, but maybe you're just touchy. If I was you, I'd drop your baggage.'

'Oh, right.' I said. 'And what "baggage" is that exactly? A shopping bag? A travelling case?'

'A truckload, honey.'

Before I could reply, Lisa drove off.

An hour later, Larry still hadn't brought Bruce back to North Canon Drive, and I was frantic. Carmelita had told me that Bruce had refused to take his pills after breakfast, and that when he'd taken off in the Bentley, she'd been unable to contact Eleanor at the Ahmanson. Larry wasn't answering the phone in Laurel Canyon, and the telephonist at the theatre insisted that my aunt wasn't taking calls under any circumstances. Desperate to speak to her, I decided to drive there in person, but crossing the city in the station wagon with Lisa's words running around my brain, I followed an impulse to return to the Canyon country store.

# Chapter Nine

> 'The performance is over. The audience gets up to
> leave their seats. "It's time to put on our overcoats and
> go home." They look round. But there are no more
> overcoats to put on and no more houses to go to.'
> Vasili Rozanov, *The Apocalypse of Our Times*

The Bentley was exactly where Bruce had left it, and I headed up the twisting roads to Larry's house without a moment's hesitation. Passing the wooden fence that bordered my father's property, there was no sign of the beige convertible, so I parked some way up the hill, ambled back down to the gate and rang the bell. My heart racing, I waited for half a minute before pressing the bell again, leaving my finger on it this time until I heard a muffled chime inside the house. Nothing happened. Taking a quick look around to make sure that nobody was watching me, I vaulted the gate and followed the stone steps down to the front door.

A bird chirped in a nearby tree but nobody came to the door when I knocked, so I went round to the deck and looked in the border for the large stone under which Larry had once hidden a spare key in case he ever locked himself out. It was a long shot, but pushing the stone aside with my foot I saw a glint of metal against the dry earth, retrieved the key, and used it to let myself in through the French windows. Blood rushed in my ears. My entry into the house had been so easy that it was only now, standing in the living room, that I realized what I'd done. Home invasion. What if Larry or a Westec patrolman found me there? And what if they were armed? Crossing the tiled floor of the hall, I glimpsed a stooped figure moving beyond a doorway set into the far wall.

My neck muscles locked but I'd only caught sight of myself, reflected in a newly installed floor-length mirror. The house contained as many mirrors as my grandfather's home on North Canon Drive so it surprised me that Larry had felt the need for one more, but then Borges' contention that 'mirrors and copulation are terrible because they increase the number of men' was never going to find many takers among the male members of the Tait family.

The place had the sharp tang of a man living alone. Newspapers, dirty plates and empty glasses were spread all over the living room, and the refrigerator was empty save for a carton of tomato juice and some browning Canadian bacon. Larry's maid hadn't dusted for a while, and I hoped she wouldn't choose to reappear while I was there. How long had Irene been in Europe? Although Larry's wife still had her own house up on Mulholland where she spent her days producing abstract gouaches, I expected to find some of her belongings in the master bedroom, but there was no trace of her, not even a photograph. The bed was unmade, crumpled clothes were draped over the furniture, and a small mirror on the bedside console was covered in white dust. I for one had never believed that Larry had stopped taking cocaine, or divorce powder as he called it, and here was more proof.

As this fresh disappointment dredged up deeper, buried discontentment, I came across a copy of *Jonathan Livingston Seagull*. It fell open near the middle: *'Earth had been a place where he had learned much, of course, but the details were blurred – something about fighting for food, and being Outcast.'* Replacing the paperback beside *Zen and the Art of Motorcycle Maintenance* by Robert M. Pirsig, the only book that I'd ever seen Larry actually read, I reacquainted myself with the back-cover photograph of the author and his son. The small, frightened-looking boy sat crammed on the pillion seat of a motorbike, his view of the road ahead completely blocked by Pirsig.

In the study, a mass of papers had spilled on to the floor from Larry's roll-top desk, and an ashtray containing a half-smoked joint stood on a pile of bank statements. Guiltily, I moved the ashtray to one side and discovered that my father was running a $50,000 overdraft on his account. This was much more than habitual mismanagement, because a recent letter from the Bank of America requested him to make an appointment to reschedule his loan repayments. Fifteen minutes later, I'd discovered that Larry was into the bank for $400,000, and that his house had been remortgaged the previous year. How much cocaine had he been taking? Larry was as broke as me, and I felt for him as I played back the messages on his antique answering machine. There were two from Eleanor, sounding characteristically keyed-up, and one from Larry's voice-over agent eager to find out if he was free the following Tuesday. Then a man's voice clicked in, saying that he'd enjoyed seeing Larry again the previous week, and asking him to make it six-thirty at the hotel bar instead of seven that very evening.

Scott Newton's voice.

In Venice, Larry had told me that he didn't know Newton. Recalling that I'd given Newton Larry's number at the Beverly Wilshire hotel, the message puzzled me. Had Larry been hiding something from me? And if Newton was simply trying a new angle to get his hands on the manuscript, why hadn't he returned my own calls? It didn't make sense. Hearing a sound, possibly a servomechanism, I went along the corridor to take a look in my old room.

Two naked bodies were entwined on the bed, snoring quietly in the darkness. The room stank of stale sweat, baby oil and dull sublunary love. Standing still as stone, I held my breath until I'd made sure they were both fast asleep. The man lying half on top of Mitzi was my cousin Danny. In need of a glass of water, my shaking hand was closing on the kitchen tap when a key turned in the front door.

'Mitzi? Danny?' my father called.

Hearing him shut the front door, I sped through the living room on the balls of my feet and let myself out on to the deck.

Closing the French doors behind me, I flattened myself against the wall, panting. My father was moving around inside the house. When it went quiet, I glanced through the window to see him sitting on the sofa with his back to me. Bruce wasn't with him. Praying that the deck wouldn't squeak under my weight, I edged past the window, replaced the key beneath the rock, raced up the steps and jumped the gate. Larry's convertible was parked under the tree, its engine making clicking noises as it cooled. Running up the hill to the station wagon, I hoped that I'd remembered to rewind the tape on the answering machine.

Still awash with adrenaline, I took a wrong turn off Wilshire in the Downtown district and got lost in a zone of corporate skyscrapers and welfare hotels. The streets were deserted save for a few homeless men, and I stopped to ask directions to the theatre from a black man sitting at the kerb.

'The Ahmanson? Save your money, dearest chuck. Thrice the brinded cat hath mewed.'

The front of house was closed, so I circled the glass building to find the stage door, which was guarded by a young gunman who was amused to hear of my urgent need to speak to Eleanor Tait. At the Ahmanson, Hermann Goering's impulse to reach for his revolver at the mention of the word 'culture' would have been a straightforward matter of self-defence, because the gunslinger's trigger finger inched towards his hip when I insisted that I was Eleanor's nephew. Before I gave him a chance to draw on me, an older guard joined us, and presented with my California driving licence, told me to come back in fifteen minutes when the technical run-through would be completed.

Waiting by the stage door, I added to the cigarette stubs pressed every which way into the sand of a Sahara-sized ashtray. Across Temple Street, a mural depicting actors performing various roles bore a paean to the so-called profession by Father Daniel Bertigan, S. J., but in my mind I kept seeing

171

Danny Tait splayed on top of Mitzi in my old room at Larry's house. The older guard finally came outside to say that Eleanor would see me, and as he clipped me with a visitor's tag, a bag-lady attempted to obtain a soft drink from a vending machine at the bottom of a ramp that led on to the stage. Failing to understand how she'd got past the guards, it eventually dawned on me that she'd portrayed one of the witches in the play, and that the rags she was wearing were her costume.

The backstage area of every theatre I've worked in has smelt much the same, a mixture of hessian, paint, make-up and dust, but the Ahmanson had the smell of an office building. Arriving at Eleanor's dressing room, the guard knocked softly on the door.

'Come in.' Flying at me in a pink robe with her hair pinned back by big steel clips, Eleanor was desperate for news of Grandpa, but told of my two visits to Laurel Canyon, she fell back in her chair. 'That's all?' she shrieked. 'You come crashing in here because you saw Larry and Bruce arguing with each other in some bloody coffee bar? And because Larry had a call from Daddy's *publisher*? Ralph, please. Give me a break.'

Struck dumb, I stood marooned in the middle of the room as Eleanor tried to call Larry. The black wig she'd worn on the advertising banners now graced an expanded polystyrene wig block on to which somebody had drawn a pair of skewed eyes in blue ballpoint. Unable to raise her brother, my aunt spoke briefly with Carmelita. Bruce still hadn't returned.

'Apparently he refused to take his medication,' Eleanor said. 'No wonder they were both upset. Larry must have been trying to take him back to the clinic.'

Of all people, I'd expected my aunt to understand what was happening. I'd been counting on her as an ally and I was desperate. 'It wasn't like that,' I said, the words catching in my throat. 'You needed to see their body language.'

'Why, for God's sake?' she cried. 'We're previewing tomorrow night and everybody's going crazy. Somebody even called my agent saying that Daddy's been killed.' Spluttering, I grasped her shoulder. 'Oh, calm down, Ralph,' she said. 'The police think it was just some sick fan who'd read the paper. But I've got a photo-call in two minutes, so if you don't mind –'

'I'm not going anywhere,' I said. 'We have to talk, Eleanor. Why did Larry and Bruce meet in secret? Answer me that.'

My aunt swivelled her chair to face me, the thirty light bulbs that surrounded her mirror on the wall serving as a makeshift halo. 'The Canyon store's hardly a secret rendezvous,' she said. 'And you've lost your mind, breaking into Larry's house. What if someone had called the police? Go back to England, Ralph.'

'But what about Grandpa?

'Sandra's following a new lead,' Eleanor said, applying a white make-up sponge to her neck. 'But don't hold your breath.'

'And Bruce? Doesn't it bother you that he's missing too now?'

'He's not missing. You said you saw him with Larry.'

At the bleep of her mobile phone, a bearded, body-built dresser appeared in the doorway, but Eleanor took the call herself. 'No, Gaby. I don't need a bloody workout, thank you very much. Call me next week, OK?' My aunt clunked the mobile phone down on her dressing table. 'Does everybody want a piece of me today?' she asked, turning in my direction. 'Would you kindly get out of here?'

As I tried to speak, she put her hands to the sides of her neck, opened her mouth and screamed to dispel her negative energy. Given the decibels involved, it was hard to believe that she was taking Prozac, but while I leapt at the sound, her dresser only rolled his eyes.

'What if Larry hit your father?' I asked her. 'You know what he can be like when he's drunk.'

'Stop trying to sabotage my work,' Eleanor cried. 'Get him out of here, Darien. I need some peace and quiet for one fucking minute.'

The tension in my stomach turned into venom. 'Do you think anybody really cares about another lousy, soulless production of *Macbeth*?' I asked her. 'Damn thee black, thy cream-faced loon!'

Darien the dresser pumped his biceps in anticipation of a tussle, but before he had a chance to test them out on me, the uniformed goon poked his head around the door, presumably in response to Eleanor's screech.

'It's OK,' I said. 'I'll go quietly.'

Battered and demoralized by my audience with Eleanor, it took all my remaining strength of purpose to drag myself down to the Beverly Wilshire hotel. By ten past six, I'd found myself a seat just inside the entrance of the bar, which was already half-filled with businessmen, Brecht's 'Jolly-looking people [who] come from nowhere and are nowhere bound.' A brass plate by my table claimed that alcohol may increase cancer risk, so I was sipping a coke and pretending to be absorbed in a menu that offered 28 grams of Beluga caviar for $95 when Scott Newton walked into the bar.

As he turned to scan my side of the room, I buried my nose in the menu, sweat soaking the collar of my least favourite shirt, until he shuffled over to an unoccupied table by the grand piano. It was only six twenty-three, and since my father had never been early for an appointment in his life, I risked a move to a free table beyond the piano from where I hoped to be able to overhear their conversation.

Larry arrived at five minutes to seven and his hip-hop T-shirt gave me a familiar jab of filial embarrassment. Greeted by Newton, my father looked anxious, but I couldn't hear a word they were saying so I went over to the bar, which at least offered me a good view of their table. Flirting with the waitress as he ordered a drink, Larry settled deeper into his armchair, chatting easily to Newton as if they were old friends swapping notes on the male menopause. Scared that I'd picked up the ball and run with it straight into a brick wall, my fears dissolved when Larry sat forward to say something in earnest, using complex hand gestures to make his point. At that moment I'd have given my return ticket to London for some subtitles. When my father was through, Newton shook his head. Crestfallen, Larry opened and closed his mouth, silent as a fish in a tank.

A woman caught my eye by the door, a blonde wearing dark glasses. Sandra Simmons. Eleanor's investigator was making a little pantomime of powdering her nose, and for a second her presence seemed to corroborate my suspicions about Larry. But was Sandra keeping an eye on my father or on me? My heart thumped as I made my way over to her table. Hearing me say her name, the former stuntwoman faked surprise, baring her capped teeth in a poor attempt at a smile.

'Hi, Ralph,' she said. 'Are you here to meet someone?'

Not for one moment did I buy her act. 'I'm spying on my father. Are you tailing him?'

'Your father? Good God, no. I'm here on another case.' Mouthing the word 'divorce', Sandra tried to get up, but I leant over her, barring the way.

'Come off it, Sandra. You're on to Larry, aren't you?'

'What makes you say that?' she asked.

'Did Eleanor tell you about this little meeting? And about the fight Larry had with Bruce this morning? I reckon Larry's terrified Bruce is going to tell somebody what happened. What do you think?'

'I've no idea what you're talking about,' she said, her beady eyes hardening. 'And nor do you.'

My guts crumpled. 'Listen to me,' I said. 'Larry may be my father, but I need to find out what happened to Grandpa just as much as you do.'

Looking beyond me, Sandra tensed. 'I have to go,' she said.

Leaving Larry to swirl his Martini at the table, Newton was walking in our direction, so I followed Sandra into the lobby and watched her leave the hotel as Newton went over to the elevators. When Larry failed to emerge, I went back to find him at the bar talking to a dark-haired young woman wearing a low-cut lilac top.

'How you doing, Pa?' I said.

Larry stood with his arms splayed for a moment before he hugged me, acting delighted. Pulling away, I asked him about Bruce.

'I had to take him back to the clinic,' Larry replied. 'He was in bad shape this morning. Stopped taking his medication. Oh, excuse me, this is Kristen. Kristen, this is Ralph.' For once, Larry didn't make a big fuss about being my father, probably because his prey was younger than I was. When I asked Kristen how she knew Larry, she revealed that they'd just that minute met, trying her best to make it sound like the luckiest thing that had ever happened to her. Larry wanted to know who I was with, and when I said that I'd come to meet Eleanor's investigator, some of his martini went down the wrong way. 'Really?' he asked. 'Is she here?'

Told that she'd left, he seemed to relax, but Kristen looked bemused. 'We saw you having a drink with Scott Newton,' I added. 'But you both looked a little uptight, so we decided not to interrupt. Was Newton asking you about the manuscript?'

'Yes. No. Not really. We're old friends.'

'You told me at Venice you didn't remember him. You're always bloody lying to me.'

Larry took me by the arm. 'I asked Newton for a loan,' he said. 'What more can I say? I've been having some problems lately. I'm sure the old man told you.'

Kristen's pupils contracted at the mention of Larry's financial difficulties.

'How do you expect me to believe a thing you say? You're such a liar.'

'Look, I helped him out once in the past so I thought he might return the favour, OK?' Larry tried to lead me aside and as I jerked free, Kristen started talking to a man in a business suit. 'I'm sorry, sonny, but I've been so stressed out about the old man that I haven't been spending enough time with you. Why don't you let me take you to dinner?'

'Eleanor thinks I should go home,' I said. 'To London.'

'Well, what do *you* think? That's the important thing.'

'I don't know. Maybe she's right.'

Larry tried to hide his relief, but it was there in a fractional relaxation of his facial muscles. He'd been lying about Newton, of that I was certain, and possibly about Bruce. My father had nothing I wanted. He never had. I left him there.

The nurse at the clinic in Anaheim refused to disclose any information whatsoever concerning a patient over the telephone and suggested that I call back the following day to speak with Dr Hendricks. When I offered to drive over with some identification right away, she informed me that visiting hours were most definitely over and that I'd be turned away at the gate. Carmelita told me that there was still no sign of Bruce, and when I called Lisa there was no reply. I couldn't speak to Eleanor until the curtain had come down on her dress rehearsal, so I tried to get Sandra's number, but the lawyers' office was closed. Thrown back on myself, I drove around the Wilshire district with all the windows open, trying to outdistance the voices in my head, until the faces of my fellow drivers began to look so reptile and corrupt, that I retreated to North Canon Drive. Up in my room, I attempted to lose myself in my memoir, but a sudden breeze dispersed my notes across the floor and I couldn't even bring myself to pick them up. Brooding until it got dark, at nine o'clock I went over to Eleanor's house.

Ilena showed me into the living area, and from the look on my aunt's face it was clear that I still 'dwelt but within the suburbs of her good pleasure'. Eleanor seemed unimpressed as I mumbled an unfelt apology for my insolence at the Ahmanson, but by that time I was beyond caring.

'Sandra's tracked Julie down to some fishing village near Cozumel,' she said, readjusting a spray of Japanese twigs in a porcelain vase. 'Through her charge card. Daddy used to go to Cozumel on his fishing trips.'

I was stunned. 'Grandpa's with her?' I asked. 'Have you spoken to him?'

'It looks as if they ran away together. Why else would Julie be in Mexico? We don't know where they're actually staying, but Sandra's flying down first thing tomorrow. I can't quite believe how selfish Daddy's being.' Eleanor's tired eyes flashed, but as she hooked her legs over the arm of the sofa, I couldn't be sure that she wasn't still performing. 'You and I got it wrong,' she said. 'We got it all wrong.'

'I saw Larry earlier,' I said. 'At the Beverly Wilshire.'

Eleanor barely raised an eyebrow. 'So?'

'Sandra was there too.'

'Give it a rest, Ralph. Sandra's convinced Daddy's safe and sound in Mexico,' she said. 'Understand this: while we've been fretting ourselves to death, your grandfather's been sunning himself on a bloody beach. But if I were you, I'd look on the bright side. Now you can go back to England and get on with your life.'

What life? It was collapsing around me, a pile of cardboard waiting to be incinerated. 'Look, Eleanor,' I said. 'Are you trying to shield me from something?'

'Shield you? Good heavens, no. From what exactly?'

I took a deep breath. 'Something Larry might have done. Something bad.'

'Actually, I'm not trying to shield you at all. Quite the opposite. I want to know what you're planning to do with yourself.'

'Well, I guess I'll wait around until Grandpa gets back,' I said. 'And help him with the book.'

My aunt chuckled. 'There isn't going to be any book,' she

said. 'Do you know why Shaugnessy King have been pushing Daddy to finish it after so long? Because John Blumenthal bought the bloody company, just to spike the thing. He's terrified Daddy's going to spill the beans about the affair he had with his wife. In 1974, if you can believe it. Roger dug around and found this out from someone in New York.'

'Blumenthal only married the woman last year,' I said. 'Julie showed me pictures of the wedding in a magazine.'

'I know, but apparently John can't bear the idea of people knowing that Donald Tait had his dear wife in the full bloom of her youth.' My worst fears about the book confirmed, my heart seemed to change places with my liver. 'Go home and go to bed, Ralph. And then get yourself on a flight. It's not doing you any good being here.'

It felt as if I was being buried alive. 'But what about Larry? You told me I needed to resolve things with him.'

'Tell me, do you *ever* think of anyone apart from yourself? I mean, I've been working my butt off for fifteen hours straight,' Eleanor said. 'Aren't you even going to ask me how the dress rehearsal went?'

'Er, how did it go?'

'Oh, forget it. You couldn't care less. "Another lousy, soulless production of *Macbeth*," wasn't that what you said? Well, what would you know, Ralph? You're a bloody amateur.' Her eyes glittered and two red discs bloomed on her pale cheeks. 'Why d'you think you avoided a career in the mainstream theatre? On moral grounds? It was fear of failure. You were scared that you weren't good enough, and it suited you to surround yourself with a group of phoneys because they bolstered your self-esteem.'

Eleanor's words drew blood. There had been value to Direct Debit's work, but it shamed me to remember how excited I'd been when someone from Andrew Lloyd Webber's company had left a message on my answering machine. And my subsequent disappointment on learning that they only wanted me to direct the third take-over cast in the Cape Town production of *Cats*. If Direct Debit had ever been invited to give a Royal Command Performance, I'd have bowed and scraped in the line-up with the best of them. I'd been lying to myself for years. The realization was annihilating.

Eleanor shook her head. 'You're the problem, Ralph. Nobody else. We're getting on with our lives, but you're stuck,' she said. 'I'm sorry to be brutal, but it's time for you to grow up.'

Demolished, I walked the gangplank back to the car and somehow drove myself back to North Canon Drive. My whole life had been a charade. An act. I was as bad as the rest of them.

That night at North Canon Drive, I lay awake in the dark despising myself. In the void. Eleanor had been right. Trapped in the prison yard of my own egotism, I'd failed to recognize that my hypocrisy had compromised Direct Debit's work from the word go. It was no surprise that I'd got it all wrong about Larry and Grandpa, because I'd got it all wrong about everything else. Some time before dawn, my thoughts turned to the atrocious way I'd treated Lisa, and as I replayed our final parting, a car pulled into the back yard: Ernesto's pick-up. Ever since Grandpa had left, I'd been sleeping in too late to see the pool man, and a glimmer of obsessive curiosity made me take a mug of coffee out to him.

Following the sound of the lawnmower, I found Ernesto near the magnolia tree, and he sucked his teeth when I asked him if he'd seen anything on the morning of Grandpa's disappearance.

'Nobody was here,' he said. 'Not until Carmelita arrived. Like I told the policewoman Simmons.'

'Sandra Simmons? She isn't a policewoman,' I said. 'She's an investigator working for my aunt.' Ernesto started to say something but thought better of it. 'What is it?' I asked. 'You saw something, didn't you?'

Setting his baseball cap on the back of his head, he sighed.

180

'I have no green card. No American wife. When the woman called, I told her I'd seen nothing, because if she took me for an interview, she'd report me to the immigration.'

Somebody was telling me the truth for once, and my ears began to ring. 'Did you see anybody come to the house that morning?' I asked him. 'Or leave?'

'Bruce was there with another guy. When I arrived, maybe six o'clock. They were putting a blue case in the back of a convertible. For travelling.' My mouth was so dry that my tongue made a clacking sound as I asked Ernesto to describe the man with Bruce. 'Guy from TV,' he said. 'I seen him here before. He drove off in a convertible.'

'Was it beige?' I asked.

'Yeah, I believe so. Look, there's something else been bothering me. You know that big head of wood Bruce carved for Mr Tait? Well, I asked Bruce what was in the case, and he said it was the head. That the guy was taking it up to Ojai to set it in the ground.'

'To the house in Ojai?'

'Sure. Thing is, that head was still out on the terrace. It hadn't gone anywhere.'

'So what was in the case?'

'Who can say?'

The thought of Grandpa's dead body dismembered in there, turning green with decay, made me feel physically sick. Throwing the dregs of his coffee into the border, Ernesto handed me the empty mug, and I staggered back up to the garage to find a clean rectangle on the dusty concrete floor where the blue trunk had stood. Larry had taken it away the morning Grandpa disappeared, and he'd been lying to me ever since, ever since the day I was born. Two hours passed before I finally got through to Dr Hendricks, who told me that Bruce had not been readmitted to the clinic.

Then I called Larry.

There was a new, over-acted message on the answering machine at Laurel Canyon, but I had more luck with his mobile number. From the croak in my father's voice, it seemed that I'd woken him, but he claimed to be glad of my call and suggested that we might meet up.

'I'd love that,' I said. 'I was going to go and visit Bruce in Anaheim. Do you want to come with me?'

Clearing his throat, I heard him ignite and inhale a cigarette. The entire performance could have served as the soundtrack to an Age of Steam exhibit in some museum. Perhaps it already did.

'Sure,' he said. 'But I don't think they're letting Bruce have any visitors just yet. He's in worse shape than he was last week. Let me call and find out. They know me there and I might be able to bend the rules a little.'

'Bruce isn't even at the clinic. I called Hendricks myself.'

There was silence at the other end of the line, and I asked Larry if he was still there. 'Yeah, I'm here,' he replied.

'Well, what have you done with him?'

There was another pause. 'What do you mean?' Larry asked.

'I told you. I called the clinic and Bruce isn't there. You're bloody lying to me again.'

'OK, you're right. Bruce has been staying here with me.'

'Great. Can I speak to him, please?'

'Not this minute. He's gone up to Ojai.'

Ojai? I almost dropped the receiver. 'What was in the trunk you took the day Grandpa disappeared?'

'What trunk?'

'Stop stalling me, Larry. The blue trunk you drove off with that morning.'

'Who told you this? Bruce?'

'Never mind who told me,' I said. 'What was in the trunk? Answer me that at least.'

I could almost hear him thinking. 'The old man's book,' he said. 'All that damn paper. When I left Mitzi's place I was still high, and I wanted to get back at Pa for throwing me out. All he seemed to care about was that damn book, so I took it. I don't know, I guess I just wanted to read it and burn it.

Would you believe, there's hardly any mention of me in it? Two references I found in the whole thing.'

'The trunk's up at Ojai, isn't it? I'm going there now.'

'Don't do that, sonny. I beg you. Let me handle this.'

'Why? Scared I'll find out the truth?'

'Don't go playing detective,' he said.

'Why not? You and Grandpa did for years.'

Larry went quiet. 'Listen to me, Ralph. Bruce has gone nuts again. He hasn't slept for days and I'm trying to –'

I hung up on him. There was no reply when I called the house at Ojai, but as I replaced the receiver, the phone rang. It was Lisa.

'Eleanor says you're going back to England,' she said. 'Is that true?'

'I suppose so. I mean, Grandpa's book's never going to happen now.'

'You want to go for breakfast? I have the day off. I thought we could maybe go back to the beach. Start over.'

Declining her invitation, I told her that I was going up to Ojai to look for my grandfather.

'Whatever for?' Lisa said. 'Eleanor told me he's in Mexico with Julie.'

'Maybe he is,' I said. There was no point trying to explain everything to Lisa over the telephone. 'But I have to do this for myself, all right?'

'You've gone crazy, Ralph. You know that?'

The emptiness in her voice made me feel cold inside, but it wasn't enough to change my mind. Across the street a neighbour was walking on a treadmill in the window of his Minimalist home, going nowhere.

'You're not really heading back to England, are you?' Lisa asked.

'No, not just yet,' I said.

Lisa laughed. 'Then maybe I'll see you tonight.'

Climbing into the station wagon, I dug out a road map. As I drove off, Ernesto watched me from the archway.

## Chapter Ten

'As the first grenades fell the order was given to go over the top, advance and dig in. While the others succeeded in advancing I did not. The commanding officer ran up to me shouting, "For God's sake get going!" "I can't!" I answered. In a querulous tone he demanded to know what I had been before the war. I replied, "An actor."'

Erwin Piscator, *Objective Acting*

The Ojai valley had been arid and dusty on my last visit, but the abundant rainfall of the intervening years had transformed it into a lush green garden, and the light was so sharp that I could make out individual trees on the distant slopes as I drove into the town past the various meditation centres and retreats that had sprung up in the wake of Krishnamurti. The main drag boasted new craft shops and coffee bars, and I turned off past the old country club, now a charmless golf hotel, to head up into the hills. After the past weeks spent in Los Angeles, the air was so fresh that for seconds on end it was almost possible to convince myself that I was making a pleasure trip. Birds swooped between the treetops, a breeze made the leaves bristle in the light, and over the next fifteen minutes, the houses thinned out as I climbed the twisting road, following my nose up to Grandpa's place. On a hairpin turn, his nearest neighbour, a retired realtor named Sieghart, shot towards me on his mountain bike, wearing fluorescent cycling clothes and a shiny black insect headpiece. Recognizing the station wagon, he waved, grinning fixedly as he flew by, a winner squeezing just a bit more from life before it finally decided to squeeze him back.

I killed the engine at the bottom of Grandpa's long stony

drive and began to climb on foot. The noise of a car carried in the hills, and anxious as to what might be happening at the house, I'd no wish to alert anyone to my presence. Pausing some 150 yards up the winding track to catch my breath, I glimpsed a car parked up ahead, blocking the drive. Regretting not calling the police, I stepped into the woods and crept towards it through dense undergrowth. Barely audible, a Beatles song was playing on the radio of Larry's convertible, and the driver's door had been left open. Had my father already been on his way to Ojai when I called him on his mobile? The car had a puncture on the passenger side, and looking in the trunk, I discovered that the spare was also flat.

When I popped the hood, the engine felt warm, but there was no way of knowing how long the car had been there, or indeed where Larry had been when we'd spoken. Unnerved, I avoided the drive and went back into the woods to make my way up the hillside. The trees gleamed in the sunlight and sweat broke out on my back as I struggled to find the best way up the steep incline. Ten minutes later, the roof of the house appeared above the ridgeline, but I still had about a hundred yards to climb before I reached the plateau on which it stood. Thorns tore at my ankles and earth got into my shoes, the grains shifting around as I clambered up the slope. Moving as quietly as possible through the trees, I used their limbs to pull myself up the final steep gradient at the edge of the wood. At the top, I slumped panting against a thick trunk to observe the house.

The storm shutters were open but there was no movement inside, so I broke from the cover of the trees and made my way across the open ground towards the front door. Half-way there, the telephone rang. Spiked by fear, I stopped dead to count twenty rings before the caller gave up. Emboldened, I tiptoed on to the porch and listened for sounds, but it was perfectly silent. I pushed open the screen door and went inside. There was a smell of fresh paint and sawn wood, and some of the mustiness of a closed-up house. Bruce had almost finished redecorating the main living room, and a paint-spattered ladder stood propped against the fireplace.

Entering the kitchen was like stepping back into my childhood, because the room had hardly changed since I'd slurped milkshakes by the sink on hot afternoons. Spidery cracks had formed in the Formica work surfaces, but the brown plastic beakers and the rainbow-coloured place mats had been there for twenty years, and they delivered a dull thump of nostalgia. There was a layered emptiness to the room and a quiet smell of dust, as if many leave-takings had left their particular sediment over everything. The refrigerator was unplugged and its door was ajar. Opening the cupboard, I found dozens of cans of chilli tomatoes, along with a stack of dry biscuits.

A sound made me jump, but it turned out to be nothing more than the screen door banging in the breeze, so I closed the latch and climbed the stairs to check on the bedrooms. Trapped underneath the roof, the air was hot and stale, but the beds had been made up in the room I'd slept in as a child. Bright Mexican blankets were tucked drumhead-tight over the mattresses, yellow knotted wood still lined the walls, and I recognized an old quilt that had smelt oddly of vanilla. It still did, and I remembered sleeping with it pressed to my face.

Opening another door, I took a step back from the sickly sweet stench of decaying fruit. The room had been turned upside down. Literally. Tables and chairs had been stood neatly on their heads, along with a chest of drawers. The twin beds were leaning on their sides against the wall. With the utmost care, hundreds of cigarette butts had been placed on end along the edges of the upturned furniture, like toy soldiers arrayed along a ridge. It was as if someone had been playing a mad game or trying to cast a spell, and I fought an urge to turn and run. Underfoot, grapes and rotten apples had been squashed on to the floorboards to form a triangular

186

design. Overwhelmed by a powerful, irrational sense that I'd already seen all this before, perhaps in a dream, and that the cigarettes had been arranged in a particular way to remind me of a message I'd once received, I felt a draught that wasn't there. The next thing I knew, I was racing down the stairs and straight outside into the sunshine.

Standing at the top of the drive, I tried to focus my attention on a dark bird circling high above the house. Was it an eagle? Did they have forked tails? I wished Lisa was there to remind me. If you look for long enough into an abyss, the abyss also looks into you, and I knew even then that the sight of that bedroom would stay with me for ever.

A full minute passed before I'd collected myself enough to continue my search. It occurred to me to call my father's name but I made my way round the side of the house instead. A pile of chopped wood had been stacked against the wall, enough to provide sufficient pulp to produce a copy of Grandpa's memoirs in the extremely unlikely event that they were ever completed. A digger on caterpillar tracks stood over by the shed, its inspection plate removed to expose its inner workings, and a trench had been partially dug by the kitchen window, roughly ten feet long by two and a half feet wide, presumably as part of some new drainage system. Its width corresponded to that of the mechanical claw on the digger, as did the teeth marks at its far end, by which lay an oily rag and a lug wrench. On impulse, I picked up the wrench, and the sun-warmed iron had a comforting heft to it.

Behind the house, a sloped pasture extended some 500 yards up to a ridge that constituted the property line. This uneven expanse of open ground was bordered on both sides by pinewoods. To my bewilderment, the black-and-silver Bentley was parked half-way up the pasture, right at the edge of the woods. The car was covered in dust and the trunk was open. Level with it, a figure lay in the long grass. I called Larry's name and Bruce's for good measure, but there was no reply, just the echo of my own voice coming back at me from the rocks above the pasture. Approaching the figure, I recognized Larry's Hawaiian shirt.

My father seemed to be fast asleep, and I relaxed a little. After all, I'd found him cat-napping many times as a child, dozing off his lunchtime Frascati in a spare bedroom. Except that this time he wasn't asleep, but lying on his side with his wrists and ankles bound with a set of faded jump leads, presumably from the Bentley. For a moment it all seemed unreal, a practical joke gone wrong. On Larry's shirtfront, a patch of wet blood had furnished a hula girl with a bright headdress and obliterated one of a sequence of palm trees that formed a major component of the shirt's design. Blood was leaking out underneath him, darkening the dry earth. Larry's face was pressed into the ground, and I couldn't be sure that he was breathing.

Instinctively calling for help, I tried to rouse my father, but he didn't respond.

I thought he was dead.

In an instant, I forgave him everything – the casual neglect, the countless disappointments – and knew that if it hadn't been love that I'd felt for him, it had been something very close. Dropping to my knees, I leant forward and held him.

'Please, Dad. Please come back.'

Larry grunted and opened his eyes. Overjoyed, I loosened the jump leads, but his breathing was laboured and uneven. In a frenzy, I told him to keep calm, that I'd get help, and he nodded and tried to smile. Failing to find his mobile phone in his pockets, I put him into the recovery position and ran back to the house to call 911, but just as I picked up speed, there was a flat snapping sound and something tore at my upper arm. Something hard and invisible.

Losing my balance, I fell to the ground and heard another abrupt snap, as if two lengths of wood had been brought together. Pulling myself to my feet, I ran stumbling back towards the Bentley, gritting my teeth against the burning pain in my arm. Had I been shot? A voice in my head told me not to be ridiculous. A voice with the clipped English accent that prevailed in British films of the inter-war period. But someone *was* shooting at me. Seconds later the gun snapped again, and the bullet ripped into the metal body of the Bentley. As I ducked down behind the car, a third round shattered the windscreen. The shots appeared to be coming from the large rocks at the top of the pasture, some 200 yards up the hill. Was Bruce up there, trying to kill me?

It was the first time I'd seen my own blood in a long while, and rivulets as red as Larry's ran down to my wrist. Craning my neck, I discovered a shallow gash in my upper arm, a flattened V much like the stripe on the uniform of a non-commissioned officer. Bemoaning my own lack of soldiering experience, I called Bruce's name and identified myself, hoping for an opportunity to parlay, but the gunman replied with another round.

Even as the absurdity of the situation struck me, I knew I had to staunch the wound. Tearing the sleeve off my shirt, I used my teeth to make some strips to bind my arm. It was a poor enough job, but at least the bandage seemed to stop the bleeding. The dark bird I'd seen earlier was now riding a thermal directly above me. Observing it, I thought I heard Larry moan in the grass thirty feet away.

Desperate to get help for him, there was no way for me to get back to the house without crossing the line of fire, and the deep sheer-sided ravine that ran down through the woods made it impossible to circle back through the trees. Grandpa's nearest neighbours, the Siegharts, lived half a mile beyond the gunman's position through dense woodland. The town of Ojai was an hour's walk away, and there was no other house for miles. Sometimes you didn't hear a car all day. Hearing Larry groan, I decided to see what I could find in the Bentley.

Crawling along the length of it, I looked inside. There was no sign of Larry's mobile phone but, opening the glove compartment, I enjoyed my first bit of luck. A handgun had been clipped to the back of the box in case of a car-jack attempt, and I plucked the weapon free of its mounting and removed the oilskin wrapping. The metal looked clean enough. Heartened, I lifted my head an inch or two, just as a bullet shattered the passenger window, showering me with crumbs of broken glass.

Flattening myself in the foot well, there was a moment of perfect, dreadful silence. I popped my head up fast and saw a glint of metal up by the rocks. Keeping the Bentley between me and the gunman, I crawled fifteen feet into the pines that bordered the pasture and decided that my best option was to move up behind Bruce or whoever it was, and to use the gun to overpower them. If this weren't possible, I'd press on to the Sieghart house. The odds looked bad, but I set off into the woods regardless. The going tough, the wound in my arm began to throb, and I prayed that I'd find Bruce up there, because I believed his precarious mental state would improve my chances in a fight. It also seemed doubtful that he could bring himself to shoot me, his nephew, at close range.

Thirty yards into the wood, the ground grew steeper. Needing my working arm to pull myself along, I was forced to stick the pistol in my waistband, and as I triple-checked the position of the safety catch before doing so, I thought of Aunt Eleanor. The cold metal jabbed into my abdomen and pain gnawed at my arm as I scrabbled my way up over rocks and brambles. Worried sick for Larry, I moved up through the woods, parallel to the edge of the pasture, and eventually reached the edge of a small clearing. If the gunman had guessed my intention, this would be an ideal place for him or her to set an ambush, safe in the knowledge that I'd no choice but to try and pass.

Imagining the crosshairs lining up on my third vertebra from behind every tree and boulder, I forced myself to circle the clearing even though it cost me extra minutes. *Stones have been known to move, and trees to speak.* Bulldozing my way through the undergrowth, I stopped to catch my breath and thought I heard men chanting. Were the members of an Iron John therapy group searching for themselves in the woods with drums and animal skins? This wasn't impossible, because old man Sieghart was a mover and shaker in the California chapter of the Men's Movement, and had even transformed one of the outbuildings on his property into a sweat lodge. If my hunch was correct, I only hoped that his merry men were summoning their 'warrior' and not their 'inner child'. The noise grew louder as I climbed, but after a few minutes it seemed that a single voice was responsible for the undulating wail. This was accompanied by a percussive, grunting beat, and the sounds were coming from the direction of the rocks at the top of the pasture. Were there two people up there? If so, I had little chance of taking them both on, with or without the automatic.

As I stepped up over a series of big boulders near the ridge that ran along the top of the pasture, the two sounds became ever more distinct from each other, almost a call and response. The massive slabs of fallen rock that lay at the foot of the ridge glowed through the trees, yellow in the sunlight. The singer appeared to be just in the lee of the ridge, way over to my right, more or less where I imagined the reserve water tanks to be. Grandpa had bought the three wholesale juice containers – gigantic plastic drums that were used to store up water from the underground spring in case of a drop in the water table – when I was staying with him aged ten. Bruce had spent two days scrubbing out the inside of the drums before they were installed, and the smell of the rancid concentrate had left me with a lifelong aversion to citrus fruit. Standing there listening to the strange sounds, it seemed incredible that my uncle had just tried to kill me. To gain an element of surprise, I needed to get up behind the gunman, so I decided to climb the rock face, which was about fifteen feet high at the point where I'd reached it. The trees would cover my ascent, and I then planned to move along the ridge to a position right above the gunman and jump down, hoping to catch him unawares. Tightening the bandage on my arm, I picked a crevasse and began to climb.

Half-way up, I lost my footing and sent several pebbles clattering down through the bushes below. The strange, wordless tune stopped as the gunman pricked his ears. Sweat mingled with the blood on my hands, making me afraid of losing my slippery hold. There was no noise save for the rustle of the leaves in the trees and the cry of an animal in the distance. If he (or she) saw me, it would be a simple matter to step out into the pasture and shoot me. A sitting target, my fingers began to ache, but mercifully the song continued after a moment or two, as did the regular bass sound that underpinned it.

Reaching the top of the crevasse, I crawled along the crest and looked down to see the top of Bruce's head almost directly beneath me. Quite alone, he was standing waist deep in a hole in the ground near the water tanks, singing his broken ditty to himself as he dug at the soil. Bruce had removed his shirt, and over the hours, the sun had burnt his upper body. A hunting rifle was propped against the rocks, ten feet from the pit in which he laboured, and his shovel was responsible for the second sound that had so puzzled me: the blade digging sharply into the soft sandy earth, and the soil making a soft whooshing noise as it flew off the shovel's face. At first I was glad that I only had to contend with my uncle, but watching him work, I could almost smell his madness. All too soon, a blue nub appeared at the bottom of the pit, and I recognized the corner of the trunk that had stood in the garage at North Canon Drive. *Safe in a ditch he bides, With twenty trenched gashes on his head, The least a death to nature.* Swallowing hard against an urge to vomit, I was convinced that Bruce was digging up my grandfather's butchered corpse.

I'd got it all wrong.

Larry hadn't killed Donald. Bruce had. Larry had simply been trying to keep his brother out of jail. To protect him. I was shot through with guilt for the resentment and suspicion I'd borne my father over the past week, but there was no time for regret. Larry would die if I didn't get help soon.

My plan was to slide down the rock face with the automatic in my hand, shooting Bruce in the leg if it became necessary. To prepare myself, I visualized firing the gun and Bruce falling down, an abominable meditation that probably sent Krishnamurti spinning in his grave faster than Eleanor's salad dryer. It did me little good. Frozen like a child on a high diving board, I felt myself begin to panic.

I jumped anyway.

As I bumped down the steep gradient on my behind, the ground rushed up to meet me. Landing with a severe jolt, I almost dropped the gun.

'Stay where you are, Bruce.' My throat was clogged with the accumulated terror of the past half hour.

Bruce rose from his task, blinking at me. Ordering him to drop the shovel, I heard the tremor in my voice and he looked right into me. His eyes were cold and empty, and the shape of his face looked different, as if the pressure of his madness had remodelled his skull. My uncle examined the shovel as if he'd never seen it before. I was expecting him to lay it down, but a second later he was up out of the hole, coming towards me.

'Hold it, Bruce,' I said. 'Or I'm going to have to shoot you.'

Perhaps my words were drowned out by louder voices in his own head, voices that his song had been intended to quiet, but he kept moving closer. I yelled at him, but still he was coming towards me, so I aimed the automatic at his legs. Trying to pull the trigger, I shut my eyes and squeezed. Nothing happened. How many times had I seen actors pull back the slide in a film, pretending to put a live round into the chamber? A thousand? More? As I struggled to do likewise, Bruce smacked the shovel into the side of my leg.

Falling back, I saw him silhouetted against the sky and then he kicked me in the head.

I blacked out.

When I came round, lying where I'd fallen by the open grave, my head was throbbing horribly, each heartbeat a new torture. Nauseated by a sharp sickly odour, it took me some time to realize that the smell was coming from me: blood from the cut on my arm had formed a gooey mess in the crook of my elbow, thicker (and stickier) than water. Some hikers were walking in single file 1000 yards away, taking a trail into the hills on the far side of the valley, but perhaps I only imagined them. On a bald patch of earth beside my face, an ant scurried back and forth like an actor in search of motivation. Dappling the valley with pink light, the sun had begun to go down and Bruce was digging at the earth around the blue trunk with his hands, talking to himself. Since my left ear was stone deaf from the kick I'd received, I couldn't make out individual words, but his monologue seemed to comprise one side of a savage argument. Or a fierce dispute between damnation and impassioned clay, as Grandpa would have no doubt had it.

Bruce strained to lift the trunk out of the hole, and when it finally came free, he heaved it up on to the ground. Facing the setting sun, he leant on the shovel with his weight on one leg and raised an arm to rub his neck. For a moment, I thought I was hallucinating. It was the exact pose that Grandpa had struck to stare down at a different valley from the site of his screen wife's freshly dug grave for the final frames of *Maclennan's Acre*. Having got his father's stance down pat, Bruce turned to me.

'You shouldn't have come up here, Ralph,' he said. 'Why did you have to do that? Why?'

The trunk lay beside him, locked and dirt-caked, and I knew I had to choose my words carefully.

'Because I want to help you,' I said. 'It's not your fault, Bruce. You didn't know what you were doing.'

'Did Larry tell you to come?'

'No, but he told me that you were here. I wanted to see you. To make sure you were OK.'

'I miss Pops so much. I don't know what I'm going to do now he's gone,' my uncle said. 'Did Larry tell you Pops wanted me to go into an institution when he passed on? Up near Santa Barbara. He didn't think I could live alone.'

Keeping the rifle within reach, Bruce sat on the pile of loose earth and picked up a handful, letting it spill from the bottom of his fist just as I'd done with the sand at Matador beach. And just as my grandfather had done long ago on a trip we'd all made to La Jolla.

'Is Grandpa's body in the trunk?' I asked.

The trunk hardly seemed big enough to contain the man, but Bruce nodded, tears appearing in his eyes, and I asked him how it had happened.

'Larry came over to North Canon Drive really late and rowed with Pops,' he said. 'I left them alone because they were talking about me. About what was best for me. Larry was drunk and they were really shouting. Anyway, I went to my apartment, and then in the morning, I found Larry dragging this trunk out to his car. He said it was the book and that he was going to sell it. But it was too heavy to be just the book, and when Eleanor said Pops was missing, I guessed Larry had killed him. By accident. Then Eleanor hired that investigator, and Larry got really anxious. He asked me if there was a place to bury the trunk up here, because he was scared he'd get found out for stealing the book. Of course, that wasn't the real reason he was worried, but I told him about the hole I'd been digging for the pump, so he came up here and put the trunk in the ground.'

Given the battering I'd received, this almost made sense. I wanted to believe Bruce, but I couldn't dispel the nagging feeling that he'd learnt his little speech by heart, and I asked him why he'd dug up Grandpa's body.

'Because it'll be discovered if we leave it here,' he replied.

'I'm going to bury Pops deep in the woods. Where nobody'll ever find him.'

'Good idea. But we'll have to get some help for Larry first. He's in a really bad way. He needs medical treatment.'

'It's too late for that,' he said. 'We'll bury the two of them together. You and me.'

'Please, Bruce. I beg you. We have to get Larry to a doctor.'

'I can't let that happen,' he said. 'Larry says the pool man saw him take the trunk away, so even if he makes it, he'll probably spend the rest of his life in jail. It's better like this. Trust me. I've been thinking it through real carefully.'

Bruce's sentences appeared lucid enough on the surface, and uncharacteristically sophisticated, but his underlying logic was so skewed that he might as well have been talking gibberish.

'What happened between you and Larry?' I asked him.

Bruce frowned. 'He's been lying to me, saying he only took the book. Trying to make me think Pops went off with Julie.'

'Hang on a second,' I said. 'How do you know Grandpa's dead? How do you know he didn't go off with Julie?'

'Pops would never do that. He'd never go away without telling me first. Not after I took those pills that time.'

For the first time I saw the manipulative side of my gentle, biddable uncle.

'Have you taken a look in the trunk?' I asked him. He shook his head like a teacher whose patience was being tried by a dimwit pupil. 'So how do you know Grandpa's in there?' I continued. 'Let's take a look inside.'

Bruce shifted his weight and I thought he was going to attack me again, but instead he just headed off down the hill through the long grass, carrying the rifle. As soon as his head disappeared below the brow, I looked around for the automatic but it was nowhere to be found. When I tried to get up, my knee gave way. Finding a stick, I put it by me to use as a weapon if the chance arose. Presently, the Bentley's engine fired and it came up the hill, bumping over the pasture with the passenger door propped open by my father's legs. Bruce reversed the car over to the hole. Two or three hours must have passed since I'd discovered Larry bleeding down by the house, and I thought of Grandpa intoning 'howl' four times, giving me his Lear on his return from Cedars-Sinai. Bruce climbed out from behind the wheel and strolled over to me, oddly calm.

'Is Larry still breathing?' I asked him. 'Tell me he's alive!'

'I'm going to stay up here for the rest of my life, Ralph,' Bruce said. 'I don't want to live in a hospital. You understand that, don't you? And Larry's going to be with Pops up in the woods, where nobody can bother them. Are you going to help me?'

'Bruce, I'd be happy to, but I need to visit a hospital myself. Can we deal with my knee first? Then we could come back and bury them wherever you like.'

'You really think I'm that stupid?'

As he glared at me, it was obvious that Bruce was not stupid at all: simply insane.

'No, but I can't move like this, I swear,' I said. 'Listen, why don't we just take a look in the trunk and make sure that it really is Grandpa in there?'

Bruce's mouth twisted as if he'd tasted something sour. 'Larry put you up to this, didn't he?' I tried to shake my pounding head. 'If I open the trunk the spirits will kill us,' he added.

'What spirits?' I asked.

'They're all around us.'

'I don't see anything.'

Bruce graced me with a smug smile. 'You see that hummingbird, don't you?' A hummingbird was perched on the branch of a tree some fifteen feet away. I asked him what of it, and he tapped the side of his nose three times. 'Look again,' he said. The hairs came up on the back of my neck, and I had the distinct impression that there was someone or something standing just behind me. *Unnatural deeds do breed unnatural troubles*. When I looked around again, the hummingbird had gone. The world began to wobble and then a groan came from the Bentley.

My father was still alive.

Larry could survive this. If Bruce came close enough, I'd have a chance to hit him over the head, drag myself over to the car and get Larry to a doctor. Bruce caught the look on my face.

'We have to get help for your brother right now,' I said.

'We can't do that, Ralph. I thought I'd explained it to you. Why do you never listen to what anybody tells you?' The whine was back in his voice, and I finally understood: Larry was the 'normal' elder brother, the benchmark against whom Bruce had always been unfavourably measured, and now he wanted him dead. It was as simple as that.

Reading each other's minds, Bruce and I stood up at the same time. I felt faint, as if I'd left a bucket of blood behind in the speed of my ascent, and my last feeble hope guttered out as my uncle lunged towards me. Even as I swung the stick at his head, I knew it was useless. Seeing the blow coming, Bruce stepped aside and tried to bring the rifle butt down on me. I turned to grab him, but my leg gave way. As I fell, I caught his ankle, tugged at it, and he twisted to drop yelling into the hole. The tumble had knocked the wind out of me, and I lay on the ground gasping for breath, waiting for Bruce to climb out of the pit and finish me off, but half a minute passed before his head and shoulders appeared above the rim. My uncle tried to pull himself out but there was something the matter with his left arm and the sides of the hole were loose and slippery, so he fell back. Wriggling over to the edge, I kicked at him with my good leg when he came within range.

'Sonny? Is that you?' It was Larry, and I rallied at the sound of his voice. Having somehow pulled himself out of the car, my father stood holding on to the passenger door, the left half of his Hawaiian shirt scarlet, and leant down to reach for something. Bruce tried to climb out of the far side of the hole, but the pile of loose earth he'd dug earlier blocked his path, and he only succeeded in pulling a load of it on top of himself. Coming back to my side, he tried to grab my foot as I kicked out to keep him back. Bruce almost got a hold, but I yanked my leg free and scrabbled over towards the rifle. I nearly made it, but he was too quick, out of the hole and heading towards me with the shovel raised above his head.

Beyond him, Larry threw something at us, something that I later discovered was a stone the size of a hen's egg. It hit Bruce on the back of his head. Looking at me in disbelief, my uncle tottered Golem-like for a moment, only to fall face down on the ground right in front of me.

Larry was slumped against the Bentley, drifting at the edge of consciousness, but Bruce was out cold, blood matting the hair on the back of his head. Finding Larry's mobile in Bruce's pocket, I called 911. My uncle was still breathing, so I grabbed the rifle and crawled over to the blue trunk, my hands shaking as I brushed the dried dirt from the latches and popped them. Holding my breath, I lifted the lid to discover the loose pages of my grandfather's manuscript all mixed up in there, and closed it before they blew away on the breeze.

Not knowing if Larry could hear me, I kept saying his name until I heard the sirens.

# Chapter Eleven

> 'I've always confused the names of my four sons.
> I'll be calling one of them Peter, and suddenly he'll
> say, "Dad, remember me? I'm Michael." It has finally
> got to the point where they don't even correct me,
> because they know who I mean, even if I call one of
> them "Kirk".'
>
> Kirk Douglas, *The Ragman's Son*

Sunlight streamed through a crack in the curtains of an unfamiliar bedroom. My knee and arm throbbed, my mouth was dry and the smell of a woman's perfume forced me to the unhappy conclusion that I'd blacked out after another night's drinking. A gauze bandage ran from my armpit to my elbow, and a second bandage circled my head, so it must have been very bad indeed, even worse than Brentwood. Playing dead, no sooner had I begun to consider my limited options for escape than somebody stirred in a chair by the side of the bed. Recognizing Lisa, everything came back to me, and my first thought was for Larry.

'Don't worry, Ralph,' she said. 'He's been incredibly lucky. The bullet passed straight through his side without touching anything.' I lay back on the pillows. I owed Larry my life. 'They gave him a transfusion and he's doing great,' she added. 'Although you wouldn't think so to hear him. There's still been no word of your grandfather.'

Mystified, I asked if Bruce had been arrested.

'No, I don't think so,' Lisa replied. 'As far as I know, Eleanor and Bob Caswell took him back to the clinic.'

I sat bolt upright. 'Bruce is in a clinic? He ought to be locked up in Camarillo! He tried to kill us!'

Lisa looked surprised. 'Really? Larry told us it was an

accident, that you guys were fooling around in the car and the gun just went off when you rolled it. You were delirious by the time you got here, Ralph. It took Eleanor and Bob Caswell for ever to sort it all out with the police.'

Too distraught and in too much pain to put her right, I asked how long I'd been in hospital.

'Since yesterday,' she said. 'They stitched up your arm and X-rayed your leg. The kneecap's bruised and you have a lump on the side of your head. That's all. They're saying you can go home tomorrow.'

A nurse came to give me my pills, and soon afterwards I began to feel drowsy. Getting up to leave, Lisa said that she had to get back to Los Angeles. When I asked her to get me to a phone so I could speak to the police about Bruce, she said that Eleanor was coming to see me and that she could answer all my questions. I tried to protest, but in a few minutes I was fast asleep.

Some hours later, my aunt appeared in my room wearing mirrored sunglasses the size of hubcaps. Kissing me cautiously, she asked if I was still in pain, but before I had a chance to reply, she complained that she'd failed to make her preview on account of 'Bruce's antics'.

'I've never before missed a performance in my life,' she cried. 'And I had to spend last night at the Ojai Valley Inn. Not a wink of sleep.'

Shaking my head in what I assumed she'd misread as sympathy, I asked Eleanor if Bruce was really back in the clinic.

'Sure, he's in Anaheim,' she replied, removing the sunglasses to check her puffy eyes in the vanity unit. 'Thank God.'

'But he tried to kill me! And Larry's got a bullet in his stomach. You can't just pretend nothing happened.'

'Nobody's pretending anything,' Eleanor said, applying some cream to her eyelids. 'But ask yourself, would you rather see your uncle in jail?

'Yes, I would!'

'For God's sake, Ralph. He only shot at Larry because he thought he'd killed your grandfather.'

Expecting Eleanor at the very least to relish the drama of the situation, her apparent detachment perplexed me. 'What about Grandpa?' I asked. 'I thought you told me Sandra had found him in Mexico?'

My aunt sighed and shook her head. 'It's been on the television news that he's missing, so we're hoping that –'

'Bruce might well have killed him,' I said. 'Eleanor, your brother's barking mad.'

'Now you're being ridiculous,' she declared. 'Bruce worships his father. He'd never touch a hair on his head.' Desperate as she was to protect her sibling at any cost, there was nothing to be gained by arguing with her, and I lay back, racked with frustration. Eleanor was intent on a cover-up. 'Look, you're angry with Bruce because he hurt you physically,' she said softly. 'But Bruce is in pain too, Ralph, more than you can imagine, and he's not responsible for his actions. You saw for yourself the state of his room up there. I know you're feeling sorry for your father just now and I understand that, but do try to remember that none of this would have happened if Larry hadn't stolen Daddy's book . . . I've only done what I thought was best, and Bob Caswell agrees with me. He took the necessary steps.'

'What are you saying? That Bob Caswell bribed the police?'

'Of course not. But Bob knows people here, and he did what he could to spare Daddy any bad publicity. Imagine what the media would make of this.'

'I don't believe it. Grandpa could very well be dead and you're worried about bad publicity? You've got to tell the police what really happened yesterday.'

Eleanor's lips twitched, her veneer of equanimity threatening to slip for an instant. 'Bruce is ill,' she said. 'And he's an innocent soul. He doesn't deserve to suffer in jail, especially after the way Daddy's treated him all his life. Try and have some compassion.'

'Don't talk to me about compassion. Where was your compassion when you spun me that yarn about Cozumel and attacked my work?'

Eleanor broke into a series of sobs, but I couldn't tell if the tears welling in her eyes were authentic or as polished as a crocodile handbag.

'I'm so sorry, Ralph,' she said. 'I was really beastly and I had no right to speak to you like that. Please try and forgive me. Sandra did fly to Cozumel, though. There was no sign of Daddy, but she found out that Julie had been staying with a couple she'd met down there. The three of them left on a boat the day before yesterday and headed down the coast. Sandra just missed them.'

'Sandra suspected Larry, didn't she?'

'I've no idea,' said Eleanor, returning to the vanity unit. 'Maybe she shared some of your suspicions, but I'd lost faith in her by then. And if it turned out that Larry was involved in some way, I thought it'd be better if you were out of the picture. Whatever you might think of me, I've had your best interests at heart all along. And Bruce's. Like I said, I only did what I thought was best for the family.'

Opening a small leather satchel which contained an arsenal of homeopathic remedies, she transferred a pill from a bottle to its cap and thence to her tongue, explaining that the magic only worked if the tiny pills made no contact with your hand on their way to your mouth. As Eleanor swallowed the pill, I glimpsed in her face the horrifying price she had to pay to hold it all together. Looking out of the window at the trees moving in the breeze, I knew that I needed to find my grandfather, and that I needed a new career.

'Daddy's photograph's on the television every hour. We're bound to hear something soon,' Eleanor said. 'Try not to worry.'

When she'd left, I asked the nurse for a pen and some

paper. At noon, I called Scott Newton to arrange another meeting with him at the Beverly Wilshire hotel in three days' time.

The nurse let me get up for half an hour after lunch, and my head swam as I sat on the edge of my bed examining the plastic brace on my knee. Hobbling down the corridor to Larry's room, I found him standing by the window in a hospital gown, attached to a bag of saline and peering through the slats of the blind with a baseball cap pulled low over his eyes.

'Quick, sonny. Come in and shut the door.' As I joined him at the window, Larry pointed to a network news van in the parking lot. 'It's been here for fifteen minutes,' he said. 'Someone's tipped them off. You've got to get me out of here. There must be an emergency exit we can use. Maybe I should call hospital security?'

'It's OK, Larry. Calm down,' I said. 'They've no idea you're here. A Country star's been admitted and it's a big news story. He collapsed on a mountain bike. The nurses told me.'

For a split second Larry looked disappointed, and I burst out laughing.

'What is it?' he asked. 'What's so funny?'

'Nothing,' I said. 'I'm just glad to see you're still alive, that's all.'

Like two members of the Men's Movement, we hugged each other, and I helped him get back into bed. 'You saved my life yesterday,' I said.

'Shhht. You're my son. I love you,' Larry said. 'And this was all my fault. I should never have taken the damn book.' My curiosity was pricked, and I asked him why he'd stolen it. 'Give me a break here, sonny. I didn't exactly steal it. I borrowed it. The truth is, Scott Newton offered to pay me for getting him a look at it. Of course, I told him to take a hike, but I got so high the night of Danny's party that it started to seem like a good idea. I thought I'd just need it for a few hours to have it copied, but then Eleanor called and said the old man had gone missing. There was talk of the police and Eleanor brought in that investigator. I was paranoid from the blow and I began to think the police were after me for stealing the book. I figured I'd better get rid of it. The trunk was in my garage at Laurel Canyon, so I took it up to Ojai and hid it. I mean, there was so much goddamn paper, where else was I going to stash it? Bruce knew what I was doing, but when the old man didn't show up, he freaked out and convinced himself I'd been lying to him. That I'd killed Pa and hidden his body in the trunk. You know how crazy he can get.' No crazier than me, I thought. 'I was hoping he'd calm down if he could see what was really in there, so I told him where to look,' Larry continued. 'But then you rang me and I didn't want you to know about my fuck-up, so I raced up there to stop Bruce digging around. That's when he lost the plot. And that's when you found me.'

In my mind's eye, I saw Larry lying in the pasture, tied up and bleeding into the grass. 'Listen,' I said. 'Whatever else you've done, you saved my life yesterday.'

Larry smiled. 'And if you forget that, I'll be sure to remind you,' he said. 'You know, the second I threw that rock, I could tell it was a perfect throw. It must have been twenty feet. Incredible considering I'd taken a bullet. A one in a thousand chance. Maybe one in a million.' Larry's chest puffed out the way it had when flattered by his fans in Venice, and he showed me the bandage that circled his thorax. Indicating the points of entry and exit above his hip, Larry tried to persuade us both how lucky he was. I asked him about Bruce.

'He's no danger to anyone when he takes his medication. They'll keep him at Anaheim for a month or so. Bruce is going to be OK. You'll see.'

This sounded like a case of what Eleanor would have called denial, but I decided to let it go for the time being. 'How come the police didn't book him?' I asked.

'I guess the lawyers would have said it was self-defence, because Bruce figured I'd come up there to kill him,' Larry said. 'Or they could have claimed diminished responsibility, something like that. The police were looking to book you, as a matter of fact. They kept referring to you as the perpetrator. But, basically, Eleanor settled everything. She arrived with Bob Caswell and they took charge. You know how my sister is in a crisis. Loved every minute. We're saying it was an accident.'

'And where were you when all this was going on? '

A young female nurse passed by the door and Larry tracked her behind the way Grandpa would have done. I repeated my question.

'I was half-dead, sonny,' he replied. 'As you know. It took everything I had to stop Bruce from killing you.'

If Larry was pleased with himself, he had every right to be, and I reminded him of the time the world had seemed to shake when I was seven years old, eating lunch with him in a restaurant in Westwood. Along with the other customers and the waitresses, Larry had listened open-mouthed to the tinkle of the chandelier and the jangle of crockery as the bass subterranean rumble had begun to reverberate in our ribcages. Then he'd grabbed me and dragged me under our table, shielding me with his body. The tremor had been short-lived, no more than ten seconds from start to finish, but long enough for me to know that he'd been terrified and that he'd put my safety before his own.

The doctors let me go the following morning, and when I'd said goodbye to Larry, I ran into Danny, who'd come to visit his mentor with Ingeborg. The golden couple were holding hands, but given that I'd last seen Danny passed out on top of Mitzi in Laurel Canyon, they'd lost some of their lustre. Although the network news team had departed following the Country star's recovery, Danny seemed jittery as I described the way that Bruce had flipped out and attacked

Larry and me. Naturally, I kept Larry's theft of the manuscript to myself, but Ingeborg's forced smile led me to wonder if she was having some understandable second thoughts about marrying into our family.

Arriving early at the Beverly Wilshire hotel, I limped out to the pool area where people were lying around in bathing costumes, trying to look like the models in the advertisements who'd been trying to look like somebody else that nobody could now remember. A girl executed a flawless swan dive, swam a couple of lengths and scowled at me as she climbed out of the water. Slashed to the knee to accommodate my brace, perhaps Grandpa's cast-off canary yellow slacks had offended her. At noon, I went to the desk to ask for Scott Newton, and the concierge invited me to go up to Mr Newton's room.

The lift hoisted me skywards, and I stepped out on to the ninth floor sick with nerves. Barefoot and sporting a surfer T-shirt, Newton opened the door and looked surprised, as if he'd been expecting someone else, but ushered me into his suite nonetheless. The sliding doors that presumably led to the bedroom were closed, and a room-service trolley bearing the remains of a meal stood by the television cabinet. The room was in a state of gentle disarray, and a sliding glass door gave on to a balcony with a commanding view of the flats. Refilling his wineglass from a bottle of Jacob's Creek, Newton asked me what Larry was after now.

'This isn't to do with Larry, actually,' I said. 'It's to do with me. I've got an idea for a book, and I thought you might be interested.'

'You're here to pitch me?' he said, scratching his armpit.

'That's right. I'm writing a memoir. My memoir.'

'But you already owe us one book, Ralph. And why on earth do you think I'd be interested in your life story? I mean, I'm sure it's extraordinary, but did I miss something here?'

I thought I heard someone moving around beyond the sliding doors. 'I know about John Blumenthal wanting to stop Grandpa's autobiography,' I said. 'My aunt told me.'

Newton reached for his wineglass. 'Yeah, well, that's as maybe, but you're still talking to the wrong man,' he said. 'I've never commissioned a book in my life.' Beginning to wonder if he was drunk, I heard a sound in the bedroom. There was somebody in there. 'Honest, Ralph,' Newton continued. 'I just work for John B, ironing out the wrinkles. What you might call a trouble-shooter.' Draining his wine, he began to laugh, and I was very alarmed. 'John only brought me out here to try and get him a sneaky peek at the book,' he said. 'And guess what? Your old man finally agreed to let me have it a couple of days ago, but when I called John to tell him, he couldn't give a damn. Turns out that the most recent Mrs Blumenthal, Jean, ran off to Europe with her therapist a fortnight ago, so John couldn't give a damn any more about who screwed her whenever. He said he's planning to dump his shares in Shaugnessy King too, and if he does, the book'll never see the light of day. And from what you showed me the other week, that's just as well. I'm no expert, but I have to tell you it was the most boring, badly written load of crap I've ever had to read.'

'You only saw a very early draft,' I said. 'Grandpa's got some amazing anecdotes and a wonderful turn of phrase. Another publishing company will buy it. I'm sure of it.'

'Really? I doubt that. In any case, it seems your grandad's got other things on his mind these days.'

'Why do you say that? My grandfather's been missing for nearly two weeks.'

Newton laughed. 'Missing? He's been up at John's place in Bel-Air. Partying.'

My jaw fell. 'Grandpa's in Bel-Air?'

'Well, he was when I went up there yesterday.'

As I sat immobilized in my chair, the sliding doors opened six inches and a young Korean-looking girl peered through the gap. Wrapped in a bed-sheet, she asked Newton if it was OK for her to get dressed.

'What the fuck are you doing?' Newton barked at her. 'You get back in there and shut the bloody door. Don't ever come out here unless I say so, you got that? Not ever.'

Fellow hell-raisers in the 1960s, John Blumenthal and Grandpa had been friends until their vanities collided following Blumenthal's last marriage. When I'd gone over to play at Blumenthal's house as a child, he'd been married to a young cello-player who had a son from her previous marriage, a pale, bloodless boy called Carlo who'd spent his afternoons trapping lizards and torturing them with a magnifying glass by the tennis court. With any luck Carlo was safely locked up in Sing-Sing, but probably he'd scaled some corporate ladder.

The Blumenthals had lived in a French château-style mansion perched on top of a landscaped hill, but I didn't have the precise address and my cab driver grew anxious as we crawled up Stone Canyon Road. Passing a pair of wooden gates that bore a sign reading 'Attack dogs on duty', he glanced at me in the rear-view mirror as if to say that I was cracked. Maybe I was, but I wasn't the only one, because a hundred yards further on, somebody had cut a section of topiary away from a tree in order to screw a security camera on to its trunk. Few of the houses were visible from the road but I recognized a pair of marble lions bracketing a set of electric gates, so I climbed out of the taxi, pressed the buzzer and said my name into the speakerphone. To my driver's surprise, the gates opened and we were able to drive on up to the main house, a three-storey structure complete with conical turrets. As I dragged my bad leg towards the front door, an African-American in a golf cart intercepted me, and when I asked after my grandfather, the man smiled.

'Oh, he's as fine as can be,' he said. 'He has such a wonderful spirit, you must be so proud of him.'

'Absolutely,' I said. Furious with Grandpa, I climbed on board the cart and we swung around the house to pass a levelled croquet lawn complete with hoops and a multicoloured winning post. Dropped off outside a low pool house with terracotta tiles on its roof, I heard samba music and a woman's laughter. Inside, another employee was mixing a pitcher of Bloody Mary behind a bar, and I asked him where I could find Donald Tait. Directed to the French windows at the far end of the room, I was making my way towards the pool that glittered beyond them when a girl in a bikini came running towards me, screaming with laughter.

The young woman shot straight past me, a blur of brown flesh and sun oil, pursued by a copper skeleton wearing a French seaman's T-shirt and the skimpiest pair of swimming trunks I'd ever seen. Cackling maniacally, the tendons in his neck stood out like cello strings from his sun-dried flesh. This ancient was at least eighty years old, but his cupped hands were full of ice cubes as he chased the girl out into the garden. Shaken, I staggered out to the pool and found my grandfather surrounded by gardenias and bougainvillea, playing backgammon with two young women in the shade of a huge garden umbrella. When I called to Grandpa, he swivelled round to greet me, looking ten years younger.

'Ralph, my dear boy. Clever of you, rooting me out like this. So good to see you.' His upper body was lathered in sun cream, and he introduced me to Kimberley and Stephanie, his nurses, who wore matching bikinis, tiny triangles of cloth with strings attached. 'The girls are meant to be on a break now,' he said. 'But they're keeping me company anyway. Isn't that sweet? Stephanie reminds me of Julie, but she's far prettier, don't you think?' And even younger, I thought. 'How did you find me, dear boy?'

'Oh, it's a long story,' I said.

'And how's Bruce? Is he well?'

'He's fine. He's in a clinic but he's getting better,' I said, planning to give my grandfather the bad news in private.

'A clinic?'

I bit back an urge to bawl him out. 'Nothing too serious,' I said. 'Just one of his turns.'

'Oh, goody,' Grandpa said. 'I've been fretting about him. Bruce is my son you see, ladies, and he can behave just as badly as me.'

The girls giggled as if they were sharing some secret joke, and I could hardly bring myself to accept the obvious: that while we'd all been so desperately concerned for Grandpa, he'd been up here frolicking with a gaggle of young women and his erstwhile nemesis. My grandfather was an absence of a man, a selfish, blinkered nobodaddy, and I wanted to rub his nose in the trouble he'd caused, but his extraordinary charm and the presence of the nurses put him beyond my reach for the time being. As the barman brought out the pitcher of Bloody Mary, the girl who'd almost bowled me over in the pool house reappeared, followed by the skeletal man.

'Welcome, Ralph. I knew you when you were knee high to a grasshopper,' John Blumenthal said, running a freckled claw over his white crew cut. 'Have you been driving on the wrong side of the road?' The question puzzled me. 'The leg brace,' he said. Grandpa hadn't even noticed it. 'What happened?'

'Oh, just a little accident. I was up at Ojai with Bruce,' I said.

'My God, Bruce wasn't hurt, was he?' Grandpa asked.

'Barely a scratch. Don't worry. Like I said, he's doing fine,' I replied. 'We all are, but we've been worried about you, Grandpa. Really worried.'

'Oh, stuff and nonsense,' he cried. 'I suspect you've been glad of a break from all my moans and groans.'

'It's been in the papers that you've been missing,' I said. 'It's on the television news. How come you didn't even call?'

'I suppose I thought I'd give myself another day or so. We've been having such a good time,' he said. 'I came over here to cheer up my old friend John, but in fact it's been the other way around. We're both single again, you see.

Bachelors. And at our age we have to stick together. We even went to Colorado for a few days.'

Blumenthal poured the Bloody Marys, Grandpa toasted everybody within range, and then lunch was served in the shade of an overhead vine. Six young women sat down at the table to eat with us, all of them employed by Blumenthal in some capacity or other, and all possessed of abnormally generous and buoyant *embonpoints*. Laughing along with the jokes, I felt angry with myself for not making Grandpa even remotely aware of the anguish he'd caused his family. Flushed with rosé, he put his hand on Stephanie's tan thigh, and to my astonishment she let him keep it there, slowly stroking her flesh. The deep red rash on the back of Blumenthal's neck could well have been a side effect of Viagra, and it seemed certain that both old men were taking the medicine.

Blumenthal was a courteous if irrepressible host, and after lunch he jumped into the pool, purposefully splashing Kimberley as she sunbathed face down and topless. Her employer cried out delightedly as she sat up in shock, and it was such unseemly behaviour in a man of his age that it was a struggle to stop myself from applauding him. While John and the girls cavorted around us, I reminded my grandfather that it was Eleanor's opening night.

'Excellent,' he boomed. 'Enough of wine and wassail. We shall attend.'

When Grandpa went inside to get dressed, I left messages for Eleanor and Larry, telling them that he was safe and well, and of his imminent appearance at the Ahmanson. Emerging from the changing room on Stephanie's arm, Grandpa complained of a headache from the sun and the wine.

'But I suppose we'll have to face the music,' he said.

By the time Blumenthal's driver dropped us back at North Canon Drive, my grandfather had enthralled me once again, and charmed by his description of a midnight snowball fight with John and the girls in Colorado, I'd decided to let someone else give him the bad news about what had really happened at Ojai. To my discredit, I'd been scared to upset him. It seemed as if Eleanor too had preferred to postpone the censure for a few hours, sending round two dozen roses to welcome her father home; overcome with emotion, Carmelita had pressed his tuxedo. While Grandpa made some calls and got ready, I went up to my room and flicked through the books by the offspring of celebrated actors that I'd borrowed from the library.

It proved an unsettling experience. In titling her memoir *Me and My Shadows,* Lorna Luft seemed to be making a gentle attempt to reposition herself in relation to her more celebrated mother, Judy Garland (indeed, I could almost hear Ms Luft's therapist exhorting her client to put herself first for once). But Ms Luft's opus seemed destined for oblivion long before her mother ran out of yellow brick road.

A glance at *On the Outside Looking in,* a book intended as an act of parricide (Chapter Seven carried the sub-heading 'Remember me? I'm your son Mike'), only reinforced my sense of Michael Reagan's subjection to his actor parent, or rather parents. It worried me that my own budding memoir would never amount to more than a bitter, aggrieved footnote to the illustrious careers of my father and my grandfather. At the time, it didn't occur to me that such speculation might itself be symptomatic of my self-centredness, but reading Reagan's prose, I received a shock. In Chapter Twenty (sub-heading 'Are you anybody?'), he'd written: '*And there I was feeling sorry for myself, sorry because I hadn't been able to spend time with my parents the way I wanted to and blaming people all my life for my problems.*' The sentence held up a mirror to my own self-piteous nature and, wrestling with this new and painful knowledge, I hurried to get changed for Eleanor's opening.

Afraid to keep my grandfather waiting for a minute (even though he'd thought nothing of keeping the rest of us waiting for eleven days), I stepped out on to the landing at six o'clock precisely. Grandpa joined me in the hall, led me out to the car Eleanor had sent for us, and steadying himself against its roof, he turned to me with a look of regret, as if he was going to apologize for, or at least acknowledge, his appalling behaviour.

'I wish we were heading back to Stone Canyon Road,' he said. 'They really knew how to look after me up there.'

The words made me gasp. Even though he'd been on the telephone for almost an hour reassuring his friends, Grandpa still didn't know he'd done anything wrong. He simply did-n't have a clue. Rocked by his blindness, I slid into the seat beside him and confessed my amazement that he'd become friends with Blumenthal again.

'Wait until you're my age, dear boy,' he said. 'And you'll find out how few real friends you actually have. John's a great chap. For a civilian.'

At the theatre, Grandpa gave a brief but winning inter-view to a local news team, explaining that he'd been on vacation in Colorado and expressing pleasant surprise at all the fuss the media had made. It seemed possible that my grandfather's disappearing act had been, on some uncon-scious level, a cry for attention. Following the red carpet past the security barriers that kept his public at bay, we made our way to the house seats where Grandpa was mobbed by well-wishers, including Lisa Mooney, who crossed her eyes and blew me a kiss. As the house lights began to dim, Larry came limping down the aisle with the aid of a silver-topped cane to make a big show of embracing Grandpa. Holding the attention of two dozen onlookers, father and son chatted for a moment as if an angry word had never passed between them, and I could only imagine that they were saving the name-calling for later.

The curtain parted on *Macbeth*, and five minutes into the play, Grandpa was sound asleep. I envied him. On page 197 of his autobiography, Peter Brook rewards his dogged reader by breaking a confidence. *'Samuel Beckett once confided in me,'* Brook confides to us, *'that for him a play was a ship sinking not far from the coast while the audience watches helplessly from the cliffs as the gesticulating passengers drown.'* Although *Macbeth* at the Ahmanson received fawning reviews in the quisling press, Beckett's metaphor captures perfectly my own experience of the production.

The curtain calls had been meticulously choreographed with an eye to billing and the vanity of the bald leading actor. Coming downstage to take a bow, he peered out at the audience, registering surprise (You mean to say that you people have been out there all along?), then wonder at the applause (Who me?), and then he sighed modestly (Shucks, I don't deserve it). It was the most naturalistic acting we'd seen all evening. Time after time the company left the stage, only to return in a new formation for another dose of approbation, the faces of the less accomplished players betraying *jouissance* as their exhibitionistic impulses were gratified. While the bald actor led Eleanor downstage to share a final palm-smarting accolade, an usher led Grandpa and I through a steel fire door to his daughter's flower-filled dressing room. By the time we arrived, my aunt was already there, having dashed from the stage to exchange her costume for her pink robe, and she flung her arms around her father in something approaching ecstasy.

'I'm so glad you're safe!' Eleanor cried. 'And it's fantastic you saw the show. I was thrilled when I heard you were coming. I've been sooo worried about you. Tell him, Roger. Distraught.'

Bursting with pride in his wife, Roger passed her a fresh white shirt. 'Donald, we can breathe again,' he said, getting into the spirit. As Darien doled out flutes of champagne, Grandpa sat himself in a chair and told Eleanor that she'd been 'simply marvellous' in the play, and that it was the best thing she'd ever done. Naturally, she pretended not to believe him.

'But, darling, you were a revelation,' he bellowed. 'You absolutely held every fibre of my attention from the moment you came on.'

Even this didn't quite meet Eleanor's requirements. Nothing ever did. 'But could you hear everything?' she asked him, stepping into a skirt with Darien's help. 'The acoustics –'

'Every single word. Every last syllable,' Grandpa said. 'Clear as a bell. You brought the verse alive, as if it was coming to you as you spoke it. I actually felt I was meeting Lady M for the first time.'

His daughter gobbled this up and it astounded me that she failed to admonish her father even slightly for his behaviour. As he went on to describe his rapprochement with John Blumenthal and their trip to Colorado, it seemed that Eleanor had forgiven, or even forgotten, his thoughtlessness completely. Standing there clutching my glass of champagne, it dawned on me that my grandfather had only been able to behave with such callous disregard for the people who loved him because for years, perhaps decades, nobody, myself included, had dared to reproach him for anything. In a *tour de force* performance of his own, Grandpa topped off his account of his most recent escapade by acclaiming his daughter's portrayal of Lady Macbeth as the greatest he'd ever seen, surpassing even that of Vivien Leigh at Stratford in 1955. Revelling in this superlative tribute, Eleanor's face shone the way Julie's had when she'd sat at Grandpa's feet in the den.

Invited members of the audience flooded the room and Larry was among them, swinging his new prop, the silver-topped cane. Snatching a glass of champagne from the tray, he downed it in one gulp and pulled me close to whisper in my ear.

'Don't tell a soul, sonny, but I'm taking the manuscript back to North Canon Drive. The old man need never find out.' Roger joined us. 'You know, Roger,' Larry continued. 'I've spent some time thinking about the difference between the hero and the celebrity. I've a feeling it'd make a great sub-ject for a play, and I want Ralph to write it for me.'

Thankfully, Lisa beckoned to me from the door. 'It's so great your grandfather's here,' she said. 'And that every-body's happy.'

With her hair up, bare-shouldered and smiling, she looked radiant. 'Grandpa certainly is,' I replied. 'God knows why we were all so anxious about him. He's seventy-six years old, but we behaved as if he was still wearing diapers.'

Eleanor brushed out her hair while Darien opened more champagne for new arrivals who were edging into the already crowded space. Macbeth's dressing room was just along the corridor, and people in dinner dress shuttled between the two rooms, gripped by a mood of fervid socia-bility as they waited their turn to water the stars' egos.

'The most exciting performance I've ever seen in the theatre,' one woman told Eleanor.

'You were sublime. Magnificent,' gushed a white-haired man wearing a blue velvet suit, and a singular diamond ear-ring.

Eleanor took such hyperbole at face value, gracing her admirers with a tight little smile that called to mind the Queen of England at her least sour. Among the crowd, I rec-ognized a number of faces from Grandpa's birthday party and others from Malibu. Danny's manager, Carl with the trapezoidal head, was ingratiating himself with the very star he'd been disparaging at the engagement party. Sporting a sequinned frock that showed off her eerily rejuvenated physique, Larry's godmother Nonie sidled up to Grandpa, and it jolted me to see her nip his protuberant lobe between her teeth as she whispered something in his ear. Finding myself squashed between Danny and Mitzi, the three of us lied about the play until Mitzi went off to congratulate Macbeth, at which point Danny told me that Ingeborg had found out that he was having an affair, and had just broken off the engagement.

'I'm having to rethink everything,' he said, long-faced.

'Join the club,' I said.

Wearing a baseball cap back to front, the tiny bald actor who'd played Macbeth parted the crowd to congratulate Eleanor on her performance.

'You were so damn truthful tonight, you blew me away,' he said. 'It was an honour to share the stage with you.'

Embracing her, he swallowed a hard lump of emotion, but Eleanor looked strained as she craned her neck to kiss a patch of air a full six inches from his face, and when Macbeth dropped to his knees to pay his respects to her father, Grandpa seemed equally disenchanted with his dwarfish admirer.

Smashed on a mixture of champagne, painkillers and antibiotics, Larry was telling Roger how he'd saved my life up at Ojai, and grabbing me as I tried to slide by unnoticed, his bear hug threatened to put us both back in hospital.

'Is it true, Ralph? Did Larry really save your life?' Roger asked me when my father had gone off to pin another hapless producer to the wall.

As I described how I'd found Larry bleeding in the pasture, the gunfire and my climb up to the ridge, the terror came back, and Roger's laughter threw me. 'What's so funny?' I asked him.

'I'm so sorry, Ralph,' he said, hiccuping from the champagne. 'But from what you're saying, it sounds to me as if you saved Larry's life. Not the other way around.'

'No, Larry did save my life,' I said. 'Later on. When I was fighting off Bruce.'

'Yes, I know that,' Roger said. 'Your father's just told me all about it. Again. But you saved his life too. Don't you see? I mean, you could have just run away.'

This took a while to sink in, and then Roger's observation detonated in my mind, illuminating it with the force of a Biblical revelation. A relative outsider had grasped what nobody in my family – not me, not Larry – had seen: I'd saved my father's life! Determined to trumpet my achievement, I pushed my way through the throng and found my grandfather discussing Laurence Olivier's *Macbeth* with a theatre critic.

'Grandpa,' I said, tugging at his sleeve. 'Listen to me. I saved Larry's life. At Ojai. Do you realize?'

'My dear boy, that's wonderful. Darling,' he cried, drawing Eleanor to his side. 'I was just saying to Saul that you brought the same comic energy to the murderers' scene as Vivien, but I really think you were just *better*. Better, better, better. More *alive*. I'm so bloody proud of you.'

Reeling, I grabbed my aunt's wrist. 'This is important, Eleanor,' I said. 'I saved Larry's life at Ojai. After Bruce shot him.'

'Not now, darling.' Shaking her head briskly, she turned her attention back to Grandpa, wanting more. The critic, a slight man in an opera cloak, swore that her performance would still be talked about in fifty years' time.

'Fifty?' Grandpa roared. 'A thousand.'

Thinking I'd go mad, I barged over towards Larry, but he was still talking at the producer, and a snatch of his prattle stopped me in my tracks: 'Even as that rock left my fingers, I knew I'd fluked the throw,' he was saying. 'A one in a million chance. One in a billion . . .'

For a few seconds, I felt giddy. As ever, it was all about Larry, but instead of getting angry with him, I experienced a pleasant steady hum in my bloodstream, and a curious peace came over me. Although I knew that things weren't right with my father, that they never had been and that they never quite would be, I saw that I could live with it, and that even if nobody else was interested, I was glad of what I'd done for him at Ojai. As a child, I'd wanted Larry to be perfect, and later on it had made me bitter to find out that he was flawed, just like me, but there in Eleanor's dressing room, I started to accept him for who he was and to let us both off the hook. Catching sight of Lisa, I led her outside to smoke a cigarette beyond the fifty or so fans waiting at the stage door for a glimpse of Eleanor or Macbeth, men and women whose faces were twisted by terrible need. When I told Lisa what Roger had said, and about the reactions I'd met with from Eleanor and Grandpa, she broke into laughter, just as her father had done, and soon I found that I was laughing too.

Roger had booked a table for the family at Le Dôme, the restaurant on the Strip where I'd celebrated my eighteenth birthday with Grandpa, and heading there in the second car with Lisa, Danny and Mitzi, I noticed Danny wet a finger and run it over his meagre eyebrow. At the restaurant, it came as little surprise that a photographer had managed to persuade Grandpa and Eleanor that we should pose for a family portrait. Grandpa had invited Kimberley and Stephanie to join us for dinner, and stitched into their flimsy dresses, they glued themselves to his side as we grouped together on the steps – everybody save Bruce, the repository of the family's madness, who was hidden away in Anaheim. As I took my place in the back row between Mitzi and Gaby, Eleanor's personal trainer, I caught myself running a hand back through my hair and nibbling my lips to give them some colour.

That photograph is in front of me now, torn from the pages of *People* magazine. Bruce is notable by his absence, and my earnest smile betrays some of my old yearning to belong. I needed, of course, to get away, and that's exactly what I've done. It's over. There's been no great tragedy, no startling denouement, and externally nothing much has changed besides Bruce's circumstances. Larry is the proud owner of two new scars, and I'll never forget that he saved my life, but the abductions and the murders were all in my mind, and perhaps this is fitting. Actors in real life are generally far less interesting than the characters they portray, and even the most successful ones tend to lead rather boring, uneventful lives.

Ten months have passed since I found my grandfather in Bel-Air. Much of his time is still spent on Stone Canyon Road, but the partying has tailed off since John Blumenthal's recent hernia operation. Stephanie is a frequent visitor to North Canon Drive, and the news of Julie's imminent marriage to a carpenter in Bakersfield barely affected my grandfather. Bruce is making slow progress in Anaheim; Eleanor and Roger have returned to New York; Larry and Irene are back together, and the three of us had dinner at her house up on Mulholland the other week. Larry's pilot flopped, but a young director has apparently offered him a decent part, and although the money isn't good, my father's hoping that it might turn his career around. Stranger things have happened. In her spare time, Lisa is teaching biology at a correctional facility for juvenile offenders near Pasadena, and when they needed someone to direct an inmate production of *The Comedy of Errors*, she put my name forward. Rehearsals started three weeks ago and so far the work proves to be its own reward. To make ends meet, I've been waiting tables four nights a week in a restaurant on Santa Monica. Lisa and I are living together and planning to quit smoking. If we succeed, perhaps we'll feel as if we belong in Los Angeles. Meanwhile, she's learning to accept me as I am, and I'm trying to change completely.

Outside my window, the traffic lights change colour on an empty street. I think about my grandfather a great deal and try to visit him at least once a week. Having long since abandoned his memoir, he knows that I'm writing my own and has given me the original tapes of his life story in the hope that they'll help me to capture his voice. I've listened to them for many hours, but although it's my grandfather who speaks the words, I sometimes have the feeling that the real man is unseen in another room, a strangely hidden soul.

Working on this story in Lisa's apartment, I've tried to purge myself of the self-obsession that riddles my kin. Change is

221

slow and it hardly bodes well for me that it never even crossed my mind to employ a third-person narrative voice, or that my manuscript should display a distinct preference for the first person singular (2,479 instances and counting) over any other pronoun. But I now know that I'm happiest when thinking of others, and sometimes I manage to do so for more than a whole minute at a time.

Having no desire to suffocate my family with their own dirty laundry, I've often regretted that I didn't have the foresight to turn my story into a novel. Not that it would have done any good: if I was to write about a group of sheep farmers in New Zealand, certain parties would still take it for a barely veiled portrait of themselves and charge that it constituted an actionable slur on their reputation. Given the levels of egotism and the appetite for the spoils of litigation that prevail in my family, I realize that I was naïve to have ever imagined otherwise.

Initially, Larry and Eleanor never asked about my writing, but when a friend of Roger offered to try to get it published, my ears began to ring with the refrain 'Is there a part in it for me?' Last week, hearing a (false) rumour that a film company had acquired the rights to my tale, both Larry and his sister bombarded me with so many deranged calls that I finally took the telephone off the hook. It was, in hindsight, a mistake. Today I received a letter from a Los Angeles law firm acting on their behalf, expressing concern that my memoir might be defamatory to their clients and demanding to see a copy. This is puzzling because if, as the letter alleges, I've merely *delivered wholesale to the page, untouched by art, the material circumstances and emotional reality* of my recent experiences in California, what have Larry or Eleanor to fear? That 'their' parts in a possible future film adaptation might go to other, more bankable, actors? It beggars belief that these so-called artists, one of whom made a very public show of support for Salman Rushdie in the 1990s, should resort to the threat of legal action before they've even read what I've written. But my dismay at their hypocrisy is far outweighed by my delight in the avid interest they're finally showing in my work, and it would be untrue if I said that I haven't had fun tormenting them. Hopefully, Larry and Eleanor won't find this book hurtful, and their lawyers' bill won't prove too crippling. After all, writing a memoir is all about being a good liar, just like acting.

STANFORD J. SEARL JR.

Mary Dyer

# QUAKER POEMS

*The Heart Opened*